Exquisite Karma

An Iron Horse MC Novel
#4

By

Ann Mayburn

The unauthorized reproduction or distribution of this copyrighted work is illegal. Criminal copyright infringement (including infringement without monetary gain) is investigated by the FBI and is punishable by up to 5 years in federal prison and a fine of $250,000.

Please purchase only authorized electronic editions and do not participate in, or encourage, the electronic piracy of copyrighted materials. Your support of the author's rights is appreciated.

This book is a work of fiction. Names, characters, places, and incidents are the products of the author's imagination or used fictitiously. Any resemblance to actual events, locales or persons, living or dead, is entirely coincidental.

Exquisite Karma

Copyright © 2016 by Ann Mayburn

Published by Honey Mountain Publishing

All rights reserved. Except for use in any review, the reproduction or utilization of this work, in whole or in part, in any form by any electronic, mechanical or other mens now known or hereafter invented, is forbidden without the written permission of the publisher.

DISCLAIMER: Please do not try any new sexual practice, BDSM or otherwise, without the guidance of an experienced practitioner. Ann Mayburn will not be responsible for any loss, harm, injury or death resulting from use of the information contained in this book.

Authors Note:

You MUST read *Exquisite Redemption* before *Exquisite Karma* or you will be lost

Dear Beloved Reader,

Due to the nature of the timeline of the first four books of the Iron Horse MC series, there is some overlap between Sarah and Swan's stories. I tried to keep those scenes to a minimum, but there were some that had to be shown so you could understand what Sarah was thinking during the time, as opposed to how Swan sees the world around her. As I'm sure you're well aware, we all look through the world through our own little personal lenses that distort what we see. So while there are a couple places where the dialog is identical, the thoughts and situations are not.

I hope you enjoy this next edition of the Iron Horse MC and as always, thank you for giving me the chance to entertain you.

Ann

PS- If you haven't read Smoke and Swan's story yet, Exquisite Trouble and Exquisite Danger STOP NOW and go back and read them first. If you skip their stories you'll still be able to understand Exquisite Redemption and Exquisite Karma, but you'll be missing a ton of the details and won't get the full story.

"Learn how to see. Realize that everything connects to everything else."

— *Leonardo da Vinci*

Contents

Authors Note: 3
Epigraph 4
Chapter 1 1
Chapter 2 21
Chapter 3 33
Chapter 4 48
Chapter 5 59
Chapter 6 67
Chapter 7 80
Chapter 8 93
Chapter 9 99
Chapter 10 113
Chapter 11 130
Chapter 12 144
Chapter 13 159
Chapter 14 177
Chapter 15 185
Chapter 16 194
Epilogue 209
Sneak Peek of Exquisite Innocence 214
    Ivan's Captive Submissive 221
ABOUT THE AUTHOR 227
Other Books by Ann 229

Chapter I

Sarah

On the Outskirts of Austin, Texas

Laughing women bustled around me in the giant communal kitchen of the Iron Horse MC clubhouse, and I let out a contented sigh. They moved around me with quick, efficient moves and managed to avoid each other, sometimes narrowly. I grinned as I thought about how close Sweet Taya, one of the old ladies I played poker with, had come to wearing a giant, buttercream frosting covered four tier cake. Only quick thinking by two nearby women managed to save the day, and the cake. We were getting the big Sunday picnic ready and we'd made enough food to feed three high school football teams going through a growth spurt. The air was heavy with the scents of cinnamon, sunblock, barbeque, fruit, and beer-an odd combination that worked none the less. If summer had a smell, this was it.

Every month, on the third Sunday afternoon, Beach had a huge bash for the brothers and their families during the day, then at night the kids and some of the old ladies left while the sweet butts rolled in, ready to party it up with the men of Iron Horse. But right now the vast yards surrounding the clubhouse were filled with hungry kids instead of hussies, and the air was rang with happy laughter as we cooked up a storm. There were towering platters of made-from-scratch golden fried chicken, heaping mounds of creamy potato salad, and more cakes, cookies, and mouthwatering pies than you'd find in most bakeries. That wasn't even counting the hogs that were roasting out back, along with a couple huge slabs of brisket in the smoker and a ton of ribs. There were even three big pots of made from scratch barbeque sauce bubbling on the stove, each destined to slather a different kind of meat.

Mouse had made one batch, Birdie another, and a twelve-year-old girl. The last one, Jennifer-Sweet Taya's daughter, had a knack for cooking that I found admirable. I'd been able to cook at her age as well, but it was out of necessity...which is probably why I order out now a lot. Anyways, Jennifer rocked in the kitchen because she was a cooking genius, and she had an adoring mother and grandmother that taught her everything they knew. So while Birdie and Mouse argued over whose concoction was better and why, my vote was on Jennifer having the best barbeque sauce at the end of the night. There was even an award for the best dish, and I bet Jennifer was working with her dad on making his ribs the winner. Yep, the men were so serious about their food they gave awards for it.

Basically the clubhouse was currently a carnivore's paradise, and it never occurred to the guys that not everyone liked to eat meat. I'd brought a vegetarian pasta salad and eggplant casserole, knowing Leah, the wife of one of the Prospects, would have slim pickings if I didn't bring something without meat in it. Because she was both naturally shy and scared of messing up her husband's chances of getting into Iron Horse, she would have rather starved than create any kind of fuss.

Fortunately for her, part of my job as the president's old lady was to make sure my girls were happy, so I paid attention and looked out for them. Taking care of others, making their lives better, fed my soul in a way I'd never experienced, and I couldn't help but surrender to a warm glow of satisfaction as I looked around the room at the organized chaos. I knew most of these women, had begun to build a history with them, and for the first time in my life I had the pleasure of really feeling like I was putting down roots.

Even at my house in Las Vegas I'd felt like I was just visiting, which is why it's been empty while my old assistant and one of my best friends, Marley her toddler Scottie, watched over my place from the guest house. The main house, where I used to live, wasn't always vacant. We frequently lent it out to close friends a lot, but it was no longer my home. I'd had all the furniture and personal possessions that I wanted to keep either put into storage, shipped to Austin, or locked away in my master bedroom that I kept secured from the rest of the house. Beach and I liked to steal away to Las Vegas when we could for a day or two of fun, and I didn't like the idea of anyone sleeping in my bed but me and my man.

A little thrill of happiness stole through me as I thought about the dangerous badass who had dragged me into this crazy, risky, amazing world. Carlos "Beach" Rodriguez, a golden-haired sexy as sin, man a good fifteen years older than me with a light Mexican accent to his English that drove me crazy. He'd dirty talk to me in Spanish every once in a while and it never failed to make my toes curl. And he was *amazing* in bed. Gifted even.

"Sarah," a sweet voice said from behind me, startling me from my pervy thoughts.

I turned to find an attractive brunette woman in her early forties who I was familiar with, but couldn't place at first. "Hi."

Giggling, a light blush reddened her cheeks as she looked at me through her long lashes and said, "It's me, Bonnie, Turtle's old lady."

Gaping at her, I shoved the bag of chips I'd been opening into the arms of a passing woman and squealed. "Shut the front door! You look fantastic! Woman, I had no idea you were such a fucking babe. I bet Turtle can't keep his hands off your tight little ass. I didn't even know you had a booty like that in those old jeans you used to wear. Damn, well done you!"

Everyone in the kitchen turned at my loud chatter and when they saw who it was, all the ladies started showering Bonnie with compliments at her new look. She'd gotten a really cute haircut that flattered her oval face, and had highlights that had been professionally and perfectly done. A little bit of sparkly pink eyeshadow brought out her deep blue eyes, and her lips were slightly shiny with a pale pink gloss.

Her old man, Turtle, had been in prison for six years, during which time Bonnie had given up on looking good. Right before he got out last week, I'd taken Bonnie on a shopping spree and hooked her up with clothes and cosmetics. I'd also given her the card to my stylist and it looked like she'd used him.

No wonder Turtle had such a big smile on his face all the time.

There was a glow about her that only came from good sex, and I gave her a quick hug and whispered in her ear, "You look so happy."

"I *am* so happy," she whispered back.

When I leaned back to comment on how cute her earrings were, a woman said in a snide voice, "Too bad she didn't get some plastic surgery to fix those tiny tits. Turtle probably needs a magnifying glass to find 'em."

I don't think Bonnie heard it, she was too busy being admired by the other women, but I did, and my gaze zeroed in on an old lady I wasn't familiar with.

Her long red hair was back in a braid and her low-cut teal tank top displayed so much cleavage I was tempted to throw pennies in it. Her coppery skin spoke of a good deal of time spent outdoors, and she had deep lines around her mouth and lips that indicated a lifetime of smoking. She'd lived a hard life and it showed. When she noticed me glaring at her, she raised one coppery brow and gave me a total "what the fuck are you gonna do about it, bitch?" look.

Oh, I knew exactly what I was gonna do about it.

See, this was the nice thing about living in an outlaw MC world, I didn't have to abide by the social rules most people did. In polite society, I would have clutched my pearls and stammered out a "Well, I never". In the world of the Iron Horse MC, I could beat the bitch out of her.

Strolling over, I gave the arrogant woman a hard look and motioned to her. "Follow me."

"You got something to say to me, bitch, you can say it right here."

The mood in the kitchen plummeted and I could feel my girls watching us with morbid fascination.

During my time as Beach's official old lady, I'd developed a bit of a reputation among the women of the Iron Horse MC as someone you didn't want to fuck with. It might have something to do with me beating the hell out of not only a couple bitches, but also a couple guys. Or it might have something to do with the fact that I didn't put up with shit from anybody, and Beach liked it that way. He gave me free rein to dispense justice as I saw fit because he trusted me to do the right thing, and so far I hadn't let him down. If I saw a problem, I took care of it. My take charge attitude pissed off some of the brothers, but I could give a flying fart that their delicate macho pride got hurt by me handling shit "like a man".

If I had to bash some skulls to take care of a situation instead of waiting for them to rescue me and hoping they got there in time, I was going to bash some damn skulls.

Morons.

That didn't mean I went around randomly beating people up. I always tried diplomacy first, but some people were just begging for an attitude adjustment and didn't respect anything except violence. I didn't know where this redhead came from, but she obviously thought she was top dog around here. The MC had an odd and ever-evolving social structure, and she was about to find out now that this was *my* territory, and I didn't take anyone's shit.

"I don't know who you are or where you're from," I said in a low voice, "but around here, we build each other up, not tear each other down. We're sisters, not strangers, and we treat each other with respect."

For a moment she seemed puzzled, then the arrogance came back into her expression and she narrowed her eyes at me, the scent of alcohol coming off her breath as the woman standing next to her smirked at me. "Awww, isn't that cute. You all sit around and eat each other's pussies then tell each other how pretty you are?"

Instead of rising to the bait, I pointed at the double doors at the back of the kitchen that led to large yard of the clubhouse, where most of the men were. "You have thirty seconds to take your negativity out of my kitchen or we're gonna have problems."

"Fuck you," the redhead sneered and touched her vest. "I'm Score's old lady."

I stared blankly at her. "And?"

"He's the VP of the Billings Chapter of Iron Horse. You're nothin' but public pussy, a little house mouse here to clean up my shit. One word from me and you're gone, so I suggest you shut your fuckin' mouth before I do it for you."

I burst out laughing as she took a step closer to me. "House mouse? Sweet butt? Seriously? Bitch, please tell me you're joking."

She raked her eyes over me, going from my super cute and trendy bob that brushed my shoulders, to my pink tank top with "Support Your Local

Iron Horse MC" on it, down to my jeans and kick-ass pink-and-black Dior sandals then back up. "Don't see no patch on your back."

It only took me a second to realize she was right, I wasn't wearing my property patch, and I inwardly groaned when I realized Beach was going to be pissed. One of his main rules, one that he was inflexible on, was that if I was at the clubhouse, I wore his property patch on my back. I'd had it on earlier, but had taken it off during the lunch prep because I didn't want to get it dirty.

Before I could look around for it, Scarlet was at my side in her cute cherry print summer dress, my vest in her hands and her gaze hard as she stared down the redhead. "Take a walk, Lisa."

"Fuck you, Scarlet." One of the women standing with Lisa tried to tug on her arm, but the redhead shook her off. "This isn't any of your business."

"Actually," Scarlet cocked her hip then held her free hand out in my direction, "it *is* my business when you fuck with my Prez's woman. Meet Sarah Star, Beach's old lady. You know, the person he'd kill anyone for insulting?"

As I slid the vest on, Lisa's face began to pale, then red suffused her cheeks as she sucked in a harsh breath. "Shit."

"Yeah," I said in a sweet voice, "shit. I suggest you move your ass out of my kitchen, *now*."

Oh, that pissed her off, and for a second I thought she might throw a punch at me, but she looked away and muttered, "Fine."

I stared at her back as she walked away, memorizing her patch so I could keep an eye on her in the future.

Most of me was glad I didn't have to kick her ass with kids around, but the bloodthirsty killer that lived deep inside me would have enjoyed a good fight.

"Sarah?" came Marley's familiar voice from behind me, snapping me out of my dark thoughts. "When do you think we should start feeding the kids?"

I turned, giving my friend a bright smile as Scarlet returned to spooning out a huge pot of mashed potatoes into giant plastic bowls.

"Ask Loretta, she's in charge of the food for the rug rats. I think she's out front at the grills with Hustler and Venom."

Marley bit her lower lip and I had to fight my instinctive urge to fix whatever was bothering her. I couldn't help it; she appeared all of sixteen years old with her very petite body and big brown eyes. You'd never know it by looking at her that she had an almost two-year-old son. She looked good in her modest jean shorts and tight pink "Support your local Iron Horse MC" shirt, but there was still a softness about her that the world hadn't been able to harden with its cruelty. While she was no longer my assistant, she did take care of my home back in Las Vegas, making sure the main building was take care of. And we had a strong bond, the kind of bond that not even distance could break.

"Okay, I'll go talk to them." She bit her lip harder before releasing it with a sigh.

Thinking she was feeling a little shy around all the brothers, I smiled at her. "Do you want me to go with you?"

She shook her head, her dark ponytail swinging behind her. "No. No, I'm okay. There are just a lot of really burly manly men here."

"Are they making you uncomfortable? I thought I made sure to let everyone know you're not only my friend, but one of my closest friends, here as Beach's personal guest, and that I'd slice the ears off anyone who messed with you."

Marley burst out laughing. "Awww, that's so sweet of you."

"Shut up, bitch."

For a moment her cinnamon brown eyes went distant, then she focused back on me with a huff. "That's why I can't get anyone to talk with me."

"What?"

"I thought something was wrong with me. Any guy I tried to talk to out there acted like I had the plague. They were chatting up the skanks hanging out by the horseshoe pit, but if I looked their way and smiled, they ignored me." She poked me in the shoulder. "Thanks for the cockblock."

A couple women snickered around me and Scarlet spoke up. "Honey, if any guy out there is worth his salt, he isn't going to let threats stop him from talking with you. Might stop him from trying to dip his spoon into your honeypot, but he won't run away if you strike up a conversation."

Marley sighed, scooting back as a woman with a tray loaded down with chicken wings hustled past us. "I thought maybe I could end my sexual drought while on vacation. I haven't been with a guy in over two years. In fact, the last time I had sex, I got pregnant. Kinda puts a damper on the idea of being intimate with anyone. I mean, I have stretch marks now and stuff. Not exactly a hot guy's version of a dream girl."

"Bullpucky." Mouse, Beach's lovable mom and one of my favorite people on earth, looked up from where she was putting plastic silverware into the containers that would go on the picnic tables. "You're as cute as a button and no good man is gonna be put off by a little softness or a few marks. Where do you think the term MILF came from? You just keep bein' you and the right man will snap you up the moment he lays eyes on you."

"And," Scarlet added with a grin, "you have DSLs. Those boys don't stand a chance."

"What?"

"Dick-sucking lips," I told my obviously confused friend along with an exaggerated blowjob motion complete with hand action.

Blushing bright red, Marley stuttered out something that I couldn't hear over the laughter around me. I couldn't help but feel love for my girls as they easily brought Marley into their fold. Maybe it was because these women were constantly judged by society for being "biker bitches", but they were some of the most nonjudgmental people I've ever met, and once they felt they could trust you, they would bend over backwards to help.

One of the women nearby, an older lady with brassy red hair piled on top of her head and a big smile, spoke up. "It's a crime a pretty little thing like you doesn't have a man at home. I've seen your boy, he's adorable, and you're a good mama. You're a treasure waiting for the right man to find you, so hold out for a good one. You listen to me, I've been married three times and my first two husbands were complete bastards. Don't settle for anything less than a patch on your back and someone your son can be proud to have as a daddy."

My friend blinked at her, then hesitantly smiled. "Uh—thank you."

"Sarah," Beach's distinctive voice bellowed from outside. "Come here, woman. Now."

"Yes, *darling*." I sighed as I looked around and said in a lower voice, "Good thing he's hot, 'cause otherwise I'd have shot him a long time ago."

"My sexy bitch," Beach bellowed, and I *knew* he knew he was annoying me. "I said bring your tight ass over here."

All the women erupted into giggles as I visibly twitched. Okay, not all of them, a few sour grapes were still pissy that I was Beach's old lady, but I paid them no mind. I had better things to think about, like the tanned and toned epitome of biker hotness waiting for me. A little tingle went through me as I anticipated the feeling of his body against mine, of his scent filling me while he held me close. We couldn't be near each other without touching in some way.

What they didn't know was that I hadn't jumped because of his bellow, but because he'd chosen that moment to turn on the vibrator held against my clit by my panties. I had no one but myself to blame for this situation. After all, I was the one who'd been online toy shopping while he was away doing club business, and had bought it for him.

What can I say, Carlos Rodriguez was a complete freak between the sheets, and I loved it.

The vibrator began to pulse gently and I bit back a moan, trying to keep the pleasure off my face. When I'd given the box containing the panties to him this morning, wrapped up all pretty with a bow, he'd given me such a predatory look that I'd been two heartbeats away from saying screw the picnic and screwing him instead. As he'd watched me slip the special black panties on, then position the bullet against my clit, his cock had been pressing against the worn denim of his faded jeans like it was trying to tear through the thick fabric to get to me. The toy combined his love of me in lingerie with something that got me off, so he considered it the perfect gift. I know my man, and the fact that he would have complete control of my arousal made him happy.

Thank goodness, because he was beginning to worry me. Something big was going on and with every passing day, the air of tension and alertness around him grew. Even now, in the middle of a family picnic, I noticed more nomads were visiting us than usual, and they were all watching the property like a bunch of unchained, territorial pit bulls.

These guys, for various reasons, didn't belong to any particular club, but they were still part of Iron Horse. They roamed the land, going where they were needed, and usually fucking someone's shit up royally while they were there. For sure they were a different breed of biker, the kind that didn't like to form attachments to anything or anyone, but they loved their president.

I just didn't know why they were here. Yeah, they all came to visit 'cause we were the national chapterhouse, like bees returning to the hive, but so many of them at once, clearly on alert, sent my Spidey sense tingling. We weren't in danger quite yet, but the potential hung in the air, gathering around the men like a deepening gloom. Not saying I can see auras like my friend Indigo can, but I felt bad shit coming over the horizon, and couldn't figure out what form that danger would come in.

Beach carried the burden of the entire MC on his broad and capable shoulders, and he'd pulled away from me a little bit over the past weeks. Nothing major, but enough that I knew he was getting trapped in his own head. If he didn't give his mind at least a little bit of rest he was going to break, and there was no way in hell I was going to let the happen.

I'd grown used to my loving, attentive man over the past ten months and I hated seeing him stressed out like this. The only way I could seem to reach him was physically, and if that's what it took then I had no qualms about seducing my man. It was only after a good round of rough sex that he would calm down enough to untie me and make love to me. If he was feeling particularly feisty that night, he might make me sleep next to him with our wrists bound together by sheep-skin-lined cuffs. Most women would balk at that, but I understood his need to make sure I was safe by his side even in sleep, that I wouldn't be taken from him when he was most vulnerable. It was kind of sweet in a slightly stalker-esque way.

The low hum of the vibrator sent tingles through me and I could just imagine the smirk on Beach's slightly weathered face.

I lifted my hand against the glare of the sun, my eyes taking a moment to adjust after the dimness of the kitchen. The shouts of children and men's booming laughter filled the air, and I fought to keep from smiling when I spotted Beach standing tall and proud with a group of rough guys. I noticed that his attention was now totally on me and couldn't help the big grin that curved my lips. Tingles that had less to do with the vibrator and more to do with the insane chemistry between us sparked to life in my belly.

Never in my life had I been this content, this secure, and this happy. All because of an outlaw biker with eyes as dark as the deepest sapphire. He raised a brow, as if asking why I was just standing there, and I started moving again, refusing to admit to myself that he affected me as much as he did.

Thanks to all the recent rain, the grass was a thick, lush green and a group of young boys were barefoot, running through it while they played with bubbles and toy trucks. Beach assigned the Prospects with yard duty and had them literally crawling through the play area for the really young kids on their hands and knees, picking up anything that could go into a curious toddlers mouth. That was Beach, always looking out for his people in ways I'd never even think of.

A few people called my name, but I gave them a smile and a small wave, letting them know I'd talk to them later.

Much later.

As in after-I-fucked-the-shit-out-of-my-man-or-vice-versa later. He'd been gone so much lately, flying across the US to visit different clubs, but he wouldn't tell me what it was all about. Not that I'd pushed him much. Truly, I was better off not knowing some of the things Beach did on a daily basis, and I was okay with that. I just wished he could confide in me a little more so I could help ease the pressure on him. Yeah, I supported him whenever and wherever I could at the clubhouse, but I wish he could see what an asset I could be helping out with the business aspects of the club as well. But nooooo. I was a girl, and girls couldn't possibly understand the oh-so-complicated work the menfolk did.

Stupid bikers.

If Beach wasn't so hot, I'd flick his balls for being a macho pig.

Today my man wore a clean white t-shirt under his cut that displayed his bunching, tattooed biceps, flexing nicely as he raised his beer and took a drink. I wanted to taste the beer on his tongue, smell the sun on his skin. His usual and ever-changing posse of men circled around their president, all of their eyes on me as I strutted across the backyard, the black spangles on my new Dior sandals twinkling with my every step. They were a gift from Beach, and I admit I might have squealed when I saw them. I couldn't help it, with their pale pink sole that had a pearl-like shimmer, they were so pretty, any woman would have gone a little starry eyed.

Beach had certainly enjoyed the stellar blow job he'd received as thanks for the extravagant gift.

He'd liked it even more when they were the only thing I wore while he fucked me.

A bandage gleamed white against his muscled forearm and my gut clenched, not liking that he'd gotten wounded while he was on his last run. The thought of him being seriously injured while we were apart constantly haunted me, but I had to learn how to live with the fact that he was a bad man who occasionally did really bad things. Since I'd killed two people…wait, make that three—no, probably more—I had no room to judge.

I was glad he was finally home, and not just for my own selfish reasons. The club felt safer while he was here, as if the malevolent presence waiting to strike couldn't compete with the Beach's formidable presence. I know it sounds corny as hell, but some people are born with extra charisma, dangerous amounts of it, and Beach had that intangible strength in spades. It made him a natural-born leader, someone people wanted to follow because they truly liked him. Some even loved him, but no one loved him like me. We'd become ingrained in each other's lives and I really needed him to hold me in his arms again and make me feel safe. The only time I didn't have to fight the world, that I could relax, was in his arms.

As if he'd read my mind, as soon as I reached him, he looped an arm around my waist and tugged me close, his lips meeting mine in a hard kiss that had my pussy clenching in need. I was so greedy for him, dying to have him inside of me again even though we'd had a quickie a couple hours ago after he'd had church with the other brothers to discuss club business. He'd been in a harsh mood and had spanked my ass hard before he fucked me, but that just made the multiple orgasms he gave me all the better. I'd take any punishment he dished out with a smile and happily beg for more. Shame had no place in our love life, and I adored every hedonistic moment of it.

"Hey, babe," he murmured against my lips before releasing me, the taste of beer hovering on his lips. "Love those shoes on you."

Some of the darkness had gone from his sapphire-blue eyes and I smiled up at him. "Hi, handsome. What can I say, my man has good taste."

Specks of lighter blue gleamed in his dark eyes. "That I do."

I couldn't help but smile wider at his obvious double meaning, and gave him another kiss before I nipped his lower lip hard enough to sting.

Abruptly the vibrator in my panties, which had been a subtle and pleasant hum, rocketed up a notch or two, and I sucked in a harsh breath while my knees went weak and I leaned into him.

Beach held me tighter to his body and lowered his mouth to my ear, tucking my hair behind it as he whispered, "Is your pussy wet for your *Papi*?"

The vibrations eased down and I had to fight the urge to bite his neck, hard. "Wouldn't you like to know."

"*I'd* sure as fuck would like to know," Sledge muttered from behind me.

Without looking, I threw an elbow into his heavily muscled sternum hard enough to make his breath come out in a huff of laughter. "Fuck off, and stay out of my personal space, you perv."

"Hey," Sledge said with a slight wheeze, a big grin lighting up his sculpted face as he stood next to a glowering Beach. "Not my fault you two can't keep your hands off each other. It's the best live sex show I've ever seen. By all means, carry on."

Sledge had, unfortunately, walked in on Beach and me one night at the clubhouse when Beach had decided to fuck me while I was chained to his desk wearing a slutty secretary outfit. It had been hot—so hot, I'd had no idea someone had opened the door. No, I was too busy writhing and begging my *Papi* to fuck me harder with his huge dick. To make his good girl hurt.

When Sledge walked in to find Beach slamming into me from behind while spanking me with a ruler, the vice president had been so shocked he'd just stood there with his eyes bugging out before he turned around and left without a word.

I'm pretty sure we scarred him for life.

I'd hoped he'd be cool about it, and he had been—to a point. I mean, he never told anyone else in the club about our little naughty secretary scene, but he'd say sly little things like that and I'd want to punch him in his smirking face. And he kept buying Beach new rulers.

Asshole.

Beach dialed down the vibrator again to a background hum as he turned to talk to some dark-bearded guy with crooked front teeth I didn't know.

Sledge chuckled and drew my gaze back to him, the thick lines of the black tattoos covering his body flexing beneath his white tank top and black leather vest. "Damn, I get a proximity hard-on just by bein' around you two."

As I glared at him, I took in his new look, having to admit it really brought out his light brown eyes beneath his thick black brows. Sledge no longer sported a mohawk, instead going for a totally shaved bald head that gave him a sinister edge. It made him look more intimidating, he had that total Latin thug look going on with all his tattoos and thick gold earrings, but he was also a good guy who worked his ass off to help Beach keep Iron Horse running in the free and clear. He also had a sweet as pie mother and five sisters he adored who I considered friends.

That meant I couldn't kick his ass, like I really wanted to at times like this. "Go away, Sledge. Don't you have some sweet butt to go bother?"

"Nah, I say suck, they say how hard. No challenge there. You're a lot more fun. So is your cute little friend Marley. Just my type with those sweet, big brown doe eyes of hers. And that tight little ass…" he whistled then licked his lips. "She's fuckin' sweet."

I snarled at him, no longer screwing around. "Stay away from Marley."

He laughed, the asshole, then shook his head at me. "Ohhh, Mama Bear is protective."

"I mean it, Sledge. Marley's had a rough life even before she became a single mom. She needs someone safe and stable in her life."

"I think she needs a man between her legs."

"And I think you need to remember that I give douchebags titty-twisters."

Sledge burst out laughing then rubbed his hand over his left nipple. "Fuck, I'd think you're just talkin' shit but my fuckin' chest still hurts from where you assaulted me last week."

"I assaulted you? Please, I was going to assault your lippy piece of ass that you let wander around the clubhouse and rub up against my man. Not my fault you got between me and her."

To my surprise, Sledge appeared chagrined and rubbed the back of his neck. "Yeah, sorry about that. I was still passed out when she decided to go hit the kitchen."

The memory of the skank trying to cop a feel on Beach while I made him and some of the brothers breakfast at the clubhouse still made me bristle. "She's lucky you stepped in."

He grinned then shook his head. "Don't I know it."

Beach, who'd been talking to the bearded man while Sledge and I bitched at each other, moved up behind me and slid my cute hair over to the side, kissing my neck lightly. "I think it's fuckin' hot when you fight over me."

"I know you do, weirdo."

"I think it's hot too," Sledge said with a dirty grin. "When that chick at the party three weeks ago ripped off your top while you were fighting, I 'bout came in my pants."

Groaning, I stared at the sky. "Why are you always around at my worst moments?"

"I'm a lucky bastard," Sledge replied with an unrepentant grin. "Somehow your clothes just seem to melt away around me."

"Watch yourself," Beach growled as his hands landed in a possessive grip on my hips.

Sledge nodded and raised his hands. "No offense meant, but your old lady is fun to get riled up and none of those situations were my fault. In fact, I believe I should be the offended party here. You've exposed me to your private life without my consent. I think I've been violated. I feel so dirty...wash me, Mommy."

"You sick asshole," I said through gritted teeth while the vibrator began to pulse against my clit. Shit. So damn good.

"What was that? You're lookin' a little flushed, *mamacita*. You need to go inside and cool down?" He studied me then his eyes widened. "You're turned on...holy shit, I think you might come."

"Am not!" I screeched, unable to control the pitch of my voice while Beach toyed with my body, a satisfied look on his face that made me wild for him.

Laughing, Beach pulled me up against him and the feel of his erection pressing into me had me stiffening. It was either pretend I was a statue or twerk like Miley Cyrus on Ecstasy while moaning like the wanton slut Beach turned me into. I couldn't help it, he totally indulged my every fetish, and I repaid the favor. In spades.

Memories of some of the rather exotic role-play we'd done raced through me and I couldn't help but bite my lower lip hard enough to hurt.

He placed his hand around my throat, gripping me lightly in a clearly possessive move that let everyone watching us know I was *his*. "What can I say? I'm blessed with a woman who has a hungry pussy. Always wants my dick."

"What?" I yelled, or tried to yell. Fucker turned the vibrator up to high and the last part of that word came out in a croak.

Running his hands up into my hair, he pulled my head back and proceeded to kiss me long and deep, my body already throbbing from the delicious torture in my panties. I nipped at his tongue, still pissed about his hungry comment—yuck—and angry that he was getting me so wound up in public. True, it was now just Sledge in the immediate area, but there were people hovering all around us, waiting to catch Beach's attention. He was well loved and respected as their president, and that meant everyone felt they could talk with him about every little bit of bullshit under the sun. If it wasn't for the Enforcers running interference, we'd be mobbed with people right now, even while we were trying to kiss each other's faces off.

As much as Beach loved his brothers, he loved me more, and my safety meant they didn't approach my man when I was around unless they had permission.

Abruptly his hold on me loosened and I sagged slightly when I realized I'd been leaning into his grip as he shouted over my shoulder, "I'm off-limits for the next hour."

Laughing, his dark eyes twinkling in a way that would make any woman take notice, Sledge nodded. "Got it. You go have fun, Prez, don't forget I put some extra rulers in your bedside table."

I flipped Sledge off as we left, which only made him laugh harder.

"Beach," I protested as we barged our way through startled-looking people, "wait—we need to eat."

In response, he turned up the vibrator to a level that had me making a startled shriek that drew even more attention to us. "Oh, I plan on eating, and feeding *you* all the dick you can take. *Papi's* home and he's in the mood to play."

I blinked at him, my body shuddering as the effects of his words and that darned vibrator were reducing me to non-thinking state. Oh fucking hell, that meant I wasn't going to be able to walk without wincing tomorrow. Little electrical darts of pleasure seemed to speed through my body as he slowed the wonderfully evil device humming away between my legs to a level that let me breathe.

My clit was so swollen, each step brought me closer to orgasm. A light sweat broke out on my brow and adrenaline flooded me, along with the need to fuck. It felt so good to press my thighs together and squeeze the humming device harder against me. I bet I could come like this if I had just a little bit more stimulation. Someone called out in greeting to us as we passed, but I ignored everyone but the man clutching my wrist in a possessive grasp that made me breathless.

Beach dragged me up the two flights of stairs leading to the third level, barking at men we passed that he'd shoot anyone stupid enough to disturb him. I got more than one smirk, and envious looks from the women, thrown my way as he dragged me to his private room.

The moment we were inside, I relaxed, taking in the décor of the room Beach had let me redesign. I'd decluttered it from the crap that had piled up over the years, then selected some of his favorite mementos to display around the room. One of my personal favorites was the huge blown up black-and-white picture of the Iron Horse MC back when Beach's grandpa had been president, complete with dramatic but tasteful lighting. His blonde-haired, Bettie-Davis-looking grandma stood next to her husband, who bore a striking resemblance to my man, his hard gaze holding the camera as he silently dared anyone to fuck with him.

Even though the picture was taken in the 1940s, the men captured forever in that moment on film could have been partying downstairs right now. Yeah, their hair styles were different and the clothes outdated, but these men all held the same predatory stare and wordless arrogance as the current group of Iron Horse MC brothers. Somehow in this photo, they'd managed to capture a little bit of the wild spirit of these men, and I marveled again at the history of the club that I was an integral part of now.

I was the president's old lady and I felt more pride about that than any other title I've ever held.

The rough scrape of Beach's weathered hands on my shoulders had me cuddling back into him, not realizing I'd moved to stand before the image.

With the vibrator now purring softly against my sensitive pussy, the feel of Beach's lips on my neck, giving me those bone-meltingly soft kisses, gave me goose bumps. "You love this picture, don't you, baby."

"I do." My voice came out in a husky whisper.

"Mmmm." His teeth nipped at the side of my throat and I couldn't help but offer myself to my *Papi* with a big smile. "Much as I love watchin' you get lost in the past, I got plans for *mi riena* in the present."

Turning in his arms, I laced my hands behind his neck and toyed with his hair. "I really missed you. Like a lot. Our bed feels so empty without you."

Pain flashed through his eyes and I felt bad for souring this sweet moment between us. Before I could apologize, Beach placed his finger on my lips. "I missed you too. Swear this shit is gonna be over soon, just a little bit longer, and we'll finally be able to just fuckin' chill. Gonna take you down to the island and kick everyone except the maid and the chef off. Then I'm gonna live inside your sweet body until you can't remember what it's like to not have me between your thighs."

"That sounds lovely." Lying my head against his chest, I ran my fingers along the edges of his thick leather vest, the heat of his body warming me. "I don't like you being so busy, but it's okay, really it is. I'm fine. It's not like I'm ever really alone, even when you're not here. The other old ladies are over at our place, or I'm visiting friends. And don't forget Marley is staying in that condo you own at the bottom of the hill leading to our house. I've seen her every morning and evening since she's been her. She even stayed later than she originally intended because you were gone so I got extra Marley and Scottie time, which is always a win."

"Not the same as havin' your man home in your bed. I know that, and wish I didn't have to be away from you for a minute, but shit I'm dealin' with right now is too important to trust to someone else."

A tiny part of me resented the fact that I knew he wouldn't tell me why he had to be away from me, or what he was doing that kept him awake at night. He worried, a lot, and his tension had begun to seep into me. It made me more aware of the world around me and had me looking for enemies around every corner even though I was better protected than I'd ever been in my life…except when I was at my dad's place out in Nowheresville, Texas. I know Beach couldn't tell me because what he was doing was most certainly illegal, and there was an unspoken oath among the Iron Horse MC brothers to not discuss certain shit with their old ladies.

"It sucks, but I've got plenty of toys to satisfy me."

"Satisfy you? You really think those pieces of plastic can compare to what I can do for you? You think they can fuck you until you cry? Make you come until your eyes roll back in your head?"

Whoops, wrong thing to say. Then again, I always enjoyed it when a tiny bit of his anger flavored our sex. Not angry in a bad way, but more in like an "I've got something to prove" way. Sometimes, a man being macho could be very, very nice.

Blinking up at him, I gave Beach my best innocent look and said, "What, *Papi*?"

His whole body seemed to swell and his gaze focused on me until I knew I was the only thing he was thinking about. A happy little glow kindled in my chest, knowing I'd managed to distract him from his worries, to totally connect with him and give him the pleasure he so desperately needed. Much like me, sex helped Beach relax like nothing else and I know he doesn't fuck anyone but me. Besides, I'm the only person he ever lets his guard go down all the way with. Even surrounded by his brothers, he's on constant alert but with me, he knows I can take care of not only myself, but both of us. That makes us equals in his eyes.

In a way, I think Beach views me more as an extension of himself than a separate person.

My arm-chair psych evaluation of my man disappeared from my mind when Beach fisted his hand in my hair hard enough to deliciously sting. "Looks like *Papi* has a brat on his hands tonight."

I gave him a totally unapologetic smile that had a dimple appearing in his cheek. "I'm always a good girl."

His snort of laughter had me grinning, but that smile fell from my lips when he gave my ass a brisk slap.

Chapter 2

"Look at you." A wicked grin twisted his lips, deepening the harsh lines around Beach's mouth. "I think my baby girl needs to fly."

Anxiety mixed with burning anticipation swept through me, pulling me deeper into his gaze. Beach enjoyed bondage, a lot, and he loved to have me at his mercy in bed. Not that I minded in the least. His possessive, borderline obsessive attention to my pleasure never failed to leave me a blissed-out mess. And when he licked his lower lip, I found myself biting my own in return.

Hot damn, he was so sexy…and all mine.

"On your knees."

I dropped gracefully before him, the response I knew he wanted to hear already spilling from my lips. "Yes, *Papi*."

"*Tienes una sonrisa muy bonita.*"

Hearing him compliment my smile in that crazy, sexy accent of his relaxed something inside of me, some switch that instantly lowered my defenses and allowed Beach deep inside my fucked-up mind, past my formidable mental barriers. Allowed him to have control of me. It was a very liberating sensation and I looked up at my man, not bothering to hide my happy smile as he stared down at me. From this vantage point, he towered over me, and I loved how gently he touched me as he stroked my hair back from my face. It was clear in his every move and look that he was totally as into me as I was to him, and I cuddled against his hand as he cupped my cheek.

"*Abre tu boca.*"

I opened my mouth as he requested, keeping my lips soft.

His nostril's flared as he switched to English and growled, "Take me out and suck me, no hands."

A hard tingle throbbed in my clit, and I didn't bother to hide the little groan of pleasure that escaped me as I eagerly undid his heavy, silver belt buckle, then unzipped and reached in to free his length.

I was careful not to hurt him on the zipper as I eased his balls out as well, knowing my man liked for me to play with all of him.

For a moment I paused, taking in the very large dick that I knew would stretch me just right.

Beach sucked in a harsh breath then muttered, "Fuck, you're so beautiful waitin' for my cock. *Abierta*. Gotta open wider if you're gonna fit this thick dick in that pretty, little mouth."

I did as I was told, tilting my head so he could slide past my lips and into the heat of my mouth. The piercing in the head of his substantial dick slid over my tongue and I struggled a little as he pushed against the back of my throat. I rubbed my tongue the best I could over the base of his shaft, my moans coming out choked as he slid deeper, now in my throat. The slight salty tang of his taste filled my mouth and my whole body seemed to hum in approval.

"That's it. Take your *Papi* deep. Fuck."

My nipples rubbed against the soft fabric of my shirt and my hands twitched to stroke the substantial length of him that I couldn't fit in my mouth. When I gagged a little, he pulled back enough for me to catch my breath, my watery eyes looking up into his hot gaze. He reached down and wiped some of the spit that had leaked out while I was sucking him.

"Love how you work so hard to please me. Now make me come."

I'd forgotten about the vibrator in my panties, but it flared to life as I sucked him back into my mouth, shivering when I widened my stance, the inseam of my pants pressing the vibrator to my aching clit. I was so turned on, so aroused, and having my mouth stuffed full of his dick while my clit was being worked was heaven. The muscles of my lower stomach tensed and I twitched as I tried to hold back, tried to keep from coming hard and long. I wanted Beach to go over with me, needed him to fill my mouth as he lost himself in me. The feeling of his hot, heavy flesh, rubbing over my tongue, drove me wild with lust.

Without waiting for permission, I wrapped my hands around his cock and jerked him hard.

Beach let out a long stream of obscenities as he grabbed my head with both of his hands and proceeded to fuck my mouth. Thank goodness he took control, because I was on the edge of my climax and my whole body seemed to freeze, to shut down and tremble as the vibrator did its job and pushed me over the edge. The rough, harsh way he thrust into my mouth was borderline violent, but it only made me climax harder, every cell inside of me glowing with the rush of pleasure chemicals flooding my brain.

My man's hold on my head eased and when I pulled off his cock, the tip was wet with his cum and my spit. I leaned forward and licked him clean, pausing to suck on his balls and make him groan. After a few minutes of my attentions, he began to harden again, a lazy kind of heat entering his gaze as he lifted his chin to the bed.

"I want you naked, on the bed."

"Yes, *Papi*. Gladly"

He winked at me, mellowed out by his orgasm, before tugging his shirt off as he made his way to the toy chest. Well, it wasn't really a toy chest. It was a locked steamer trunk filled with all kinds of fun stuff for when Beach and I were feeling kinky. Which was most of the time.

When he pulled out a length of smooth, dark rope, my already aroused body went into overdrive.

Sometimes when we made love he was Carlos, my adoring man, sometimes he was Beach, dirty, fun, and kinky. Then there were the times when *Papi* came home to play, and that rope was always an indication which side of Beach's personality I'd see tonight. My butt clenched tight as I realized what else that meant. I'd be having some really good anal orgasms. *Papi* always liked to play with my ass. He hadn't taken me back there yet, his dick was almost too big for my pussy, let alone my ass, but he enjoyed plugging me while he fucked me hard.

"Spread for your *Papi*, hands and knees," he growled out, sending shivers of pleasure over my sensitive skin.

I went to all fours then lowered my head until it rested on the soft fabric, the faint scent of Beach's delicious cologne wafting out. Taking in a deep breath, I raised my ass higher and tilted my hips, giving him a good view of the pink between my thighs. His harsh grunt sent a bolt of energy through me that fed my lust, like throwing gasoline on a fire.

"All this *belleza*...all this is mine."

It wasn't a question, but a statement that he owned my beauty, so I didn't bother to answer. Instead I let the feeling of the pride in his voice warm me from within, filling those empty spaces left inside of me that craved an authority figure's love. And even though I was self-aware enough to realize this, I didn't fight the joy suffusing me. I may be crazy, but I'm not stupid. When the universe gives you pleasure like this, you enjoy it to the fullest. Karma doesn't like it when you ignore her gifts.

His rough hands smoothed over the globes of my rear end, his voice thick with need. "You want your *Papi's* mouth on you?"

More than eager to have his talented tongue playing with me, I spread farther. "Please lick me, *Papi*."

His thumb grazed my anus and I moaned, softening to his touch. Now, anal isn't the easiest thing in the world to enjoy at first, unless your partner has a teenie weenie, and it takes practice to get into the groove of having your butt played with. Thankfully, Beach was completely gentle with that part of my body, never rushing, always awakening me slowly. And he always worked me over good before putting anything inside that tight ring of muscle.

With a soft groan, he rubbed his long dick between my ass cheeks, clutching them together over his shaft as he teased me with his length. I shamelessly rocked against him, enjoying it when he spanked me hard on my right cheek, then my left. I panted and fisted the sheets, rising up onto my arms so I could push back against him harder, then tried to twist my hips and get his thick dick inside of me. Unfortunately, Beach was having none of that.

"Bad girl," he spanked me firmly enough to make me squeal and try to crawl away. "Arms behind your back, brat. Tryin' to make me fuck that seriously wet pussy of yours before I'm ready...naughty. You know better than that."

I had to close my eyes to keep him from seeing my glare as I reluctantly allowed him to pull my arms behind my back and loop the rope around my forearms. When I'd been part of the show in Vegas, I met all kinds of cool people. One of them was a shibari rope master who did this amazing display with his submissives. Very artistic and beautiful. Beach wasn't a shibari master, but he sure as hell knew how to tie a girl up in an efficient, if not pretty way.

It was like redneck shibari.

With my arms pulled behind me, I remained still as he checked the fit, loosening it until I was comfortable. I wouldn't call Beach my Dom, I certainly wasn't his submissive, but we had some kind of D/s vibe to our relationship. Putting my scattered thoughts into words was beyond me, but the best way I could describe the feeling of giving over control to Beach was that it was freeing. And I knew he'd never hurt me in any way, that he would take care of me so well, all I had to do was be happy.

He knew me, knew how my mind worked, and usually anticipated my needs. The rough scratch of his stubble against my bare shoulder sent a shiver through me as he leaned forward to kiss my neck. While he assaulted the sensitive bundle of nerves where my shoulder and neck met, he placed the end of the rope in my hands. "You pull this and you're free in less the two seconds."

See, the man understood just how far to push me, how much he could take from me, before he'd give just enough control back to melt me like butter.

I totally relaxed beneath him and he flattened me to the bed as he gave me some of his weight. That only had me going deeper inside myself, pinned beneath him and seemingly helpless. Even though I held the end of the rope in my hands, and could free myself in an instant, I struggled against my bondage, a dirty part of me enjoying the thrill of giving him a little mock reluctance.

Wiggling my butt, I lightly set my nails against his stomach and said in a breathy voice, "You're too big, it's going to hurt."

Oh man, the sexy purr Beach gave as he ground his cock between my ass cheeks lit me up inside when he murmured, "Baby wants to play."

With a tilt of his hips, he had the head of his cock teasing my wet entrance in a way that stole my breath.

"It'll only hurt for a moment. Let me fuck this pretty pink pussy, little girl."

Mindless with the need to have him push inside of me, I gave an ineffective bump with my hips. "Leave me alone!"

"Mmmm, don't think you want me to leave you alone." He slipped one arm beneath me and tweaked my hard nipple. "I think you need to be fucked, badly."

He was right about that, but I loved role-playing with him, and got another dirty thrill as I whispered, "Please, your dick is too big, mister, it won't fit."

Moving quickly, Beach straddled my legs so they pressed together, making an already tight fit excruciating as he worked the head of his shaft into me. My body clenched down and I let out a stuttering moan. His cock pulsed inside of me and that blessed piercing of his rubbed me deep. Shit, he had so much dick to feed me, and I let out a squeal when he went as far inside me as he could, balls deep, so tight it stung.

"Fuck," he whispered into my ear. "See, you little slut, fits just right."

With my toes curling I moaned my agreement as he began to fuck me nice and deep, stroking me so well I forgot my own name. The only thing I could do was feel the length of his muscled body against mine, the soft brush of his body hair as he moved over me. My pussy began to clench and release as his pace increased to the point where the loud clap of our bodies slapping together filled the room. His harsh breathing matched my own, and right before I could come, he slowed down.

My whine of protest died a quick death when the familiar sensation of his lube-covered fingers toying with my bottom rushed through me.

"No," I rasped out, "not there."

"Gonna fuck you everywhere. There won't be an inch of this sweet body I don't take. And you can't do shit about it."

The inner muscles of my sex quivered, making Beach groan. "Bad girl."

Cool metal pressed against my anus and I tightened involuntarily, then relaxed. It was a small, smooth butt plug and it eased inside of me as Beach began to move again.

So full, I was so damn full like this, too many sensations bombarding me with pleasure and tension. The coil deep inside of me wound tighter, and when the butt plug began to vibrate, I lost it, coming all over Beach's cock. My pussy grabbed on to his length and as he fought against my inner muscles, I thrashed beneath him, the vibrations traveling through my bottom and into his cock, which made his piercing vibrate hard.

Another orgasm came on the heels of the first and I screamed his name while he fought to keep fucking me hard and deep, using his weight to hold me down while I bucked beneath him, the constant stimulation driving me wild.

With a rough shout, Beach pulled out of me, then yanked the rope, freeing my arms. I was limp as he pulled out, his cock so engorged with blood it looked painful. Licking my lips, I tried to sit up so I could take him in my mouth, but he had other ideas. Collapsing back in bed, his body covered in sweat, Beach smacked my ass.

"Ride me, baby girl. Make your *Papi* come, fuckin' ride it outta me."

More than up to the challenge, I placed my hands on his chest and allowed him to guide his first few inches into me. The anal plug was still inside of me, though no longer vibrating, and I had to catch my breath on the initial descent down on his length. His groan of pleasure echoed my own, and I moved so I was on my feet, crouched over him in a straddle. A faint smile curved his lips and he closed his eyes, his head arching back as he settled in.

With a twist of my hips, I took him all the way, then rose back up, working him like a dockside whore on Navy payday. Every downward stroke rubbed my engorged clit against his stomach and brought a gasp from my lips that he echoed. The air was thick with his scent and I moaned low in my throat as the most exquisite tension filled me.

Our bodies moved together and he fucked me through another orgasm before he couldn't hold back any longer. By this point my legs were shaking but I rode him hard and fast, practically snarling at him as I watched him fight his orgasm. Squeezing my pussy, I released as I came down then squeezed on the way back up, tearing a shout from my man.

He grabbed me by my hips as he sat up and captured my lips, using his strong arms to grind me against him until I had to tear away my mouth so I could scream out my pleasure.

The moan he gave as he began to climax sent a full-out shiver through me, drawing answering noises of male satisfaction from Beach as he released inside of me with pussy clenching grunts of raw male lust.

I collapsed on his chest, the ringing echoes of my intense orgasm still making me twitch. For a long time we lay there, my thighs shivering every once in a while, which always made Beach give me a smug smile. I'd bitch at him for being an arrogant ass later, after my body stopped squeezing his semi-hard dick still inside of me.

With a soft laugh, Beach palmed my ass then gently worked out the plug before setting it on the table next to us. "Good to be home. Not gonna lie, I missed you like crazy."

After placing a kiss on his damp chest, I put my head back down with a sigh, utterly relaxed as he caressed me. "Me too."

His voice still husky with the remains of his orgasm, Beach growled out, "Tomorrow night I'm takin' you out. Wanna show the world what a lucky man I am with such an amazing woman on my arm. Have a spa day with a couple of the old ladies, my treat."

"I wish I could, but I've got lunch with Swan tomorrow. After that, I'm all yours."

He tensed beneath me. "You gonna bring me with you?"

Shit. He'd been hinting—okay, outright *telling* me that he wanted to meet my sister, but so far I'd been able to put him off. It wasn't that I didn't want him to meet her; I think they'd get along—eventually. She just wasn't ready for Beach, and everything that came with him.

I'm not a fool. I know that a couple of the brothers who are keeping an eye on my sister have expressed interest in her in a way that had me threatening to slice their dicks open. As soon as Beach met Swan, those men would consider it open season on making her their old lady. My sister was a recluse by choice and if she became part of the Iron Horse MC, she'd be thrust into a world that might scare her enough to send her back to my parents' house to live. The thought of her weird but sweet personality broken beneath the weight of the violence that was part of Iron Horse made me sick.

I couldn't do that to her.

So even though I knew this would start a fight, I forced myself to say, "Maybe next time."

And that went over like a lead balloon.

"It's always fuckin' next time."

"Beach..." How could I defend myself against him? He'd be hurt to know I didn't want my sister around the club. "I just need more time to break her into the idea. She's been pretty adamant that she doesn't want to meet you. My, um...track record with men hasn't been too good. I've been with some not-so-nice guys in the past and she has every reason to not trust my choice in men."

Fisting his hand in my hair, he pulled my head up, forcing me to make eye contact with him in the golden, shimmering light filling the room. "Baby, you need to let go of that stupid fuckin' guilt about that fuckin' child molester who took advantage of you in Reno. For once, listen to me. I don't know the particulars of what happened because you haven't told me, but the basic truth is, at fifteen, you were a child, he was an adult, and he took advantage of you. As if that wasn't bad enough, he got you all screwed up on drugs then pulled one hell of a mind fuck. None of that shit was your fault. He took advantage of you."

Talking about Morrie always made me feel terrible about myself, ashamed beyond belief, and I tried to roll away, but he held me tight and a whimper escaped me. "Let me go."

"No, *mi Corazón*, you're mine, love you too much to live without you."

His grip loosened on my hair and I snuggled up close to his body as I resisted the urge to blurt out the truth to Beach. A truth I'd been hiding from him out of fear and shame. I had indeed been trained to feel self-loathing and guilt, I'd been manipulated and used, but it was by my mother, not Morrie.

For as long as I could remember, everything was my fault, in one way or another. Hell, she even blamed me for Swan being autistic. My mom said I was the bigger twin at birth, that I'd hogged more resources in her belly, took them from Swan, and that's why she was born just a little different than me. Despite my best efforts, a tiny bit of blame managed to pierce its way through my heart, leaving behind a familiar, sharp burn.

"Please, let me go."

"So you can run away and try to convince yourself you're not worth loving? No way. You're stuck with me, Sarah. You're my old lady and we belong together, were made for each other. Wish you could see that as clearly as I do. Now, we're gonna take a nap, then we're gonna go back out there and party. You need a night to cut loose and have fun, get rid of some of this tension ridin' you. I'll keep watch over you, so go as wild as you want. Poppy's in town with some new product, and I know Marley is dyin' to be naughty and try it out."

I couldn't help the giggle that escaped me, glad for the change in subject. "She's mad at me."

"Why?"

"She figured out that I'd cockblocked her from the entire club."

He grinned at me. "Told you it would piss her off."

Linking our hands together, I studied his battered and scarred knuckles and the tattoos covering all his fingers and hands. This wasn't a man who hid who he was, or how he lived his life. One of the social quirks that most Americans had was to shake hands when meeting someone new. A person's hands say a lot about them. Are they married? Do they work outdoors or indoors? Are they healthy or frail? And most important of all, at least to my mother, are they rich? She could size up a man in a matter of seconds and give you a pretty good ballpark figure of his net worth. It was almost scary how fast she could read people...well, when she was sober. When she needed a fix, everyone became her friend, even men she'd normally refer to as scum.

His deep chuckle rumbled through my back and snapped me out of my dark, racing thoughts. "Babe, I hate to say this 'cause I know you see her as someone who needs protection, but Marley is a grown woman who can make her own decisions. Yeah, she fucked up in the past with her ex, but since the moment she found out she was pregnant with that little boy of hers, she pulled her shit together and made sure her son always had the best life she could provide him. Let her have a little fun."

"But I don't want her to get hurt."

"Not your decision to make...but I can't say I totally disagree that she needs someone to watch over her. I let it be known that she has my personal protection, and if a brother approaches her, he'd better be ready to put a patch on her back. He comes to me first, and if I give him my blessing, he has my permission to try to win that sweet girl's heart. It's a shame the piece of shit man she had didn't respect her or see what a treasure she is. Good woman like that who's also a great mom to a cute as shit kid? You pull out all the stops to win her heart, do whatever it takes to make her and her little boy happy. I see a guy treatin' her like gold and they'll have my blessings."

"Beach, you're not her dad and you can't just marry her off." I gently bit his thick wrist, tasting the faint hint of sweat and wind.

The timbre of his voice deepened and he pulled me tight to his long frame. "Minute I saw you, knew I wanted to lock your high-maintenance ass up and get my patch on you."

"Oh please."

His scruff rubbed against my bare shoulder as he nibbled on my skin. "It's true. Knew your ass would be high maintenance—"

This time I bit his wrist hard enough to make him growl. "I am not high maintenance."

He was silent for a long moment. "Honey, it takes you two hours to get ready every day. Thirty minutes of that time is spent trying on different outfits while you bullshit on video chat with your girlfriends."

I looked over my shoulder and glared at him. "That's only for special occasions. I'm sorry I don't know the biker etiquette on what to wear when meeting a new chapter president."

His snort of laughter irritated me and I elbowed him in his solid ribs, but he only threw his heavy thigh over my hip. "Didn't say I don't like the results of you bein' all girly. Hell, the way you get your pussy waxed perfectly smooth is an art."

"You did not just say that."

"Edible art."

That startled a laugh out of me and my emotions flipped, warmth soothing me now as I basked in his attention, his playful mood pulling me from my worries. "Perv."

"Love you, *mi riena*."

I wanted to say it back, to tell him I loved him, but I was fucked in the head about admitting it to Beach out loud. My therapist and I are working hard to help me relearn how to deal with life like a normal person, but right now I hated more than anything the fact that I couldn't tell Beach how much I loved him in return. Some weird nervous tic in my brain insisted that if I told him, he'd leave me. No, it made no sense, but that was the default mind setting that I had to deal with.

It wasn't that I didn't love him; every moment we spent together made me feel so damn good, it was addictive. I always slept like shit the first few days that he was gone doing club business, and missed him fiercely. He was the first thing I thought of in the morning and the last thing at night.

That thought brought my busy mind back to the present and I smiled then cuddled close. He pulled the sheet up, the fabric caressing my skin as it floated down over our bodies. Maybe I couldn't easily say those three words, but perhaps I could say something else to let him know I cherished this time alone with him. "Do you know you're the only person in the world, other than my family, that I feel safe with? You're the only person I can relax and be totally myself around. It feels really good to know that no matter what, you'll take care of me if I need it."

The warmth of his breath tickled my face as he sighed. "Go to sleep, *mi amor*. I've got you. *Quiero estar contigo para siempre*."

He continued to whisper to me in Spanish, sweet phrases about love and adoration, complimenting me on my beauty and grace, telling me in no uncertain terms that I was his woman and he was my man.

Slowly my thoughts stilled until one thing began repeating in my head.

I was safe. Safe in his arms, safe in a way I'd yearned for my whole life.

Maybe I couldn't tell him how much he meant to me, how I wanted to spend the rest of my life with him as well, but I could show him.

Chapter 3
Carlos "Beach" Rodriguez

My woman sat beneath a wide bronze umbrella on the patio of a nice restaurant in downtown Houston. Today her short hair was slicked back in a way that made her look sophisticated and hot. My dick agreed, and I had to fight getting a hard-on as I sat in the SUV, spying on Swan and Sarah. We were parked down the street but I had a perfect view of her long, spectacular legs as she crossed them.

After Sarah shot me down for meeting her sister yet again, I had to see for myself what Swan was like, something I'd avoided so far. I'd given Sarah a chance to make things right, to introduce us, and even though Mimi told me I needed to be patient, I had to see this mysterious sister of hers. It wasn't that I didn't trust Sarah, I just felt like there was more to her relationship with her sister than what she was telling me, and I needed to watch for myself how they were together.

Smoke offered to do some surveillance on them with me and we'd made the drive to Houston, him at the wheel and me in the passenger seat, doing business on my phone the whole way down. I needed to be back at the clubhouse handling shit for the big shipment we were going to run for the Russians, and maybe the Israelis, soon. This was in addition to all the other runs we were doing, protection we were providing, and territories we were controlling. It was enough to drive a man crazy, but even with all that on my mind, the only thing I really cared about was Sarah. I was so fuckin' whipped it was pathetic, yet I couldn't find one shit to give.

Any man who had the glory of Sarah melting in his arms would do everything he could to make her happy.

Clearing his throat, Smoke said, "Seen enough?"

Yeah, I'd seen enough to know I was an asshole for pushing Sarah on meeting Swan. From the moment the sisters had stepped out onto the patio and into my view, I'd watched my woman turn into a lioness intent on protecting her cub. I'd seen pictures that Sarah had shown me of her and Swan growing up, and heard plenty of stories about their exploits together, but watching them in the flesh was totally different than staring at photos.

Sarah escorted her sister around like Swan was the President and Sarah the head of her Secret Service. If anyone got too close to Swan, Sarah would let them know real quick to back off in a subtle way that I don't think Swan noticed. Interesting. Heads had turned to track the sisters' movements and I couldn't blame everyone for staring when they had followed the hostess. Seeing a woman as beautiful as either Anderson twin was a once-in-a-lifetime thing; seeing two of them was like spotting a fucking unicorn.

My need to guard my old lady's back poked at my self-control as I watched some douchebags in suits eye-fucking my woman. I'd have been a little more concerned if I hadn't watched Sarah strap three different blades to her body before she slid on her conservative but sexy black suit. She had them seated at a table where Swan was in the corner, out of reach and as isolated as she could get on the massive patio. That meant I didn't get to see much of Swan, but I had a good view of Sarah.

Right now the girls were sharing a pitcher of margaritas and laughing about something. Smoke and I sucked in an identical breath, as did every male around them. I didn't like the way the men watched my woman with such hungry expressions, and I had to tamp down the urge to go up there and stake my claim again. The main deterrent of that being the fact that my woman would pin me to the wall with her knives before I made it halfway across the room. She would not like the fact that I'd invaded her private time with her sister, especially when she'd asked me not to.

My heart was both heavier and lighter thanks to my recon. "Yeah, I've seen enough."

Smoke pulled out of the parking spot from where we'd been watching the women and I leaned my head back against the leather seat, relief filling me. For a moment I'd been worried that she wasn't meeting her sister, that she was really meeting some fucker I'd have to kill. She's never given me any reason to think she would cheat, ever, but living the life I've lived, people ain't exactly known for being loyal. Sarah would kill me if she ever found out, but I'd needed to see them together to understand how shit worked between them.

All bullshit aside, Sarah loved Swan with her whole heart; it was obvious to anyone with eyes in their head.

"She always that protective of her?" I asked Smoke as he eased into the busy downtown Houston traffic.

"Yeah. Anywhere they go, Sarah has a table reserved that gives them privacy. When she walks with Swan, she's always makin' sure no one touches her." He blew out a harsh breath. "I saw some asshole take Swan's hand once. Swan went super pale and I thought she was going to throw up, but Sarah flipped out on the guy and Swan had to keep her from beating the guy up. Anything ever happened to Swan, Sarah would lose her shit."

"What're you tellin' me, Smoke?"

His hands flexed on the steering wheel in an unexpectedly nervous gesture. "I'm just sayin' that I've been keeping an eye on Swan over the last few months and I can understand what Sarah said about her being fragile. Whatever her issues are, they keep that young woman a prisoner inside her own home. She comes out to work, shop, and on very rare occasions has a few female friends over. I'd say she's an introvert, but it seems more than that. It's almost like she doesn't know how to react to people."

My gut tightened as I turned to fully look at Smoke, who avoided my gaze by staring at the road. "You're watchin' her pretty close, brother."

Smoke gave a stiff chin lift. "Case you hadn't noticed, I like Sarah—as a friend, but a good one. I look at her, then I look at Swan, and I wonder what happened to make a woman that could be as wild and free as Sarah all quiet and withdrawn like Swan. At first I felt sorry for her, until Sarah explained how special Swan is."

Unease stirred through me as I leaned back into my seat. "You talk to Sarah a lot?"

"She's desperate for any news about her sister, Beach. That's it. You know I would never betray you like that," he said in a low voice, and I felt like an ass—again. "When I check on Swan, Sarah always wants to know as many details about her sister as I can remember. Look, I don't know what happened between them, but Swan doesn't trust her. Sarah wasn't bullshitting you when she said Swan isn't ready for the MC life."

"Shit." I rubbed my eyes. "I know that, and I agree with you. Sorry, man. Losin' my fuckin' mind over here tryin' to keep everything goin' right."

"I hear ya, man."

One thing was now crystal clear to me—Sarah loved Swan, deeply, and if anything happened to her, Sarah would lose her mind.

The sudden need to protect Swan filled me and I grabbed my phone, already sending out instructions to my other Enforcers. "I'm steppin' up security on her. I want her checked on once a day, maybe more if you're feelin' uneasy for any reason. You got that house near hers, right?"

"Yeah."

"I want someone watchin' her house overnight."

"Got it."

"Who's on Sarah today?"

"Dragon. He's got eyes on the girls right now."

"Good. All right, let's head back to the clubhouse. Hustler needs to talk about some inventory issues he's havin' at the store."

"Fuckin' Veronica," Smoke sighed. "I told him not to let that crazy bitch into his bed but he never fuckin' listens to me. They are not fuckin' good together, and the last thing I need is my fuckin sister-in-law causing drama between Hustler and me. Damn that bitch is a pain in my ass."

I patted his shoulder. "Can't choose who we're related to, *mi amigo*."

"Got that shit right."

Five hours later, safely back at the clubhouse in Austin, I looked up from the paperwork I'd been going over and stared at Vance, praying I hadn't heard him right. "Did you just say my old lady is missing?"

Running his hand over his short, dark hair speckled with grey, Vance looked away. "She's not with Swan, Prez. We got a guy watching Sarah's sister right now, and he says Sarah never showed up and Swan hasn't left her house since she got back from lunch. We had Dragon following Sarah, but she managed to lose him in traffic on the way home."

Now, I normally have no problem keeping my temper, my reign as president of the Iron Horse MC would have been pretty short if I didn't, but all my self-control went out the fucking window when it came to Sarah. "How long has she been missing?"

"Only an hour or so."

"She's been gone for an hour and no one told me?" The need to shoot Vance in the knee was burning at my self-control. "What the fuck!"

"Prez—"

"Shut the fuck up, Vance."

I tried calling her but it went right to her voice mail. That unease had my gut tightening again but this time it wasn't that I was worried about Sarah cheating on me. I was worried one of my seemingly endless number of enemies would hurt her while she was out of my sight and my protection. I pushed away from my battered desk, an endless pile of work waiting for me that needed to get done, but I couldn't concentrate on shit until I knew Sarah was okay. To the rest of the world it might seem irrational to be so worried about my woman, but people have tried more than once to kill my ugly ass, and I worried they'd view Sarah as easy prey.

They couldn't be more fucking wrong.

Though Sarah may look like the former *Playboy* centerfold that she was, my woman was also raised by an ex-Special Forces crazy-ass survivalist father who taught her how to kill a man a hundred different ways without chipping a nail. "Track her phone. I want her found, and get Smoke."

Vance opened the door to my office and relayed my instructions to one of the Enforcers standing guard outside.

Sarah would be pretty pissed off if she knew I'd had her phone hacked, but I needed her to be safe. Since she officially became my old lady, Sarah's become an essential part of my life, someone I can't, and won't, live without. Not only does she keep me satisfied in every way possible, she's also taken to her role as the president's old lady like she was born for it. And maybe she was. She keeps me sane, gives me balance, and both my personal and professional lives had grown stronger because of her presence. The thought of something happening to her drove me wild and I began to pace.

A woman's voice came from outside my door, and a second later Scarlet, the raven-haired beauty that was Thorn's old lady and Sarah's buddy, as well as my old friend, stuck her head around the corner. "Beach, I know where Sarah is and she's okay, but it's a secret."

Liking this less and less, I moved from my desk to where Scarlet was hovering around the doorway, the smile wilting off her face. "What do you mean, it's a secret?"

Hesitant, Scarlet nervously smoothed her hands down her tight jeans. "Uh—it's a surprise. She'll be back soon."

I lowered my head so I could look her right in the eyes. "What the fuck is goin' on, Scarlet?"

Movement came from behind Scarlet and Sledge strode in with murder in his dark eyes. He shrugged his cut on, covering up the shoulder holsters and spare ammo clips. "Any word?"

"Scarlet here was just sayin' that my woman is okay, but it's a fuckin' secret where she is."

Frowning at Scarlet, Sledge growled, "Have you lost your damn mind? Did it even occur to you that the last fuckin' thing we need right now is havin' the president's old lady without an escort? Jesus, woman, use your fuckin' brain."

"I-I didn't think…I mean, she's not doing anything bad. It's—it's a surprise."

Striving for patience, I clenched my jaw then ground out, "She take any brothers with her? Any protection? She out there a-fuckin'-lone?"

The pulse in Scarlet's throat began to beat faster as her cheeks paled. I've known her for over twenty years and she never could lie to me, so I knew she was being honest when she said, "She's in a safe part of the city."

"Who does she have with her?"

"Um...no one. She—she didn't trust your guys not to run their mouths to you. Really, she's okay."

My anger, along with my fear, grew by the second. "You mean she's out there *alone*? That you fuckin' knew she'd be unprotected, and you didn't fuckin' think to tell me about it?"

"Easy, Prez," Sledge said in a low voice while Vance watched us with an intense look that irritated me. "I'm sure she's okay. Probably just went grocery shopping or doing some chick shit."

Turned to face the windows, struggling against my temper. "She fuckin' knows better than to leave without an escort. When I find her, I'm gonna—"

"You're gonna do what, darling?" came Sarah's husky voice from behind me.

I turned to face her and at the sight of my gorgeous woman safe and sound, everything inside of me relaxed, right before I got angry again. "Where the fuck were you?"

Her blue eyes sparked as her temper flared to life. Beneath the elegant cranberry silk blouse that she wore beneath her black suit jacket, her breasts rose and fell as she took a deep breath, distracting me. Fuck, having a hot-as-ballz woman is both a blessing and a curse. It was hard to stay mad at her when she looked so damn good. Every time I saw her, I felt a little bit like it was the first time, my attention totally focused on visually devouring her. Contentment mixed with lust burned through me and I fought against getting hard. She still wore the conservative outfit she'd had on during lunch with Swan, letting me know she hadn't gone home first.

My gaze was drawn off the tight fit of her shirt and back to her angry face as she growled out, "Whoa, whoa, whoa, back the fuck up. I don't need an 'escort' anywhere. I can take care of my damn self."

I struggled for patience, reminding myself that I needed to be the calm one. "Babe, you don't got eyes in the back of your head."

"Babe," she snarled back at me, "I'm not some stupid bitch blindly skipping through life in my Chanel heels without a care in the world. I can protect myself."

"I know you can, but you can't keep fuckin' leavin' without an escort." I grit my teeth, terrible mental images going through my mind of all the ways Sarah could be hurt. "Fuckin' Los Diablos would love to get their hands on you. All it takes is one second of you being distracted. They could be sneaky about it, trick you into putting yourself in harm's way before you were even aware of it."

"Stop treating me like a child!"

"Then stop fuckin' acting like one! Shit, woman, I do not need the stress of you only thinkin' of yourself."

"Oh no you fucking didn't."

My heart chose to beat a little faster as our gazes locked and I was momentarily taken aback by how pissed off she was.

Aware of everyone watching us closely, and Smoke grinning like an asshole as we bickered, I kicked them out, slamming the door on the curious faces watching us.

When I turned around Sarah pointed her finger at me and said, "You are such a dick!"

I'd tried to be patient with her, to take into account her young age and how new she was to the MC world, but if she didn't stop running off by herself she was going to get hurt. "You can't fuckin' take off by yourself, Sarah, you know this."

"Jesus, I was gone for less than two hours and I told Scarlet where I was going. I don't need a babysitter, and I sure as fuck don't need to tell you my every move. And I don't appreciate you yelling at me in front of everyone."

"Yeah, you fuckin' do need me yellin' at you 'cause aren't getting it. I've tried to tell you this in private, but you obviously weren't fuckin' listening. This is a bad time to be anywhere, *anywhere*, alone."

Instead of looking contrite, my stubborn woman rolled her damn eyes at me like I was some kid throwing a tantrum. "I'm not an idiot, Beach, and I'd like to remind you that I've saved *your* ass more than once."

This was true, but my own temper was rising to the surface despite my best attempts to remain cool. We were both passionate, opinionated, and stubborn people, so when we fought, we fought hard. I couldn't let her think this taking-off-on-her-own bullshit was okay, I had to make her understand the consequences of her actions. This wasn't just about her and me, but the club as well. Iron Horse would have my back, no matter what, and I'd scorch the Earth around any motherfucker stupid enough to harm her, but I'd rather avoid the bloodshed.

Holding her gaze, not giving in an inch, I stared her down. "Do you have any idea what I would do if anything happened to you?"

"Considering you cut the pinky fingers off that Los Diablos member that tried to roofie me at the bar last month, yeah, I do."

"He wouldn't have tried that shit if you'd been wearing your patch."

"Oh for fuck's sake. I was at a popular dance club for Scarlet's birthday party with a bunch of women and the Enforcers who were babysitting us. We were having fun, I had a great time, and the moment something started to go wrong, your boys were there to make sure I was taken care of." She shook her head. "I'm not wearing your property patch everywhere, Beach. You just have to trust me. I trust *you*."

This was true, and her words soothed me. "I do trust you, it's the rest of the world I don't."

Striding across the room, I pulled her stiff frame into my arms, loving the way she fit against me even in her anger. Her slender fingers curled into my hair and when she tugged, I rubbed my face against hers, grinning when she squealed because of my scruff. Her small nose rubbed against the side of my neck as she nuzzled into me for a moment, breathing me in before she drew back with a sigh. For whatever reason, my touch soothed her, and it always gave me a sense of pride to know this strong woman needed me. Her pale eyes searched my face as she stroked her hands through my hair before tightening her grip enough that it stung a little bit.

"Beach, you have to give me a little bit of freedom. I shouldn't have to sneak out like a kid trying to break curfew. That kind of bullshit will not stand with me, and you know this." She had to clear her throat a couple times before she could speak again, and worry flooded me since I could feel her emotions seething below the surface of her skin. "Honey, I have to feel free to come and go as I please; when I don't, it triggers the need to run in me."

"Need to run?" Shit, Mimi had talked about this, and I tried to remember the conversation we'd had months ago.

"Yeah." She closed her eyes and looked away, her expression filled with pain. "My mom, well—let's just say when the goin' got tough, she got goin'."

"That's not you."

"What?"

"You won't run."

"How do you know that?" Her lower lip quivered and I cupped the back of her head, resting her cheek against my chest, wishing I could take away the self-doubt that was radiating from her.

"Simple, you're not a runner, you're a fighter. I haven't seen you run from anything or anyone. And trust me, there have been times that I'd wished you'd used your brain and run, but instead I had to bail you out of a gun fight."

"That wasn't my fault," she huffed out. "There was no way I was letting the asshole at that gas station shoot the attendant. How was I to know that a bunch of his gang member buddies were waiting in the car with guns? Besides, I had the situation under control when you arrived, and if I hadn't stepped in, they would have never found that police chief stashed in the trunk—and we both know his death would'a been long and painful."

"Babe, you shot them all in the kneecaps."

"They couldn't run anywhere and it was *under control*."

"Then you shot them in the head, execution style."

Her lips thinned out and a merciless expression hardened her face. "There were other customers in there with me, Beach. Two of them, a young guy and his girlfriend, were killed by those gangbanger fucks. The scales had to be balanced."

Having seen my woman go into avenging angel mode more than once, I understood her cryptic statement at the end.

I rubbed my lips over the silken strands of her hair, then cupped the back of her neck so I could make her look up at me. "You're lucky Chief Massie made sure no one questioned your story about some vigilante cowboy."

"Hey now, it was believable. Not my fault their security cameras didn't work. And all the witnesses even described the guy who saved us."

A chuckle escaped me as I thought back to that crazy day. "You told them all to describe Clint Eastwood."

"Yeah...how was I to know some of them had no idea who Clint Eastwood was?"

"Maybe the fact that they didn't speak English."

"They have movies in India," she muttered. "Anyway, all's well that ends well. Point being, I can handle myself and I need you to give me the freedom to do what I think is right. I'll never be the kind of woman who can walk away from an injustice like that. It's not right, and I know karma puts me there for a reason."

I knew better than to even try to argue with her about karma being an actual real force in the universe. It's all coincidence and bullshit, but Sarah and Mimi both believed it; now they've got my mom and Birdie believing it as well. Shit'll happen and they'll all look at each other with these smug expressions, like they somehow knew what was going to occur.

I didn't want to admit it, but I found myself doing stuff to stay on the right side of karma lately. Not saying I'm off doing charity or any of that bullshit, but I try to show a little more patience with my brothers, and it's had a positive ripple effect throughout the club.

It was time to use some more of my hard-earned patience with my woman and give her the room she needed to not just fly, but to soar.

Stroking her cheek, I sighed. "I'll back off, but right now it's not safe for you to go out without at least one of the brothers at your back. It just isn't."

She rested her head against my chest, the soft floral scent of her shampoo rising from her hair. "Beach, how much longer is it going to be like this? I can't live my life at DEFCON 1."

I rubbed the calloused tips of my fingers over the smooth perfection of her cheek, pleasure sparking through me. My cock thickened from having her so close to me and I wondered if there would ever be a point when I wasn't starving for her. Some long-suppressed need to mate urged me to fuck her, to claim her, to own her in every way possible. But first, I needed to reassure my woman. "Things will calm down, but right now there are special circumstances that make it more dangerous than usual. I was worried about you. Can you imagine how you'd feel if I pulled a vanishing act?"

"You're right, I'm sorry. I handled this badly." She sighed. "I didn't know I'd be gone so long. I thought I'd be back before you noticed I was gone, but it turned out to be a longer process than I'd anticipated."

"You didn't think *what* was gonna take so long?"

"Honey, it's your birthday tomorrow. I wanted your present to be a surprise."

Damn, I'd totally forgotten about that. With all the shit going down around me with legal issues, a brother headed to jail, and a missing shipment of guns, I had no time left to think about myself. But Sarah had remembered, and a warm glow flared in my chest as I gazed down at her earnest face. With her hair swept back, she seemed so corruptible, and I ran my lips over her forehead, needing to touch her in a fundamental way that was beyond explanation. Yeah, we fought, but we always made up, and each fight shaved some of the rough edges on our relationship, brought us closer together. My trust in her was absolute and I fucking adored her.

"You got me a present, huh?"

"Yep."

"I told you I don't need anything but you." Nuzzling her temple, I drew her scent into my lungs and let the warmth of my love for her run through me.

Her body grew tight and she leaned back enough so she could look up at me with a nervous expression that set me on alert. "I know. That's why I got you what you asked for."

"What?"

A vulnerable expression came over her, one I'd never seen before that made her look young and unsure, far different from her usual hard-as-nails mask she wore to face the world. "You've made me happier than anyone ever has in my entire life, Carlos. I don't think you understand just how precious you are to me. I wake up every day, unafraid, safe and content in a way I'd only dreamed I could be. The love you give me so freely…you have no idea how good it feels to know you love me. To know you mean it. I've been starved for affection and now I have so much I don't know what to do with it."

"You're easy to love."

Her gaze darted away and I inwardly cursed. Even though I'd told her plenty of times that I loved her, she hadn't been able to say it back yet. Something about her past had fucked up that phrase for her, but she hadn't shared with me what it was yet. While she was an old soul in some ways, in others she was still a scared child who was terrified of the dark and weary of anyone getting too close. It hurt that she couldn't tell me those words back, but I know she loves me because she shows me every single day in every way that matters.

I was used to her arguing that I couldn't love her, that it was too soon and all the usual deflective crap she liked to spout out when she was emotionally uncomfortable, so I was surprised when she murmured, "Thank you."

"What?"

A pink flush raced over her cheeks, making the blue in her eyes stand out more. "Thank you. I'm—uh, well, my therapist and I have been working on my…issues, and she pointed out that when I try to talk you out of loving me, I'm hurting you. So instead of arguing with you that I suck, I'm going to try to accept it and say thank you instead."

It did hurt that she seemed to find herself so unworthy of being loved, but I didn't say that. "Baby doll, you're too hard on yourself. Can't you see that I'm the one unworthy of you?"

She blinked rapidly as her eyes grew glassy with unshed tears. "Stop, I'm going to cry."

I lightly brushed my lips over her forehead. "*Mi Corazón.*"

"Are you still mad at me?"

"Yeah, but I'll get over it." I grabbed her wrists with the intent of bending her over my desk and showing her how much I loved her, but her yelp had me releasing her quickly.

She cradled her wrist to her chest and I noticed that her shirt sleeve had ridden up enough to reveal a bright white bandage wrapped around her wrist. "What the fuck?"

Chewing her lower lip, she tried to hide her bandaged wrist behind her back. "It's nothing."

"Nothing?" I stalked closer to her while she backed away. "You disappear and then show back up hurt and you don't tell me? That's not fuckin' nothing!"

"Calm down."

"Let me see your wrist."

"No."

"Sarah, let me see your damn wrist."

"No!"

We were facing each other across my desk know, and while I could have reached over and made her show me, there was a high likelihood she'd have her gun out of its concealed holster and up against the side of my head before I could draw a breath.

Trying for tolerance, I said in a low voice, "Please."

To my shock, she stamped her foot like a kid having a tantrum and said, "Dammit, this isn't how it's supposed to happen! I had this whole thing planned out how I would show you and you're ruining it."

Completely confused now, I gripped my hands into fists and tried to be patient with her. "Woman, you better start making some sense, and soon, or I'm gonna come over there and spank that pretty ass until you can't sit down."

Tapping her foot in a pissed-off rhythm, she crossed her arms and glared at me. "You're such a dick."

"I know, now show me your wrist."

She glared at me, but when I didn't look away, she finally huffed out, "Fine, but my way would have been so much better. It was awesome, and you're going to totally miss it because you have no patience."

Jerking up the sleeve of her shirt, she picked at the tape holding the bandage to her skin with her red-painted nails, muttering unflattering things about me the whole time. I ignored her, focused on the injury that she was trying so hard to hide from me.

At first I didn't understand what I was seeing, but as she turned her wrist to me, my heart seized in my chest then I couldn't breathe, couldn't force my lungs to inhale past the happiness filling me.

All I could do was stare at her beautiful, delicate wrist, forever marked with my darkness.

Suddenly shy, Sarah went to withdraw her wrist, but I gripped her by the forearm as she whispered, "I wanted to show you that I'm yours, Beach; that you don't have to worry about me wearing a patch. That I may be younger, but my commitment to you is as solid as your commitment to me. We belong together, and though I may not have waited as long, I have waited my whole life for you."

I raised her wrist higher, my lungs finally filling with oxygen as I let out a slow breath at the sight of "Beach" tattooed onto the pale skin of her inner wrist in elegant script.

Words failed me and I could only stare at the permanent mark of my name on her body, of my brand on her flesh that would let everyone who saw her know she was mine.

"Baby…"

"You don't like it?"

"I love it. I love *you*." I lifted my gaze to her shy one then gave her a soft kiss before saying, "You're never gonna regret being mine, Sarah, I swear it to you."

"When I first came to Austin with you, you said you'd make the rest of my life nothing but happiness, and you have."

Without another word, I hauled her over my desk, not caring that the careful stacks of papers were now scattered on the floor. Our lips met and that electric zing shot through me that I always got when I kissed my woman, a fire that burned through my blood right into my soul.

As she melted against me, I swore that no matter what happened in the future, I was never letting her go.

Chapter 4

Sarah

I stared at the computer screen, forcing my tired brain to absorb the words before me. While I loved my modern art appreciation class I was taking online, right now my brain was in freak-out mode over the events of the last few weeks.

Bad luck had come to visit Iron Horse, then decided to stay. My gut was telling me something bad was going on, that the predators were circling our home, but Beach was so overwhelmed with running the club that he came home exhausted and the last thing he needed was me talking about some illusive bad feeling I had.

At first it had been little things, houses being robbed, vague threats being made, and then it had escalated to a club sweet butt being raped and beaten then left on the road leading to the Iron Horse MC clubhouse.

It was a message, and an insult, all rolled up into one.

Not that I gave a fuck about any of that. I was far more concerned with the woman who had been taken, a girl scarcely older than I was whose only crime was partying with Iron Horse. The girl, Ashley, had paid dearly for that sin. They'd cut up her face, and while we had a plastic surgeon who would work miracles on her, it would take time. I'd set her up with a job on the Caribbean Island Iron Horse owned to get her away from the bad memories.

I hadn't been to the island yet, but Beach promised me when things calmed down we'd go there for two weeks. While we wouldn't have the whole sixteen-mile island to ourselves—half of it was rented out to people willing to pay obscene amounts of money for a private beach—the other half was Iron Horse's official vacation club.

Yeah, it seemed weird that one of the perks of belonging to the MC was vacationing for free in a tropical paradise, but I'd seen where the island was on the maps and realized it was in a very good position for smuggling. Not that I'd asked Beach about it, he'd just give me blank face and tell me the less I knew the better, but I wasn't stupid and I was the daughter of a gun smuggler. I'd seen enough of my father's work to know how most supply routes operated, and that island was perfectly positioned for smuggling stuff from South America.

For the tenth time, I tried to process the words I was reading, then gave up with a sigh and kicked my chair back from my white-wood computer desk. The whole room was done in shades of white, ranging from a bright crystal to a deep cream. The space wasn't huge, but it did have large windows that looked out over the gated front drive of our home, and down the steep hill beyond to a great view of the majority of Austin. Our place was on top of one of the ridgetops, so on a clear day like today, it felt like I could see forever. The view was surprisingly green thanks to the recent rains and I allowed my gaze to take in the beauty, hoping it would soothe me.

My emotions were all over the place as a knot of worry grew in my belly that left me feeling slightly nauseous. I knew from my intelligence network, aka the old ladies of Iron Horse, that a couple of the brothers had gotten busted during a run, but we didn't know who yet. Only thing anyone had heard was the club's kick-ass lawyers had been called in to arrange bail. My man was handling stuff behind the scenes, no doubt greasing the right palms and calling in favors to get his boys out. I'd had no idea how corrupt the government was until I got together with Beach. Anyone, and I do mean anyone, has a price, and my man often knew just what to offer to get what he wanted.

Still, I worried. I worried so much I was exhausted with it, and considered going to sleep on the small daybed in my office, but my rumbling stomach reminded me I'd skipped breakfast.

I made my way downstairs to the bright blue and steel-grey kitchen, where one of our maids, Juanita, hummed as she bustled about the kitchen. Her well-rounded hips shook as she danced to whatever music was playing on her headphones. I loved to watch her move; she still did salsa with her husband a couple times a month, and you could just tell by watching her that she was having fun. When her dark brown eyes met mine, she flushed, then laughed and pulled her earbuds out.

"How are you doing, Ms. Anderson?"

"Good. Tired and hungry. Do we have anything you could heat up real quick?"

"Of course. What are you in the mood for?"

"I don't know…my stomach's kind of off."

She gave me a considering look that I didn't understand, then smiled in a way that softened her whole face. "How about we do grilled cheese again? I will even cut the crust off for you."

Laughing, I made my way over to the sleek, circular ebony table that occupied a large breakfast nook. "Deal."

We chatted while she worked about her massive family; she was the oldest of eleven children and had four grown children of her own, and they all lived in Texas. Hearing her stories was better than any Spanish soap opera, and I laughed until my cheeks hurt as she talked about her youngest son, who liked to think he was a Lothario, and how two girls he was dating found out about each other and beat his butt at a nightclub.

As amusing as her tales were, my stomach kept scrunching up as I checked my phone what felt like every minute, but was probably every ten seconds.

"Put that thing away," Juanita scolded me as she placed my plate before me, the scent of the warm bread and cheese making my mouth flood with saliva. "Always checking for the text, always staring at the little screen like it holds the secrets of the universe. What is important is what's here, right in front of you, right now."

Shaking my head, I reluctantly pushed my phone away then thanked her as she handed me a big glass of milk.

She left me to eat and I scarfed down the sandwich, grinning when she returned with a second one for me, along with some pills.

"What are these?"

"Your vitamins."

"I have vitamins?"

"*Sí*, you do now. I see you looking tired all the time, how hard you work and how busy you are taking care of others. You need to keep your body healthy, and you will not give it the rest it needs, so take your vitamins. Then maybe you should take a nap."

"But Beach—"

"If he calls, I come wake you up. Mouse asked me to look after you, and I love you like one of my own, so you will take your vitamins and you will go take a nap." She gave me this…this mothering look that made me feel four years old. "Am I clear?"

I merely nodded and took another bite of my sandwich, mildly surprised at how stern Juanita could be. Then again, with her hellion sons, I guess she needed to have some brass to her. That, and the fact she worked for the president of an outlaw MC. She gave me a wink then put her headphones back on and began to clean up the kitchen, humming to herself under her breath in a slightly off-key way that had me turning away to hide my smile.

Knowing she'd hassle me until I gave in, I went upstairs to the master bedroom and collapsed face first on my massive four-poster, black iron bed. It was a monstrosity with chains and cuffs hanging from all the posts. I'd fussed at Beach when he'd added them, not wanting the maids to know our sex life, but he'd merely laughed then went about showing me how wonderful it could be to have cuffs and chains on one's sturdy bed. A soft breath escaped me as I rolled onto my back and stared at the ceiling.

Daylight streamed through the big windows facing the valley and I squinted before saying, "Gloria, darkness please."

Beach always laughed at me for addressing the house computer by name, and for being polite, but I didn't care. To me, the magical being that made things happen when I spoke could have some sort of artificial intelligence, and I figured I'd be better off if my house liked me. After all, I loved it. This ninety-five hundred square foot mansion had been designed back in the 1980s by one of the nation's premier modern design architects at the time. It had taken a little bit of work to restore it, but I'd taken full advantage of having a clean slate to work with for designing the interior of the home. Beach let me pick out and do everything, from ordering the fabric for the couches, to haggling with the masonry guy about the shit job he was doing on our fireplace.

Happy memories eased the knot in my belly and I grabbed Beach's pillow, holding it tight and inhaling his scent.

I must have fallen asleep, because I woke up to Beach shaking my shoulder. "*Mi Corazón*, you need to wake up. Got someone here you need to see."

Turning over slowly, I blinked up at him, still feeling like I could sleep another fifty hours. The sleek black marble nightstand lamps were on and the warm illumination made Beach's face seem older and worried. Without thought, I reached up and smoothed back his hair, my fingertips threading through the hints of silver streaking the gold here and there. "Hi, honey, who's here?"

"Babe, brace yourself."

Instantly I sat straight up, all thoughts of sleep gone as I reached over the edge of the bed and clutched Beach's wrist. "What?"

A million terrible things went through my mind, everything from something happening to the club to finding out my parents were right to be paranoid and the world was crashing down around us.

What I didn't expect him to say was, "Your mom is downstairs, and she's been beat pretty bad."

"Oh my God, Mimi?" I released his arm and started to roll out of bed, but he stopped me.

"No, Billie."

Instant, raw, visceral fear had me wrapping my arms around myself in a protective gesture. "Billie?"

"Yeah."

"Is downstairs right now? In our house?"

"Yeah." He frowned at me. "Sarah, you okay? You just went pale as a ghost."

Before he could say another word, I gagged, a heavy wave of nausea churning the remains of my lunch in my stomach. When my mouth filled with saliva, a sure sign I was going to puke, I shoved a concerned Beach out of the way and managed to make it to the toilet. I barfed so hard, and for so long, my stomach ached by the time I managed to calm down. An icy sweat covered my body and I slowly became aware that part of that cold came from the wet washcloth a very concerned Beach was holding against my neck.

With his cut off, and just wearing a pristine white t-shirt, his broad shoulders seemed even bigger, and I had to fight back tears as I stared into the face of the man I loved more than anything in the world.

"Water, please. And a cup with some mouthwash."

After making sure I was propped up against the wall, he hustled over to the sink, leaving me to stare at my reflection in the floor-to-ceiling mirror that made up the far wall. My reflection was less than flattering and I wondered what my mother would see when she looked at me.

I haven't seen her since she'd broken into my house and stolen a bunch of stuff—then tried to blame it on Marley—close to three years ago. She'd tried to contact me from time to time, but I think she believed me that if I ever saw her again, I was going to the police with everything I knew about her, personal consequences be damned.

Why the hell would she show up now?

Something really bad must be going on if she'd sought me out.

Or she wanted something from me.

Beach crouched before me, his faded jeans tightening around his thick thighs as he squatted down so I didn't have to strain my neck looking at him.

"Thanks."

I took the cut-crystal glass and drained it, forcing my stomach to accept the liquid. After I was sure it would stay down, I rinsed my mouth out with the mouthwash really well before spitting it into the empty cup. Even as freaked out as I was, I didn't want Beach breathing in my vomit breath.

"You okay?"

"Yeah, I was just...upset." Closing my eyes, I rubbed my temples and tried to get my shocked brain to focus. "Did you really say Billie's here?"

Frowning at me in concern, he nodded while cracking his tattooed knuckles in agitation. "That's right. She's downstairs with Vance."

"What? Why?"

He held my face with both his hands, ignoring my still sweaty skin. "Sarah, honey. Your mom…well, she's hurting."

Despite my best attempts to harden it, my heart instinctively ached at the thought of my mom being in pain even if I knew she deserved to burn in the fires of hell for all eternity for some of the shit she's done, the people she's coldheartedly ruined, and even killed.

"Oh."

"She's okay, had a doc look her over, but with her broken ribs she isn't going to be able to do much for herself for a few weeks."

"How did she get here?"

"She showed up at your house in Las Vegas, barely walkin'. When she started banging on the door, begging you to let her in, it tripped the cameras. The security system we set up on your place sent out an alert and one of Smoke's men at his security company saw your mom slumped against the front door then called it into the club. I was busy dealin' with shit in another state, so Vance handled it for me."

"And his first instinct was to bring her to Austin? To our *home*?"

Beach gave me a funny look, the tone of his voice almost scolding. "You don't want her here? I know you two are fightin', but Sarah, she's your mom and she needs your help. I busted my ribs years ago spillin' my bike on a slick road and I can tell you that she won't be able to care for herself like she'll need. It's too painful and she says she doesn't have anywhere else to go."

Shit, could did I say? As far as Beach knew, my mother was a fuck-up who'd been married a bunch of times, and was a harsh disciplinarian. I hadn't told him yet the more sordid details of my past, my shame making me wish that part of my life would just disappear. If Beach knew some of the things I'd done…the marriages I'd destroyed, the good men I'd brought low while helping my mother, he'd be disgusted with me.

Trying to buy myself time, I rubbed my face with my hands. "Sorry, my brain isn't working. I'm kind of in shock here. How did she get here again?"

"Vance went out to Vegas and got her. He said she refused to go to a hospital, but that she needs our help. She left her current boyfriend after he beat the shit out of her and she needs a place to lay low and heal. Someplace safe. I know you'd do the same for my mom in a heartbeat if she ever needed it."

He loved his mom, and he loved me, so that was all the reason he needed to bring the viper to his bosom…if guy's had bosoms.

Beach's mom, Mouse, was super amazingly awesome and down to earth; she loved me and her love was fierce. If his mom had ever shown up banging on our doorstep, beat to shit, I'd move heaven and hell to make it right. But Mouse was a good woman, salt of the earth, while my mother was nothing but poison.

If only he knew how being around her had been slowly killing me for years, how she'd risked my life again and again without thought, manipulating me until I didn't know up from down, left from right. Beach thought all my issues came from Morrie, having no clue just how bad my childhood was.

I'd fucked myself with my own lies, painting myself into a corner that I couldn't think of a way out of.

Mistaking my silence for worry, Beach pulled me into his arms and held me close. "Seriously, baby, I've got this handled, but I'm sure you want to see your mom. Just brace yourself 'cause someone beat her up good."

I merely nodded, standing then momentarily considering changing and straightening myself up. It wasn't because I wanted to look good for her, but when I was growing up, if she was in a bad mood and caught me dressing in a slovenly manner, she'd make me do chores until bedtime with no supper. Knowing that she was going to see me in pink sweatpants and an oversized Def Leppard t-shirt with my hair all fucked up had triggered my old litany of things I had to do to keep my chaotic yet OCD mom happy.

Beach tugged my arm. "Come on, you look fine."

I didn't even attempt to smile as I followed him out of our bedroom, steeling myself for the shit storm that had turned up on my doorstep.

As we came down the stairs, I could see a group of Iron Horse men talking in our foyer, their black leather cuts a stark contrast to the pure white perfection of the two-story room. When they spotted us, they grew hushed, and I found a bunch of really mean bikers giving me openly sympathetic looks. I suppose I should be crying or something, like a normal girl would if her mom was hurt, but I couldn't allow myself any emotions right now. With each step I raised my internal walls higher, then reinforced them with steel, then raised them again and reinforced them with titanium.

I couldn't let her back into my life, no matter what happened.

This wouldn't be the first time I saw my mother black and blue, and probably wouldn't be the last. In a very fucked-up way, my mom liked being hit, liked douchebag men who treated her like shit emotionally but spoiled her financially. Eventually she'd have enough of their garbage, or they'd have enough of hers and they'd part ways, but not before she'd come home with a split lip and a black eye more than once. It used to make me angry, made me want to go kick those guys' asses for touching my mother, but as I'd grown older, I realized my mother sought these men out, looked for ones who would abuse her.

My stomach twisted again as we walked past Smoke, who reached out to touch my arm as I passed.

"Need me to get Swan?"

"No!" The word came out in an aggressive shout and I had to dial my bitch back by about a million. "No, please, don't disturb her. You know how she is, how hard it is for her to be around people. Promise me you'll keep her away from all of this, please. My mother…they don't have a good relationship and it would be stressful for them both."

Smoke frowned. "Not sure if that's the best idea. If it was my mom, I'd want to know."

I let my head fall forward, my slightly tangled, light blonde hair hiding my face almost to my chin. Jesus, another mama's boy. How in the world this bunch of degenerate fucks had some of the world's best moms was totally beyond me. I must have *really* done something bad in a past life for karma to stick me with *my* birth mother.

Beach waited for me, but I could see he was impatient so I cut to the quick with Smoke, needing him to understand me.

I took a step closer, the dark wood floor cool beneath my bare feet, and lowered my voice. "Do not make Swan face the club, please. Once, when we were younger, I was at the mall with her and some bitchy girls were giving us shit because we were attracting all the male attention. While I had no problem cutting them down to size, one of them grabbed Swan and she threw up all over the girl. Swan was so embarrassed, she refused to leave the compound for nine months."

"What?" Smoke barely breathed.

"I didn't tell you the full extent of her sensory issues because she hates for people to know how much it bothers her, hates pity and appearing weak." I gave him a humorless smile, aware that Beach was behind me, but that the rest of the men had stepped back, no doubt warned away by my man's rabid-tiger glare. "I'm not saying she's an invalid. Through therapy she's gotten to the point where if someone touches her clothing, it's okay, but if someone touches her bare skin, any skin, it pains her. Now, think about what would happen if you brought her here, all these people, unfamiliar place, to see a woman she doesn't particularly like?"

"Shit," Smoke muttered, and I was surprised by the way his gaze strengthened as it met mine. "She doesn't like your mom?"

I looked him dead in the eye and let him see all the things I couldn't put into words. "Not at all. They don't really get along; my mom doesn't know how to handle Swan's eccentricities so Billie gets all weird and awkward with her. It's difficult for them both to physically be around one another so they just avoid each other."

Not looking particularly happy about the decision, Smoke nodded. "Might not be the best idea to throw Swan into the clubhouse face first, might be better to ease her into it. But Sarah, you're gonna have to tell her at some point. I seen a lot of beatings and your mom took a hard one about a week ago, and is still hurtin'. We've made her as comfortable as we can, so she might be a little loopy."

Right away, acid burned my throat and I forced myself to nod. Right, my mother was loopy? When was she *not* fucking stoned out of her mind? And I do mean out of her mind. The woman is no longer sane, her brain fried on over twenty years of indulging heavily in everything from coke to heroine. I just wondered if she'd be coherent enough for me to figure out why she was here and what she wanted.

"Right."

Beach squeezed my shoulder gently and murmured, "I'm here for you, baby, whatever you need."

I closed my eyes then drew in a deep breath, channeling every ounce of personal strength I had to face the woman who, right before she tried to rob me, had been blitzed out of her mind on PCP and had, in a psychotic rage, tried to stab me.

She was dangerous, and there was no way in fuck I was going to let her harm my family, new or old.

Chapter 5

At the sight of my mother's black, blue, green, and yellow bruised face, I froze, blinking hard. Her long, blonde hair was held back in an elegant, low ponytail and her lips were so swollen she looked like a grotesque parody of herself. One of her blue eyes, so like my own, stared back at me while the other was hidden behind a swollen-shut eyelid. Big diamonds, which I knew were real, glittered in her ears. She'd never wear fake, and I realized she was doing better than when we'd last seen each other. Her body had filled out a little bit, no longer stick thin and ravaged by heroine.

Now, I'd seen her beat up before—her taste in rich, violent men who liked to use their fists on her had led to more than one week spent hiding from the world while she healed. I have no idea why she sought these men out, but obviously some sick part of her craved their viciousness.

It fucked with my head to think about the reasons she'd been attracted to my father, and I started walking again as I realized what would happen if he found out she was here. My father loathed Billie, with very good reason, and she knew better than to get any closer to him than she had to; it wouldn't be good. And then there was Mimi, who'd burn down the world for me to keep me safe and do it with a smile. I think she'd like an excuse to carve up Billie's face. A giggle almost escaped me as I thought about Mimi's favorite threat against Billie, to cut out her implants and beat her with them.

I shook my head to clear my thoughts as the room fell silent and everyone either looked at me or Billie, who was watching me closely. She knew coming here was a risk, and like some kind of fucked-up adrenaline junkie, she was waiting to see if her gamble payed off.

While I had no idea what in the world she'd gotten herself into this time, I forced any feeling of pity away. "What happened?"

That got me some odd looks, but I focused only on her. Reading her face with all those bruises was next to impossible and I gazed above her right shoulder, an old trick for appearing like I was looking at her, when I really wasn't. My eyes focused on a lovely, smooth crystal vase full of bright red, orange, and—of all things—blue tulips that added a splash of color to the pale, textured gold of the wall behind my mother.

She reclined on my white velvet fainting couch wearing a shirt that managed to show a lot of cleavage and a pair of tight yoga pants. Even though she was close to rocking her sixties, my mother still had an amazing body, and it wasn't lost on me that a couple of the older brothers seemed to notice.

Shit.

The absolute last thing I wanted her to do was hook up with a member of the Iron Horse MC as her next conquest.

"Sarah." Her husky voice broke my wandering thoughts and I reached out, grasping Beach's hand in my own for strength against whatever bullshit she was about to throw at me. "I'm sorry, I didn't know where else to go. I'm so sorry to be an imposition on you. I told them to let me go to a hotel and I'll be fine, but they wouldn't listen."

As she talked, the glittering rings she wore flashed on her long, artistic fingers. Every movement she made was a dance, even when she was covered in bruises. Always preening for a male audience. I ran my gaze down her body, noticing she wore sandals with a high, thin heel. She couldn't be hurt too bad if she was strutting around on stiletto spikes. The sight of her ridiculous, bright yellow shoes made me want to take them off her feet and hurl them, and her, out the door.

Beach spoke before I could, which was probably a good thing, considering my temper was prodding at my self-control. "Billie, you're always welcome here. I'm Carlos, Sarah's man."

My mother let out a soft, fluttering sob that would have been perfect on one of those terribly overacted Spanish soap operas. "Oh, Carlos, thank you. I-I'm so scared. My fiancé and I have fought in the past, but nothing like this. Walt is rich, and I'm afraid he'll find me if I use any of our bank cards."

"So you need money? How much?"

The brothers stared at me but I ignored them, hoping I had enough in my savings to make Billie go away without leaving me bankrupt.

"No, sweetheart, I don't need your money. I gave Hustler some jewelry to pawn for me. I'll use the money to get safe. Please don't worry about me. I knew my being here would make you uncomfortable and...well—I brought this on myself. I shouldn't have pushed him so much."

I clenched my teeth so hard I was afraid they were going to crack as I choked on her martyrdom act. "Gentlemen, I would like a moment to speak alone with my mother. All this attention has to be making her uncomfortable."

"Oh, no, Sarah," my mom gave me a pathetic look, "these men don't scare me, I feel safe with them."

I glanced out of the corner of my eye at Beach and had to hide my disgust at the soft expression warming his rugged face. God f'ing dammit, he'd fallen for her shit—hook, line, and sinker. She knew just what to say in order to have all these men feel responsible for her somehow. It was a popular manipulation of hers that she used often because it worked so well on macho men. I wanted to sock Beach in the kidney to stop him from giving my mom any kind of attention, but knew I'd come off as a psycho.

She wanted to play games, fine. I let my lower lip tremble, then made a soft noise of sadness, tears filling my eyes. Yep, I could cry on command, a skill my mother had taught me when I was barely seven years old in a way so fucked up I still didn't think about it if I could help it. Let's just say I'll never have a pet again. Those acting skills came in handy now as I let fat tears spill from my eyes.

"They're good men, and Beach is the greatest." I looked at him, then leaned up on my tiptoes and pressed a soft kiss to his lips. "Mom, you can trust them, because I do, completely. They've proven over and over again that they have a code of honor like you wouldn't believe. Might be a little twisted, but they're one of the rare breed of men who give their word, and mean it. I'm so blessed to have them in my life."

I meant every word I said, so it made the words ring true in my voice and gaze. While I hated playing with the men's emotions, I'd do whatever I could to keep her away from them. Giving Beach one more kiss, I smiled at him and blinked back tears.

"Honey, I need a moment to speak to my mom alone, okay?"

"Whatever you need," he murmured just low enough for me to hear, his gaze warming for a moment before it turned cold again as he looked at his men and gave them the oh-so-eloquent chin lift that seemed to have a thousand different meanings in biker culture.

As soon as everyone was out of earshot, I put on my big-girl panties and strode over to the couch, the anger open on my face. "What the fuck are you doing here?"

Shrinking back as if she was afraid I would hit her, which was ridiculous, because the only times I'd fought her had been in self-defense, Billie whimpered, "I'm sorry, I'll leave as soon as I can. Please, I'm sorry."

Memories of her saying that exact phrase to the monsters of my past as they beat her pulled an unwilling sympathy from me. Shit. If only I could truly be as coldhearted as I pretended.

Sucking in a deep breath, I forced my eyes to meet hers. "What happened?"

Shame, or at least I think it was shame—with her swollen face it was hard to tell—twisted her battered features. "I tried to leave my pimp, but he found me. I didn't want to work the street, but he said I was old so men wouldn't pay top dollar for me anymore."

Closing my eyes, I prayed no one was close enough to have heard that. Embarrassment filled me as if I was the one who had sold my body for money. She'd escorted before, but she'd always gone to one of those high-class brothels out where it was legal. I knew this because when I was thirteen, one of my friends' older brothers went to the brothel and said he'd seen her there. To say I'd been devastated was an understatement, and that's the year I'd started smoking pot, something I quit last month so I could focus my attention on my classwork.

I felt dirty; just being around her was like standing in a ditch full of sewage.

I could only imagine how my mother felt, having to say those words. At one time, so long ago it felt like a century, my mother had been a vibrant young woman. According to what I'd learned from my dad and Mimi, Billie had doted on me and my sister before my parents divorced, an amazing mother in every way. That was why my dad hadn't been worried about her moving to a new house across the compound with me. He had no reason to believe she'd take off in the middle of the night—and take me along with her. I've wondered if their divorce, or just the strain of being married to my crazy dad, had been the proverbial straw that broke the mental camel's back and began Billie's descent into narcissistic madness.

To see how far she'd fallen down the hole of mental illness and drug addiction struck me like a blow, and against my will, a couple of tears escaped. "Why are you doing this to yourself? Why can't you just be normal?"

"I'm sorry," she whispered again, her tears joining my own. "I'm so sorry."

The guilt in her voice disturbed me. She must have fucked up really bad to be feeling guilty about anything. "Just tell me, are you putting me in danger by being here? The truth, Mom."

"Yes," she whispered. "If my old pimp finds me, he'll try to bring me back. I might have stabbed him while I was trying to escape. They had me chained to a bed—"

I took a step back, as if I'd been slapped, and if felt like I had. "They chained you to a bed?"

"It doesn't matter." She tried to sit up and groaned. "I'll leave."

"No," I said quietly. "You can stay until you heal. But not here. I'll set you up with a furnished apartment and get you what you need, but you have to leave once you're well enough. I don't want you living here. Don't contact me, don't talk to me, don't even use my name. Understood?"

Billie nodded eagerly then winced. "I will, I promise."

Even though I felt like the world's biggest bitch for what I was about to say, I knelt down and stared into her face, needing her to know I was completely serious. "If you do anything, and I do mean anything, to hurt my family—blood or club—I will make sure you can never hurt anyone ever again. Do you understand? If you came here with any ulterior motives to somehow fuck me over because you're a selfish bitch, you better wipe those thoughts from your mind right now."

"Yes," she whispered then curled up on the couch. "You really love him?"

"More than anyone."

That struck deep, and I could tell when her voice came out hollow. "Oh."

Only my mother would be surprised that her constant abuse had killed my affection for her.

Without another word, I rose to my feet and kept my attention locked on the floor before me, my heart heavy and my mind racing. Was she telling the truth? I knew from personal experience she was a chronic liar and did it with ease, but those bruises…the pain she must be in. I've been beaten up once or twice in my life and it fucking sucked, your body aching for weeks as it tried to heal all the broken bits. An echo of remembered pain overtook me for a moment and I paused, gathering myself, before I hit the foyer where the men stood talking.

The scent of coffee hung heavy in the air as I took in the tired faces around me. For the first time, I wondered what else had happened tonight, my mind too preoccupied with Billie to focus on anything but her drama. It had been so nice, so freeing to not have her in my life, and I wanted to return to that state as soon as possible.

The guys gave me those stupid sympathetic looks again, and more than a few patted my shoulder as I walked past.

Beach spotted me coming and held his arms out. "Come here, baby."

I gratefully burrowed into his embrace, allowing his strength to become my own.

He kissed the top of my head and rubbed my back. "You talk to her?"

"Yeah."

"She tell you the name of the guy who beat her? Vance tried to get it out of her but she refused to give him up."

My mind spun as I debated once again lying for my mother, or telling the horrible truth, that I was the daughter of a drug-addicted whore. "No, she wouldn't tell me."

"Why is she tryin' to protect the fucker who did that to her?"

I shrugged, my throat filling with bile.

"Doesn't matter. We'll make sure she's taken care of."

Eager to get her out of my house, I blurted out, "Hey, don't we have medical equipment at the club?"

"Yeah."

"Let's take my mom there. That way she's close to medical care and figure out where she'd be best off. She might need a rehab if she's badly injured."

Beach pressed a kiss to my forehead before pulling back. "I'll get her any private nurse she needs, babe. We'll put her out in the pool house."

Our "pool house" was actually a three-bedroom home that sat at the back of our property near the infinity pool. I'd had it built with Marley in mind. I missed her like the dickens and was trying to talk her into moving out here from Vegas. The house had been built with her in mind, and I did not like the thought of my mother soiling it with her presence. Then again, that was better than having her actually inside the house. Chewing my lower lip, I wondered if I could set up surveillance cameras in there without anyone noticing.

The fact that my gut was telling me to keep an eye on her pushed me to tell Beach at least a little bit of the truth.

"Can I talk to you for a second, in private?"

"Of course." He said a few words to the men lingering around us before I took him upstairs to our bedroom.

Once we were inside, I turned on him. "Honey, she can't stay in our pool house."

Looking completely confused, he frowned. "Why not?"

"Because…because I don't want her living here."

"What?"

Running my hands through my hair, I let out a frustrated noise. "I haven't seen her for over two years for a reason, Beach, and it's not because I haven't had time to call her. Honestly, if she hadn't shown up on our doorstep tonight, I probably never would have seen her again. I don't *want* to see her again."

"I know, babe, but I also know you'd feel terrible if somethin' happened to her. I'll set her up in an apartment and have the boys keep an eye on her, okay?"

I wanted to tell him to send her to a rehab in Siberia but managed to choke those bitter words back. "Okay. Just…don't trust her."

His eyes narrowed and he took a step closer to me. "Somethin' you need to tell me?"

"What? No, no, I just don't trust her, and I don't want you to fall for her shit. She's very good at manipulating men to get what she wants."

He smirked at me. "Babe, she's not gonna get anythin' over on me or my boys."

I wanted to shake him and tell him about all the brilliant men she'd conned, but I was trapped in my own lies and had to stare at him in mute misery.

With a sigh, he closed the distance between us and tucked me into him. "I'll have someone keep an eye on her."

"Thank you."

"You okay?"

No, not in the least, but I couldn't tell him that.

"Yeah, I'm fine."

"It'll be okay, Sarah. You'll see."

While I highly doubted that was true, I prayed he was right.

Chapter 6

Seven Weeks Later

Carlos "Beach" Rodriquez

My hands shook with anger as I gripped the handlebars of my motorcycle, unable to believe the sight I was seeing across the street.

One of the bars we owned was going up in flames, the second property of ours this week that had met a burning end. Firefighters did their best to keep the flames from spreading to the other businesses on the south side of Austin, but I knew our place was a total loss. I'm sure they'd find signs the fire had been professionally set, just like the last one, and I had to grit my teeth to try and keep my calm.

Someone was fucking with us, hardcore, and so far we'd been unable to find out who it was.

Sledge stood a few feet away talking to one of the firemen, nodding as he pointed to the building. My VP's family members were all firefighters and Sledge had a ton of contacts, as well as a knowledge of fires I didn't possess. The headache that I'd been nursing all night throbbed harder and I lifted one hand from my motorcycle to rub my eyes. It was six a.m. and I hadn't been to sleep yet, called away from my bed and my woman by emergency after emergency.

It was making me irritable as fuck and when Sledge came back to me, I snapped, "Let me guess, they don't know shit."

Looking equally haggard, Sledge ran his hand over the minute stubble on his bald head while staring at the fire. "Got that right."

"Yo, Prez," Vance called from somewhere behind me.

I turned to find him coming up to us holding cups of coffee, the chain on his wallet chiming softly with each step. While the guy could be a major fucking prick, he had his moments. I gratefully took one cup and sipped through the small hole in the lid, just the scent of the brew waking me up a little. Thankfully Vance got me a super dark roast, 'cause I needed every ounce of caffeine.

"*Gracias.*"

Lifting his chin in the direction of the smoking building, he asked, "Learn anything?"

"No, other than it looks like it was deliberately set just like the last one."

"Fuckin' hell," Vance muttered. "Can't seem to catch a break."

"Ain't that the truth," Sledge sighed. "At least we haven't had any more sweet butts turn up dead."

Guilt at not being able to protect those women clawed at me but I shoved the emotion away. I didn't have time to feel guilty, not when I had to put an end to this shit. For the past month or so someone had been for sure fuckin' with the club, and I was pretty sure I knew why. In two days, we were gonna do a major run with cargo that included fuckin' missiles for the Russians and a bunch of shit for the Israeli mafia—including a bunch of fuckin' plants, of all things. The trucks carrying the load were in Louisiana right now, that part of the transport being handled by a different group. Once it arrived at our warehouse, our leg of the journey would begin.

"Go home," Vance said in a sympathetic voice while he looked at his phone. "Me and the boys will deal with this shit. You need to get some sleep."

"I'm good."

"Beach," Sledge interrupted with a yawn. "They've got it handled and he's right, we both need to grab some shuteye. Know I'm gonna grab myself a couple sweet butts to keep me warm then sleepin' for about twenty fuckin' hours."

I only wanted to sleep with one woman, and I wondered if she was even home. As busy as I'd been, Sarah had been even busier. She was gone as much as I was, helping out with club issues, and I missed her.

We barely saw each other and I needed to spend some time just breathing her in. This past month had been hectic as shit and I knew it was stressing my girl out. I wasn't so blind that I didn't notice she'd been dropping some of the weight she'd put on during our time together, and even with her makeup on I could see the dark circles beneath her eyes.

While I knew havin' her mom around stressed her out, so far Billie had been nothing but nice and helpful, and as far as I knew she'd stayed away from Sarah. The guys keepin' an eye on Billie said she kept to herself, other than work. We'd set her up with a job at the pawnshop and Hustler said she was one of his best salespeople. I didn't see her much, was too busy with other shit, but the few times we had interacted she'd been nothing but grateful. She'd asked about Sarah, but I wasn't about to get in the middle of a mother/daughter fight.

No fuckin' way.

"Right, I'm out. Tell Smoke to keep me updated."

"He's in Houston right now," Vance said with a small frown.

"Again?"

"Yeah."

Smoke's growing obsession with Sarah's twin sister, Swan, was beginning to worry me, but I had so many other things that needed my attention. "Tell him after this shift, I need him back in Austin."

"Got it."

It took me about an hour to get through the heavy traffic to my place up in the hills, but as I passed through the big iron gates and waved to the guards patrolling the grounds, a couple nomads I'd called in for extra protection, something inside of me settled. The big white, two-story 1980s home dominated the hilltop and had amazing views from all sides. I'd never really given a shit about architecture or any of that crap, but Sarah fucking loved it and I'd given her free rein on our house to make it our home, and she'd done an amazing job.

I drove right up to the front door, the big engine on my Harley loud in the early morning quiet, before turning my bike off and dismounting with a groan.

Damn, some days my body barely felt older than twenty, and others I felt more like I was quickly approaching eighty.

"Beach!"

Sarah bounded out the black steel front door, still in the pink cotton shorts and tank top she wore to bed. The sight of all her smooth, exposed skin had my dick twitching in interest before she threw her arms around me and hugged me tight. "I missed you. Is everything okay?"

I hugged her back before tugging her toward the house. "Not really. I'll tell you inside. I'm fuckin' beat."

Once we were up in our bedroom, Sarah took my hand and pulled me towards the bathroom. "Come on, you need this."

"Need what?"

My answer came at the sight of our huge tub filled with steaming, fragrant water. "Get naked, I'm going to wash you."

"You gettin' in the tub with me?"

"No."

"That's no fun."

She laughed and helped me out of my clothes, her hands running over my body, tracing my tattoos as she sighed in appreciation. "You're so pretty."

Laughing, I grabbed her by the back of the neck and pulled her close, loving how she smiled up at me. "Pretty?"

"Absolutely. Any woman would want to hang life-size portraits of you on the wall to stare at while jilling off."

"You're a goof."

"Yep, now get in the tub."

"Sure you don't want to join me?"

"I've got an appointment with a new gynecologist today for my yearly pap. I want to be all fresh and clean down there. Now get in the tub."

I did as she told me, vaguely wondering what exactly a pap was. Our tub was big enough that I could stretch out all the way, and I did with a low groan, my head falling back onto the curved edge of the tub as the heat soaked into me. While I didn't want to admit it, my sore lower back needed it, along with a myriad of other small aches and pains. I've lived a rough life that hasn't always been good to my body and the older I get, the more I pay for it.

Sarah proceeded to wash both me and my hair before she gave me one hell of a hand job. I wanted to return the favor but she got all weird again about her pretty pussy showing any signs of use.

Women.

As I threw myself on the bed, the chains on the posts jingled. "What time's your appointment?"

"Two, but I have a bunch of stuff to do first."

I reached out and yanked her down onto the bed with me. "It's barely seven a.m. Come back to bed with me."

She yawned, hugely, and I knew I wouldn't have to fight her too hard. "Okay, but just for a little bit. I'm still tired even though I slept eight hours."

After getting us both beneath the soft red comforter, I hauled her body next to my sated one and kissed her smooth shoulder. "Love you, baby. So fuckin' much."

She tensed for a long moment, but I waited her out, knowing those words were still so hard for her to say. Some part of her feared the power those words would give me over her, and I could only wait as patiently as I could while she battled her inner demons.

This time the silence only lasted eight seconds before she whispered, "I love you too, Carlos."

Hugging her tight, I showered kisses on her warm face. "I know you do, baby. I know."

Later that night, I attended a meeting where I went through what would happen on the run one more time with my some of my top men and a few civilians. Smoke ran a security company partially owned by the private corporation the club used for its legit business dealings, and he had some men and women on his staff who were scary good at what they did. Good enough that they were being included in this high-stakes run without wearing patches on their backs. We were at my house in what

Sarah liked to call my war room, a massive space I'd planned out for myself in the basement, right next to the panic room Smoke's company had put in here for us, one of five in the house.

What can I say? I'm a little paranoid about Sarah's safety.

The thought of my woman momentarily distracted me from looking at the hologram in the center of the table, a detailed map of how the run was going to work, our backups, and our backup's backups. This entire thing had to run as smooth as butter, and if it did, it would cement Iron Horse as the go-to club for runs in the US Southwest. Shit, we might even get some of Mike's business. So far we'd managed to avoid crossing paths in a professional context, but I knew it was only a matter of time until I started moving some of his guns.

My gaze focused in on the moving red dot that represented the transport and my pulse sped.

Missiles.

Cutting-edge weapons.

And a bunch of massive vials of some kind of silver liquid.

And a dozen saplings.

Those vials, which resembled titanium pills the size of fifty-gallon drums, were added on by the Israelis last minute, and they'd demanded an additional layer of protection. They wanted Poppy to ride with the trees. I have no idea why they wanted this, but they were adamant and swore she would be protected and returned safely to her home a much richer woman. Without a doubt, I felt guilty as hell for involving Poppy in this run, but true to form, once I'd mentioned it to her, she'd agreed without hesitation. When I'd asked her why she was okay with it, she'd merely shrugged and said, "Curiosity."

The large black leather chair creaked beneath me as I leaned back and willed my body to relax. Walking around in a constant state of readiness was going to grind my nerves into dust, and I couldn't afford that. Nine to ten hours from now, those trucks would be rolling into our warehouse, passed off to us from a group I was assured was "competent" for the transport. Considering it was the Russian fuckin' mafia sayin' that, I wondered if I should have Tom Sokolov, one of Smoke's best friends from childhood—who just happened to be related to half the fuckin' Russian mafia—with us to see if he could identify them.

Then again, I didn't want to piss off any of the Russians. The *Bratvas*, what they called their organizations, were ruthless to the bone after fighting for centuries to get to the top. Not only did they have to fight other families, they'd carved out their criminal empires against a background of war, the Soviet Union, and back-breaking hopelessness. I'd found them to be fair men, but if they had a hit out on me, they'd shake my hand then shoot me in the face.

A memory of watching a man's head explode as he was shot at close range flashed through my mind, and I willed it away.

"Smoke," Hustler called out from across the room, "Checkpoint D is a go."

On the hologram, a dot turned bright blue as the final group called in to affirm they were in position. I was taking no chances, so I had everyone out a few days early to scout and secure their positions. With everyone where they were supposed to be, I relaxed marginally, then leaned forward and placed my hands on the table before speaking over the din, "We got a long day tomorrow and we've done everything we can to make sure the run goes smooth, so I want you to go home and get some sleep."

It took me another twenty minutes to get everyone out the door, and by the time I secured the house it was past midnight.

I took the stairs to my bedroom, passing the kick-ass chandelier Sarah had found for our foyer. The giant slivers of red, blue, and yellow crystals looked cool, but somehow dangerous, like shards of razor-sharp glass would. The iron railing was smooth beneath my hand as I climbed the steps, more than eager for the treasure awaiting me in my bed.

A low amber light burned from a nightlight across the room, giving me enough illumination to see by so I didn't trip over anything in the dark. Not that I would; Sarah was almost a neat freak and would often pick up my shit before I could get to it. Still, I tried to not be a slob and took a moment to strip down and throw my shit in the hamper, then brush my teeth before I came to bed. The minty taste in my mouth reminded me of that cooling, then warming gel I'd used on Sarah a few weeks ago. That made me take a detour into our closet to grab it before I finally got to our massive bed.

Sarah was sprawled out in the middle, awake and watching me.

"Hey, beautiful." I smiled as I tossed the tube onto the table next to the bed before sliding beneath the covers with her. "You're a sight for sore eyes."

Her lower lip trembled and tears filled her eyes. For the first time I noticed how puffy her face was from crying and how she clung to me. I couldn't see anything physically wrong with her, but worry filled me nonetheless. "Babe? You hurt?"

"No…" She sucked in a breath and buried her face against my neck. "Just a long day."

"Wanna talk about it?"

"*No.*"

She said that word with such vehemence, I rolled her onto her back so I could see her face more clearly. "Who upset you? I'll fuckin' kill 'em."

For some reason that made her burst out into semi-hysterical laughter and I *really* grew worried.

"Oh, Carlos," she finally sighed once she'd calmed down then studied me with a solemn expression. "Everything okay with you? I know tomorrow is that big thing I'm not supposed to know about."

"You sure you're okay? Doctor appointment go all right?"

She stroked my cheek, then nodded. "Perfectly healthy. Just a little stressed out."

I took her hand and kissed her knuckles, the skin smooth and perfect beneath my lips. "It'll get better, I promise. Few weeks, you'll have a break from school and I'm takin' you to the island. You've been amazing and I have no idea what I would'a done without you. I love you, babe, so much. Never gonna let you go, ever. Me and you, Sarah."

She instantly softened and tears filled her eyes as she whispered, "You mean the world to me."

I took her wrist where she had my name tattooed and placed a gentle kiss there, licking softly at the sensitive skin until she started to squirm against me. She was so responsive to me and I gloried in how easily I turned her on. It gave me a sense of power that went straight to my dick and pushed me to wring orgasm after orgasm out of her. Just the thought of her pussy squeezing down on my dick while she climaxed had me eager to bury myself in her, but first I had to have a taste.

Giving her a grin that made her pupils dilate further, I grabbed the tube of gel and scooted under the blankets, where it was dark and the air was saturated with our combined scent. She helped me shimmy her out of her shorts and panties before eagerly spreading her legs wide. Always so impatient for me, always so desperate. I could smell her sweetness before I tasted it, her slick arousal already wetting the bare lips of her sex. I gave her a few strokes of my tongue and she arched her back, silently asking for more. I squirted some of the gel onto my finger then spread it over her labia and clit before rimming the entrance to her body.

Her harsh cry had me flipping back the blanket enough to look up at her passion-dazed face, so soft with need and desire. Christ, she was beautiful enough to bring me to my knees over and over again. The fact that she was mine still sent a thrill through me, and I blew gently on her sex, my fingertip tingling from the gel. Her pussy visibly clenched and I chuckled before taking another lick of her sex, my tongue and lips buzzing from the gel. I gently parted her lips, then gave her hip a sharp slap when she squirmed.

"Still."

"Yes, *Papi*."

Her sweet voice had my balls drawing up tight and I pressed my dick against the mattress, needing something to soothe the ache while I ate her pretty little pink cunt. I pushed my tongue into her, fucking her with it while she began to tremor and arch her neck. Needing to be inside of her, I rubbed her clit with my thumb while tongue fucking her, loving how she was soaking my face with her wetness. Sliding into her was going to feel soooo fuckin' good.

Without removing my thumb from her clit, I rose onto my knees between her wide-spread legs.

"Play with your clit for me, sweetheart."

She immediately took over so I could lift her hips up and set her butt against my thighs. Her legs draped over my hips, giving me a clear view of the tip of my dick pressing against her, the piercing shining for a moment before being hidden inside her hot sex. Sliding into her pleasured me inside and out, my heart filling my chest until I had to close my eyes against the intensity of my love for her. She flexed her internal muscles and I moaned then began to move, slowly, deep inside. Our gazes met and I stared into her eyes while I made love to her, sharing this amazing experience and loving that she got off on me as much as I got off on her.

Leaning forward, I grasped her pink nipples and pinched them.

"Too hard, *Papi*," Sarah gasped with a wince.

Normally she liked it a lot rougher, but I had used the nipple clamps on her a couple days ago so maybe she was still sore. Mindful of her sensitivity, I stroked those tight pink nubs gently and was rewarded by Sarah grinding her hips against me in a move that made me see stars. Shit, my girl could fuck.

Plucking at her nipples, I rode her hard and deep, the need to come filling me while Sarah began to climax beneath me. I grit my teeth and held back, continuing my punishing pace as she gasped and twisted, pulling her hand away from her clit. Leaning down, I sucked her nipple into my mouth and she plunged her hands into my hair, responding once again to my thrusts.

"It's so good, Carlos, so good," she gasped.

Releasing her nipple, I grabbed her hands and held them over her head while I thrust, our bodies pressed tightly together while I licked and bit at her neck.

Once again she began to tighten around me, and I whispered encouragements to her to come again, to get my dick all nice and wet.

Thank fuck she did, because I was pretty sure I was going to black out if I didn't bust a nut soon. The moment her eyes began to roll back in her head, I let go, my shout loud enough to be heard by the neighbors down the hill. No doubt my brothers standing guard outside had heard it, but it wouldn't be the first or last time. I didn't give one rotten fuck who heard me making Sarah scream my name.

I collapsed on top of her, needing a moment to gather my strength before I could roll off to the side. As soon as I could catch my breath, I reached into the drawer next to the bed and pulled out the baby wipes. Sarah didn't bother to try to fight me anymore as I cleaned up the evidence of our passion. At first she'd been a little disturbed by my need to care for her after sex, but now she understood it was just a part of who I was.

I would always, always take care of my girl.

The first indication we had that the world was about to go to hell was the frantic phone call from Scarlet. She'd been over visiting with June, my brother Tink's wife, helping her get the kids ready for school, when someone had shot the shit out of their house in a drive-by. Considering they lived outside of Austin in a really nice and safe community, there was no way this had been a random crime. June had gotten grazed on the biceps, but other than that was all right. Thankfully none of the kids got injured, but everyone was flipping out.

I'd ordered all the women and children to stay on lockdown in the clubhouse until this shit was over.

It would be a hell of a lot easier for me to protect my people if I knew who the fuck I was fighting against. So far no one had claimed responsibility for the beatings, murders, fires, and deaths, which pissed me off. Not being able to put a face to my enemy had me operating in the dark, and I fuckin' hated it.

Though it tore me apart, I had to admit it was looking more and more likely that we had a traitor in the clubhouse. The thought of one of my brothers trying to destroy us like this was like a wound to my heart, and I hoped like fuck I was wrong. Tink was supposed to go on the run, but I pulled him off so he could stay with his kids while his wife was recovering. He still would have gone, Tink was about as loyal to the club as they come, but his family needed him and his head wouldn't be focused on the run.

Now it was just after ten p.m. and I was leaving my office at the clubhouse, intent on finding Sarah. She'd tried to talk to me about something important earlier, but we'd been interrupted time and time again until she gave up and told me we'd talk about it later.

Soon I'd be leaving with a handpicked group of my brothers to transport the cargo, and before I took off, I needed her love. The shooting incident had shaken us all and the sound of voices filled the clubhouse, instead of the usual party. All the sweet butts were gone and we'd cleaned up a couple areas for the kids to hang out in. Up on the third floor it was quiet, and I nodded to Dragon standing guard at the top of the stairs before continuing on to my room.

After a quick knock—with Sarah as tense as she was, I didn't want to surprise her—I came into our bedroom and found her sitting in the middle of the bed wearing a silky white nightie, which had an almost virginal look to it, and a worried expression as she hugged her knees.

"Everything okay? How's June? Does she need help with the kids?"

Shrugging off my cut, then my shirt, I crawled across the bed to her and gathered her warm softness against me, forcing her stiff body to relax into mine. "Everything's good. June's been discharged and Scarlet and Birdie are helpin' Tink out with the kids."

"Okay, good." She chewed on her thumb in an uncharacteristic display of nerves.

"Sarah? You wanted to talk about something?"

Her gaze darted to mine, then away, and she clasped her hands together. "Oh, yeah."

I waited for her to say something, but she was so nervous she began to tremble. Starting to get seriously worried, I sat up. "Babe, what's going on?"

"Well…y-you know how I went to the doctor yesterday?"

Jesus, she was about to shake to pieces and the fear in her eyes terrified me. "*Mi Corazón*, are you sick? Is that what all the throwing up's been about? Oh Jesus, tell me you're okay."

She took a deep breath and let it out in this weird, almost giggly sound that totally threw me off. "No, no I'm not sick. Well, I am, but not in a bad way."

"What the hell are you talk—"

Before I could finish my statement, there was a hard banging on my door followed by a frantic Dragon yelling, "Beach—Beach open up! We got a huge fuckin' problem."

I leapt off the bed and ran over to the door with Sarah at my heels. When I opened it, an ashen Dragon stumbled in, with Sledge not far behind. Both men were wide-eyed with shock, and I knew whatever was going on, it was *really* bad.

Flipping on the lights so I could see them better, I barked out, "What?"

Rubbing his bald head, Sledge growled out, "The warehouse where we were storing the stuff was hit. All the guards are dead and the trucks are gone."

A ringing filled my head as I tried to comprehend what had happened, and how badly it put everyone and everything I loved in danger. *"How?"*

His gaze turned to Sarah, and with a blank face, Sledge said, "We got video of them; no one we recognize, except for one—Billie. She distracted the guards long enough for them to get ambushed."

Sarah made a terrible moaning sound—and I turned just in time to catch her as she fainted.

Chapter 7

Sarah

The rotten taste in my mouth woke me up and I stared up at the ceiling, wondering why I felt like shit warmed over—so weak and tired I could barely keep my eyes open.

The last time I felt this way was after I'd accidentally OD'd on heroin when I was sixteen.

That was a long time ago and even as out of it as I was, I knew I didn't do drugs anymore.

At least not the kind that could leave me feeling more than half dead.

Then it came to me in a nauseating flash.

I wasn't hung over after a drug binge, I was pregnant.

As soon as that thought burst across my consciousness like a blazing rocket, I clutched my stomach and rolled out of bed, jerking to a halt when I noticed Hustler, Vance, and Smoke all watching me with dead eyes from the other side of the room, blocking the door. Confused, I frowned at them then looked around to see if anyone else was here. The lights were on all the way and I had no idea what time it was, but the world outside the bedroom windows was still dark except for the glow of security lights.

A disgusting sweat broke out over my skin and I gagged as a hot, greasy wave of sickness raced through me.

Clasping my hand to my mouth, I darted into the bathroom before any of them could say a word, sliding on my knees to the toilet just in time to puke up what little food I'd managed to eat earlier. Bitter acid burned my throat, coated my mouth, and I wanted to cry out at how terrible it felt. This wasn't just throwing up; my morning sickness had me dry heaving to the point I was afraid I was going to start throwing up blood. The doctor had written me a prescription for some anti-nausea pills, but I hadn't had a chance to fill it yet.

As I heaved, my stomach cramped hard and I cried, worried I was harming the tiny little life I was now in charge of keeping safe.

A firm hand landed on the back of my neck and for a moment I hoped it was Beach, but as the memories of the last few hours began to surface behind my morning—fuck, all-day sickness, I couldn't help the sobs that poured from me.

I must have looked a sight, draped over a toilet full of puke, snot and tears dripping down my face while I moaned as the agony of my mother's betrayal raced through me, burning away any love I might have had for that woman, once and for all.

The man's hand left my sweaty neck and a familiar woman's voice said, "Sarah, honey, sit up. You need to calm down before you pass out again. Just breathe with me. Deep breath in…let it out. Now do it again."

I had to clutch my abs as I did as ordered, blinking my tear-swollen eyes to see Scarlet watching me with a very worried, sad, and angry expression. Her hair was pulled back into a tight braid and she wasn't wearing any makeup, leaving her looking strangely young and innocent. They must have woken her up to come deal with me, or maybe she was already awake. She looked as if she'd been crying, and being Thorn's old lady, she probably knew what had happened.

"I'm—I'm so sorry!" I bawled while she handed me a cool, wet washcloth to clean myself with. "I didn't know, I would have stopped her, I swear it."

Her eyes softened and she squatted before me, her voice low as she whispered, "I believe you, but a lot of the brothers aren't so sure. There's talk that this was all a big scam from the start, that you've been planning to rip this club off from the beginning. How long you been settin' this up with your mom, huh?"

"What?" I gasped as I held the towel to my chest. "That's not true. How can you even say that to me?"

His gaze was dark and serious, not a trace of my loving man looking back at me in those cold deep blue eyes. "Look, you need to stay in the room right now. The sentiment downstairs isn't very happy. Beach is dealing with the Russians and the Israelis, trying to buy us some time to find Billie and our shit. Do you have any idea where she might be?"

"No." I swallowed hard, my eyes once again filling with tears. "I didn't know anything about her bullshit, I swear. The only time I saw her was at my house that first night. I wanted nothing to do with her, and I let her know on no uncertain terms that I wanted her out of my life. I tried to tell Beach but…" Guilt swamped me and I closed my eyes. "I should have tried harder."

"Did you…did you know she'd do something like this?"

I hung my head in shame. "No, I never thought she'd go this far. Are they sure it was her? I mean, my mom has no morals at all, but I can't see her pulling off something this big, or even helping to plan it."

"Billie distracted one of the guys guarding the outside then a team covered from head to toe in tactical gear moved in. I watched the tape with Thorn, just to make sure it was her. I didn't want to believe it. She's been nothing but nice to me, to all of us, and honestly I was wondering why you were being such a bitch to her by not even acknowledging her existence. Last time I saw her at Hustler's store, she actually teared up when I asked her if she'd had a chance to talk to you yet. I felt so bad for her, crying because you wouldn't have anything to do with her."

"That manipulative bitch can cry at the drop of a dime." I took a deep breath, deciding to just lay it all out. "The last time I saw my mother, she stole my grandmother's heirloom jewelry from me and pawned it for drugs. The time before that, she cut me with a knife on my arm because I was trying to help her detox and keeping her from her drugs. And that doesn't even touch on the first sixteen years of my life being raised by a selfish, remorseless, mentally disturbed drug addict who basically stole me from my dad. For as long as I can remember, my mother has lied to me about what would happen if he ever caught us. Terrible things, like he'd kill her and make me his work slave out on his farm, where I'd be beaten daily."

Scarlet sat back on her heels, her jaw slack as she stared at me. "That's fucked up."

"Yeah, but she's done worse. This is also the woman that hooked me up with a thirty-year-old married mobster when I was fifteen, just so she could get a free hookup for good coke. She got me a fake ID and everything, taught me how to dress and act, and got me into the hottest clubs in Reno, where she proceeded to make sure Morrie knew I was available." I let out a bitter laugh as the cruel memories washed over me. "So yeah, maybe you understand now why I wanted nothing to do with her."

"Oh, Sarah." Scarlet brushed my hair off my sweaty forehead. "I'm so sorry."

God, she was such a nice woman. She had every right in the world to be furious with me for my mom's actions, but her face was filled with love and sympathy. I didn't deserve a friend as good as her. A sweet soul in a dark world. I had to protect her from the shit my mom had rained down on us.

A sense of purpose began to fill me, pushing away the crippling despair.

"This is my fault. I should never have allowed Beach to take care of her. I should have fought harder, but I was weak, and now I have to pay the price." I drew in a deep, hitching breath. "I'll find her."

Standing, I moved over to the sink and brushed my teeth while Scarlet watched me with a worried gaze, wringing her hands together so tight her knuckles turned white. "Honey, we're not allowed to leave the clubhouse. We're all on lockdown. They got this place surrounded by men and you're safer here than anywhere on Earth."

I shook my head, the determination setting in even as a tiny, unfamiliar part of me worried that I was putting the baby inside of me at risk. I was about three months pregnant, and I had a hint of a bump going on, but my long torso hid it nicely. Since I've been on birth control for years without an issue, it never occurred to me that I should be worried about the potential consequences of fucking the hell out of Beach every chance I got. Guess when you consider how much sex we have, we were bound to get lucky—or unlucky—eventually, since no birth control was one hundred percent. That little pudge that I thought was the result of too many fudge brownie ice cream shakes was instead a new life coming into existence inside me.

Holy shit, I'm going to be a mother.

A shiver of fear had me gripping my hands into fists as I lowered my head and fought the anxiety that tried to take hold.

No—I can't think about that right now. I have to focus. There's no other choice. They will never find her without me, and if I don't get the Israelis and Russians their stuff back, there is a chance my baby will never even be born.

The very thought sent a feral rage through me the likes of which I've never experienced, the thought of someone denying my child their first breath. I looked at myself in the mirror and promised that I would be a better mother than my own.

Tears filled my eyes, and fear pierced my heart, but I decided on my course of actions.

"Scarlet, I have to do this." She started to protest but I held my hand out, my expression starting to harden as I rebuilt the walls around my shattered emotions. "It's the only way, and you're not going to stop me, or talk me out of it. You know me, you know what I'm capable of, and you know I'm not fucking around. Stay out of my way so I can get this done."

I pushed past Scarlet and walked back into the room where the men were still watching me with open distrust. Ignoring them, I pawed through my drawers until I found the clothes I wanted, then went to the closet and grabbed the bag holding my guns and my bug-out backpack before slinging them on the bed. Turning to look at Smoke, I read the confusion on his face before he closed his expression down again.

The distrust in his dark eyes hurt me and I tried to keep myself from letting it show. "I need to go to wherever my mother was staying."

"What," Hustler asked with a faint sneer in his voice, "you never been there before?"

I jerked on my jeans, sliding them on under my nightgown that I'd worn special for my man, my back to them. "That's right."

"Bullshit," Vance said. "Your mother said you visited with her."

"Bullshit," I spat back at him as I glanced over my shoulder, done with his crap. He didn't like me and the feeling was mutual. "She'd tell you whatever you need to hear in order to manipulate you."

His eyes narrowed. "Like mother like daughter."

I was about to let him have it when Smoke held up his hand. "Enough. Sarah, you can't leave. End of story."

Ignoring him, I stepped into the bathroom long enough to change my shirt, then came back out and began to pull guns out of my bag. "Don't make me fight you on this. I'm going to her apartment. I know how she thinks, what her habits are, and I might be able to find something."

"We've already searched the place." Vance glared at me with so much hatred I was taken aback for a moment. "Tore the fucker apart."

"And you found dick, right?"

"We didn't find much," Smoke admitted with a frustrated grit to his voice. "Maybe you can see somethin' we didn't, but Sarah, the place is trashed."

"Why do you wanna go so bad? You wanna destroy some evidence? Your ass belongs here, in the clubhouse on lockdown, where we can keep an eye on you," Vance spat out.

"Look, asshole, I had nothing to do with any of this. I love Beach, I love this club, and I would never do anything to endanger it. My mother is poison, and while I regret allowing her to stay, I truly thought she was trying to get clean and sober." I began to load bullets into the clip for my Sig Sauer 9mm. "You don't have a choice; if we don't find her, we're all dead. Hell, probably everyone we love as well. So stop being a dick and help me."

Running a hand through his hair, Smoke took out his phone. "Fuck, you're right. We don't got a lot of options. You really think you can find something there? We already searched the place and couldn't find shit—and we *looked*."

"I sure as fuck hope so."

"That's a bad idea," Vance argued. "She could get hurt and Beach will kill us *all* at high tide. Or maybe she'll lead you into an ambush."

For a moment I wondered what the hell he was talking about with the whole "high tide" thing, then dismissed it and began to load myself up with knives and weapons.

"Anyone that tries to hurt me is going to be in for a big fucking surprise."

I casually flicked a knife past Vance's head, where it embedded itself in the wall with a hollow thunk, startling a yelp out of him.

Vance's lip curled as he took a step towards me, but he stopped when Hustler let out a low chuckle while Scarlet said, "Honey, I don't think it's a good idea. There are people out there right now trying to hunt down any Iron Horse members they can. The men whose stuff got taken are very unhappy, and very powerful. They could flip out and order hits on all of us, but especially you. It's no secret how much you mean to Beach, and if they want to hurt him, killing you would do it."

"All the more reason for me to get out of here. I'm a target, and being around me is dangerous."

Smoke sighed. "I can't get through to Beach. He's meeting with the Boldins right now."

The mention of the Boldin *Bratva* made my stomach cramp, and I had to fight away a worry that I was once again hurting my baby with all the stress I was under. "It can't wait. The more of a head start she has, the better chance she has of vanishing into thin air."

Vance threw his hands up in the air. "I want no fuckin' part of this train wreck."

"That's fine. Hustler, Smoke, you coming with me?"

Scarlet began to swear softly, but both men nodded.

Cracking his neck, Hustler took out his phone. "Quicker we get this done, better chance we have of Beach not realizin' you're gone."

"Sarah, Beach is going to lose his mind," Scarlet said in a tight voice.

"Then you need to convince him to chill out." I closed my eyes, gathering myself, and when I opened them again, I knew the ruthless survivor my family had trained me to be had risen to the surface. "I have to do this."

She took a step back, her face going pale as her eyes grew wide. "Okay."

Grabbing my stuff, I tucked my hair behind my ear then nodded at Smoke. "Let's go."

Twenty minutes later, I stared at the destroyed apartment before me, my dim flashlight revealing the destruction. The place had been absolutely shredded, and I had to walk carefully through the debris of torn-up couch cushions, tattered books, emptied cupboards, and broken shit everywhere. When Smoke had said they'd already searched the place, I didn't know they meant down to ripping open every pillow and smashing everything to splinters. Hell, there were even a couple holes in the drywall here and there where it looked like a gigantic fist had gone through it.

With my heart pounding in my throat, I took another step forward as broken pottery crunched beneath my boot.

"Sarah, you gotta hurry," Smoke said while standing in the doorway, looking down the hall of my mother's apartment complex, his large frame tight with tension.

"Right."

For a moment I just stood there, looking at everything as I swept the beam of my light back and forth, not even knowing where to start. Another step into the living room and I scanned the refuse, waiting for something to jump out at me, but nothing did.

Moving into the bedroom, I found it in a similar state of chaos, clothing strewn everywhere, the mattress destroyed, the dresser drawers lying empty and broken around the room. The mirror had been ruined and the sharp slivers of glass still stuck in the edges of the frame gleamed in the low light of the small flashlight I held.

A tremor went through my body as doubt filled me that I could ever find anything in this mess, even if I had days to do it instead of minutes. Danger hung in the air like a thick smog, smothering me with the need to get the fuck out of here. The ride over had been tense as hell and Smoke had done some fancy driving to ditch a tail we'd picked up. They both kept in constant contact with the clubhouse, and the word pouring in was not good. Beach had bought us some time with the Russians, but the Israelis were super fucking pissed and threatening to wipe the club off the face of the earth.

With a harsh sigh, I glanced at her bathroom before Hustler gave a sharp whistle. "Time to go. Beach found out you're gone and has lost his damn mind."

I winced then hurried back to them, trying with all my might to keep myself from losing all hope. My flashlight reflected off the stainless steel fridge and I paused for a moment, a memory tickling my mind. Something my mother would do when she was getting ready to move, a habit that she was OCD about.

A compulsion that might help lead me to her.

On the side of the fridge, there were three magnets holding up what looked like a shopping list and other crap. One was for Las Vegas, one was for Austin, and one was for Colorado.

Past. Present. Future.

My heart thumped hard enough that the pound roared in my ears and I wondered if it could be that simple.

She always got a magnet for whatever place she planned on moving to next, something I finally figured out when I was a kid and noticed a new California magnet on our fridge a few weeks before she announced we were leaving. Too bad it was only a state, not a city, but it was better than nothing.

I needed one thing to start me on the path to her, one clue, and I was hoping this was it, because I had nothing else to go on.

"Sarah," Smoke growled, "we gotta go, now."

"Right."

Once we were safely back in the SUV, Hustler turned around from the passenger seat to look at me, his lip ring winking in the amber glow from the streetlights we passed. "You find anything?"

I almost said yes, but held back at the last moment. The more I thought about the situation, the surer I was that it was some kind of inside job. It had to be, all the clues pointed that way and I knew Beach had been considering it, but he didn't want to believe one of his close brothers would betray him like that.

I blinked and stared at Hustler for a moment, wondering if he was the one betraying us, before shaking my head. "No, I'm sorry."

Smoke let out a tense breath. "It's okay. We knew it was a long shot."

"Thanks for letting me try."

Turning back around, Hustler looked at his phone then said, "Thank fuck. Beach managed to get us some time with the Israelis. Now we just need to find their shit, return it to 'em intact, and we'll all be golden."

I rested my head against the cool glass of the window, my thoughts racing as I tried to figure a way out of this mess.

When we pulled up to the clubhouse, the lot was packed with cars and we had to park farther away than usual, on the grass. A new minivan was parked next to ours and I absently looked at the little stick-figure family on the back, my gaze going to the car seats inside. Shit, I'd need to get one of those in the near future for the little life inside of me.

In a surreal moment, I wondered if I'd have to trade in my new, super awesome Jaguar F-Type that Beach had bought me, with no backseat, for a mom-mobile that could fit the massive car seat for our baby. My reflection stared back at me in the tinted glass, illuminated by the rising sun. I looked as tired as I felt, with deep circles beneath my eyes, and I stared at my reflection as I braced myself for Beach throwing a fit. I knew I'd fucked up when I left without his knowing, but the information I had was worth whatever verbal lashing he was about to unleash on me.

Sure enough, Beach bellowed out behind me, "Sarah!"

Whipping around, I winced as Beach came thundering past the parked cars to get to me, the fury on his face making me take a step back. Unwelcome memories of men stalking towards me with similar looks of rage when I was a child triggered my fight-or-flight response, and as usual, my default setting was fight. So instead of deescalating the situation and talking to my man, I snarled at him.

"I'm right here."

His lip curled up in response, and if I'd been a rational person in any way, shape, or form, I would have recognized it for the bad sign it was. "You manage to destroy any evidence your mom left behind?"

His harsh words hit me like a blow and I took a step back, shocked out of my anger. "What?"

Vance followed close behind, a slight smirk tilting his lips before he smoothed his expression.

Beach ran both of his hands through his dark blond hair, the veins on his forearms standing out. "Were you workin' with her, Sarah? Tell me right fuckin' now."

"Of course not!" I screamed, loud enough to draw the attention of everyone who had backed away from us while we were arguing, everyone except Vance. "I can't believe you would think that I'd do something like that."

"I can't believe you lied to me about that bitch! You never fuckin' told me about all the scams she pulled. I had to hear it from Vance about all the people she's ruined. Bitch is slick, I'll give her that, but she made a mistake leavin' you behind. Tell me where she is!"

I had to wrap my arms around myself to keep from hitting him, his betrayal striking through me. "You think I'm in on this. After all our time together—"

"It hasn't been that fuckin' long," Beach spat out. "And obviously I didn't know shit about you. I was also clued in on all the scams you helped her run. Shit, you've been connin' people since before you could even read."

My heart ached and I swallowed hard, but my voice still came out pinched. "I see. Your mind is made up."

He paused, squinting as he stared at me. "Did you help her?"

"Does it matter? You've already decided." My world started to crash down around me, but I was a survivor and I managed to build a bubble of indifference surrounding my heart, trying to force him out. "If you're done accusing me of being a traitor, I'd like to leave."

"Get her out of my sight," he snarled.

I held his gaze for a moment, willing him to see the truth in my words. "I never betrayed you, or the club, but you just betrayed me."

Smoke took my arm and urged me with him. Without another look, I turned my back on Beach, and it hurt, but I forced myself to do it. Every step felt like a blow and I ignored the looks thrown my way, some sympathetic, some pissed, others sad. By the time we made it to the building, I was holding on to my pride by a thread, refusing to cry as I was marched up the stairs to Beach's room, where I assumed I'd be locked in.

Not that it mattered, I already had an escape plan that I'd formulated the first time I spent the night here.

So I didn't protest when Smoke sighed then said, "Give him time to cool down, Sarah. I'll go talk some sense into him."

I shrugged and made my way over to the window, looking out at the ground three stories below. "Whatever."

"Sweetheart—"

"Just go, Smoke. I'm tired and not feeling well."

I didn't watch him leave, but let out a soft breath as he shut the door tightly behind him. I *was* tired, but I didn't have the luxury of indulging in a nap. The sooner I left, the better. At the moment, most of the guys were probably still on the other side of the building with Beach in the parking lot. That meant I had to go, now.

With my heart beginning to race, I grabbed my backpack and gun bag, glad I'd kept up with my workouts as I settled the heavy gear next to me on the floor.

Next, I jumped up onto a chair and pushed up a ceiling tile above me. I pulled down the coiled rope ladder I'd stored and secured it to the sturdy handle of the steel-reinforced door leading out of Beach's room.

The climb out the window was surprisingly easy and I jumped the last few feet, landing in a crouch and trying not to grunt as my gear shifted.

"What the fuck? Sarah?" came a man's voice to my right, and a burly nomad that I kind of knew stared at me as he started to draw his gun.

With a small internal wince of regret, I took a step forward then swiftly kicked him on the side of the head, hard enough to knock him out.

As he fell, I waited for someone to sound the alarm, but we were situated at the corner of the building, where the shadows were thick. I dragged him against the side of the clubhouse, scanning the yard before I made my next move. Uncertainty nipped at me and I held my breath as men's voices began to draw closer, talking about someone named Chief.

Knowing I faced greater odds of getting away from two men than just one, at least without anyone getting seriously hurt, I made the decision to move. I had to admit, it had been over a year since I'd last done any running with a full pack, but my muscles warmed as I sprinted across the yard in the pre-dawn light, my lungs expanding as I still waited for someone to raise the alarm behind me. Hopefully I'd moved the guy I'd knocked out enough that they wouldn't fall on top of him.

I had to do this quick, had to get to my secret storage unit I'd rented under a false name and get the paperwork for my new identities. I had four deep-cover ones that I would use over the coming days to set myself up with a home base. Part of me wanted to go to Colorado right now, but I couldn't just drive around the state, hoping to run into her.

No, there had to be something or someone here who could help me narrow it down. For a moment, I considered going to my dad and Mimi, but my mind shut that shit down almost instantly. First, my dad would go ballistic and lots of people would get dead. Second, Mimi would go ballistic and lots of people would get dead. Like enough to start a war. She'd go after the Russian and Israeli mafias on her own if she felt it was needed to keep me and Swan safe. If she knew about the shit storm raining down on us right now, she'd lose her mind.

So going to them for *help* was out of the question, but maybe not for a visit if I couldn't find anything down here in Austin. I had friends with some impressive resources on the compound, and one brilliant man who saw me as an enemy but could help me, only as a last resort. The taint of my mother seemed to spread to anyone who had contact with her, and I didn't want anyone hurt for helping me out.

No, I'd try to do it on my own first. I could only hope that Beach didn't tell Mimi and my dad what was going on. There wasn't a doubt in my mind that they'd torture then kill my mother for this on principal alone. Even as much as I hated her, I couldn't knowingly sign her death warrant.

My breath came out in soft huffs as I reached the old tree that had been struck by lightning without any alarm going up behind me at my disappearance. A dozen steps to the north of the burned wood brought me to a thicket of bushes that held my means of escape.

As I uncovered the ATV that would lead to a safe house with a car nearby, I prayed to God in all his divine glory to watch over Beach while I was gone, and help me keep my baby safe.

Chapter 8
Carlos "Beach" Rodriguez

AUSTIN TX

My neck itched, and I had to resist the urge to scratch it to allow the new tattoo going from the back of my neck to the middle of my throat time to heal. I'd gotten it the day after Sarah had left, almost two weeks ago, and prayed I'd be able to show it to her someday. For all I knew, she was already dead.

No, can't fucking think about that. Thinking of my beautiful woman dead in a field somewhere, or captured, would lead to a madness I could not afford.

Every member of the Iron Horse MC was depending on me pulling our asses out of the fire and I couldn't let them down, no matter how fucked up my head was about my old lady.

I stared at Sledge standing across from me in my big office at the clubhouse as he talked quietly with a group of brothers on the other side of the room. I absently noted the drywall needed to be replaced, again, after I'd punched some holes into it in an effort to channel the rage that tried to burn me alive into a non-lethal release. Sledge had played a big part in helping me hold my shit together. He'd really stepped up in the past few weeks, and he had Marley and her little boy on lockdown at his mother's house, taking one big worry off my hands. Sarah loved Marley and her son Scottie, and we weren't taking any chances with their safety by sending them back to Las Vegas.

A hollow pang hit me from deep inside my gut as, for just a moment, I imagined having to break the news to Marley that Sarah was dead, and I banished that evil thought.

No, my baby was strong, brilliant, and lethal—she could take care of herself. I just hated that my epic fuck up had sent her running.

Guilt swamped me as I recalled our last conversation, when she looked at me with cold, dead eyes and told me I'd betrayed her. In that moment, my stupid ass had known she would never fuck the club over and steal from us, but I'd been exhausted and my head had been filled with shit by a few brothers I was still pissed at. Not that I could blame them for their suspicions, after all, Billie was Sarah's mother, but even when it looked like all the evidence pointed to Sarah, I should have known better, should have listened to Sledge and Thorn when they told me Sarah had no part in the heist. I'd been so fucking pissed that Sarah had lied to me about her past with Billie that I let that anger consume me. Instead of having my woman's back like I swore I would, I fucked up and drove her away.

It was my fault she felt the need to go after her mother, that she felt like she had to prove herself. I was the one who'd betrayed *her*, who drove her to such a rash action, and it haunted me. She'd left me a note telling me she was going after the bitch, and reassuring me she'd make this right. That was it, no talk of where she was going, what she was going to be doing, or when she'd be back. If only she'd contact me, let me know she was okay, I'd tell her immediately how sorry I was for those terrible things I'd said. And I would spend the rest of my life making it up to her if she let me.

That is, if either of us made it out of this bullshit alive.

Darkness tried to overwhelm me and I swore the lights in the room dimmed as despair moved through me.

My phone rang, drawing me out of my fucked-up thoughts, and I saw that it was Smoke. He was watching Swan, Sarah's twin sister, tonight down in Houston and kept me updated on her status. So far the people waiting for us to retrieve their merchandise had kept back, but their patience was wearing thin. And we weren't the only ones looking for it. Word had gotten out about the value of the run and we had bounty hunters searching for it as well. Basically we were fucked six ways from Sunday, and I had to stay here in Austin and do everything I could to control the situation instead of going out and looking for Sarah.

I'd never regretted being president of the Iron Horse MC before, but the fact that my duties were keeping me here gnawed at my already shredded patience.

Standing, I answered the call while stretching out. It was late, after Swan's shift at work had ended, and as usual Smoke was calling to update me on her day, which was usually spent inside her home. Sarah was right, Swan was a total recluse, and I knew bringing her into the club would be akin to torture for her. If—no, *when* Sarah came home, I didn't want to greet her with a twin sister who had a psychological breakdown while she was gone.

More guilt added to my already overtaxed soul and my voice came out thick. "What's up."

"Swan's gone," Smoke spat out in a hurried rush. "Someone was fuckin' with our bikes and I went out to deal with it. She went out a different exit and we didn't notice until she'd left."

"You have GPS on her car, right? Find her."

"We did. Her car's in the parking lot of a bar, but she's not inside and no one's seen her. Beach, a big group of Los Diablos was here earlier, but they cleared out before we arrived. They…they probably have her."

"Fuck!" I shouted at the ceiling and dropped my phone before I started smashing it in a fit of rage.

Sledge scooped it up and talked to the phone while I strained to control myself, to not give in to the fury that wanted me to scorch the Earth.

I growled at Sledge, "How long has she been missing?"

He relayed the question to Smoke and responded with, "Not long, maybe an hour."

"An hour? She was gone for a fuckin' hour and no one fuckin' noticed?"

Sledge didn't bother to repeat that one, but his gaze shifted to mine as he listened to whatever Smoke was saying. "Right…right. Do it."

After he hung up, he came over to me and grasped my shoulders, making me meet his gaze. "We'll get her back."

"Los Diablos." I closed my eyes. "You know what they do to women."

His grip on my shoulders tightened to the point of pain. "Breathe. Swan's unique, they won't physically harm her. Fucked up, but true—they won't wanna damage the merchandise. We both know that to those flesh-peddling motherfuckers, a prize like her will fetch a big price, but only if she's looking her best, which means they won't hurt her."

Hustler burst through the doorway of my office, his hazel eyes wide with shock. "I just got a phone call from Sarah."

"What?" myself and just about every guy said at the same time, along with a couple "thank fucks".

That made Hustler blink, then he continued. "She said she found Swan. She's being held at a warehouse in Buda. I tried to get her to talk but all she would tell me was that she was okay, and where Swan was, and she let me know Los Diablos had her, then she hung up on me. The call came from a fuckin' pay phone—no idea they still had those things—near Buda off the freeway."

"Let's go."

"Prez," Hustler began, "you sure it's a good idea for you to go? Hate to say it, but could be a trap. We got no idea if someone was holdin' a gun to her head to make her say those words."

I gave him a look that let him know exactly how I felt about the situation and he blanched before nodding. "Right. Then let's get this shit done."

By the time we reached the warehouse, Smoke was already inside searching for Swan. It didn't take long to secure the building, they only had four men on her, but I kept two of 'em alive for questioning and sent them back for interrogation with Hustler. The bastard was a master of fucking with a person's head and could get the truth out of anyone…if he didn't kill them doing it. My temper was threatening my self-control as I waited for Smoke to bring Swan up from wherever they were holding her. He said she was okay, but I needed to get a grip on myself before I met her for the first time.

Despite the utterly fucked-up circumstances of our meeting, I wanted us to get along. Sarah said her sister was hypersensitive to violence and angry men, so I needed to get my shit on lockdown. I sat on the edge of the desk that probably belonged to the foreman of this place before it got shut down and ran my finger through the thick dust coating the moisture-warped surface. I had hoped when we pulled up that, by some miracle, Sarah would be here, but she wasn't. At least I knew she was alive. Hustler said the only thing she'd tell him was that she was safe and working on finding her mom. No mention of me, no message for me, and that shit stung.

Voices came from the hallway leading to the office and I took a deep breath then let it out in a rush as I got my first close-up look at Swan.

For one brief moment, my fucked-up brain thought I was looking at Sarah, and my entire body froze. Then her pale blue eyes met mine and I could instantly see the differences in the two women. Besides having hair down to her waist, Swan was a little curvier than her sister, and just as muscled, but her gaze and the way she held herself were entirely different.

There was a softness, an innocence about her that Sarah didn't have, something that hinted at the kind of vulnerability that could draw a man in. Give him the urge to protect her and keep her safe. Smoke certainly seemed to feel protective over her. He stood close enough that his tall frame dwarfed her, a wall of muscle and leather at her back who would protect her with his last breath. My jaw clenched as I noted what looked a fuck of a lot like beard burn on her face from kissing someone with scruff, someone like Smoke.

Motherfucker.

I'd have to be deaf, blind, and dumb not to see that my Master at Arms was head over fuckin' heels in love with Swan.

This could either be really good or really bad. A man like Smoke was a lot to handle and I didn't know if putting Swan into his care would be too much for her. He was intense, used to women who knew the score, and if I had a sister, I'm not sure I'd want her with him. Swan seemed to be gravitating towards him now, but she needed a taste of his hot temper.

Perhaps *here*, where I could intervene if need be.

With that in mind, I mentioned what I'd learned so far from Hustler's interrogations. It was indeed Los Diablos, they were going to sell her to the Russians, and as suspected, Smoke lost his fucking mind.

He roared and raged and threw shit, all while venting his anger in an epic display of pissed the fuck off. While he smashed a chair, I watched Swan, taking in her terrified expression.

I was about to end this shit show and take Swan home with me when something in her stance changed. Her shoulders straightened, she took a deep breath, and then displayed a rare inner strength as she visibly mastered her fear and proceeded to talk Smoke down.

The moment Smoke realized he'd scared the shit out of her, he let out a groan like he'd been shot—and chilled out in record time. I was actually shocked at how quickly he pulled his shit together, and the look that came over his face as he reassured Swan let me know he'd live and die to keep her safe. And the way she stared back at him with a sweet wonder made even a cynical bastard like me bite back a grin.

Good enough for me.

Still, I gave her a chance to make her own decision and wasn't surprised when she grasped on to Smoke like a drowning victim. Then she got nervous and began to babble in a way that made me want to laugh for the first time since Sarah took off. Thank fuck my baby had somehow managed to save her sister. The thought of how close Los Diablos had come to destroying the sweet young woman now being gently dragged from the room by Smoke curled my stomach. Before they left, I let Swan know that she'd never have to worry about these particular dirtbag motherfuckers ever again.

I was gonna make an example of their deaths, vent my rage on them, and do what karma had put me here to do—balance the scales of vengeance.

Chapter 9

Sarah

The hot summer sun beat down on me as I drove through the Texas Hill Country with the top down on my brand new Shelby Mustang. It was a beautiful opalescent white, and Beach had gotten it for me a month ago instead of the motorcycle I wanted. While Beach was liberal in many ways, for a biker, he was dead set against me ever riding a motorcycle without him. A woman belonged on the back of her man's bike, in his narrow mind, and that was it.

I'd been pissed at the time, but now I'm glad I hadn't learned how to ride a motorcycle while pregnant.

Just the thought of what could have happened sent a cold shiver down my spine, and I fought back the panic that was getting closer to the surface every day.

In an effort to calm myself, I switched the music from the hard rock I'd been listening to in an effort to stay awake, to something a little smoother.

When the soft strains of classical music spun through the air, I let my body ease into the soothing melody.

In the past three days I'd managed maybe nine hours of sleep, constantly on the move as I'd narrowly avoided being caught again and again. It was like as soon as I stopped moving, they'd catch up to me. So far I'd only caught a glimpse of them, but it was the same group of four men, all wearing dark clothes, all with dark hair, and all moving with the trained grace of professional killers. When they'd shown up at the first hotel I'd stayed at, I'd been lucky enough to have been on my way out, but I'd noted them as they'd strolled into the lobby of the hotel, looking completely out of place.

Then I saw them again a day later. I told the sympathetic receptionist at the front desk that my ex-boyfriend had been bothering me and I was staying in the hotel in the hopes he'd get the hint and leave me alone. She promised me if anyone came asking about me, she'd let me know. Sure enough, after I'd been there for less than five hours, they'd shown up again.

I never stuck around long enough to try to figure out who they were. Sure, Beach could have sent them to find me, but I had a feeling deep down in my gut they meant me harm. After all, I had a bounty on me that would tempt even a saint to kidnap me. I'd contacted old friends who'd informed me, with great sorrow, that some anonymous asshole had put a price on my head. They'd also told me that word on the street was someone had attempted to kidnap one of Sledge's nieces from school, but had been thwarted by a pair of armed fucking soccer moms with big guns who'd been at the school and seen the attempted abduction. God bless Texas.

A broken laugh escaped me and I gave myself a mental slap, needing my brain to function before I arrived at my parents' survivalist compound—aka, home.

It was the one place in the world I knew I'd be completely safe, and I needed a few days to rest up for the next leg of my journey and gather intelligence. That meant I'd have to talk to Stewart, the selfish fuck my sister had almost married.

Just the thought of that smug, arrogant little shit made me want to punch him in the face.

I had a special hate set aside for him because of what he'd done to Swan.

See, Stewart, the man who'd professed his undying love for my sweet, naïve sister, was gay. I knew this because I'd caught him having a threesome with two guys from the massive hippie compound on the other side of my parents' place. For months I'd known something was wrong, but I couldn't put my finger on it until I watched with disgust as he got spit roasted at a hippy party. Just hours before he'd been at my house with Swan, watching a movie with her on the couch, as sweet as can be. The perfect boyfriend. Lying fuck.

As the smooth pavement rolled beneath my tires, I waved to one of the sentry cameras on my dad's property and let out a deep breath. I didn't care who was after me, there was no way in hell they were getting near my dad's place without being eliminated. There were all kinds of nasty surprises, and back-up surprises, and back-up backup surprises waiting for anyone stupid enough to cross into my dad's kingdom. Woe be the foolish mortal who took on the man some called, and not affectionately, "The God of War".

Mike Anderson only sold weapons and information to causes he believed in, and his support was enough to have aided more than one rebel group, or government, overthrow the enemy. It was well known throughout the criminal underworld that Mike Anderson was a man you did not want to fuck around with.

Beach was the one who'd filled me in on that, and I hoped like hell he hadn't told my parents that I was missing. If he had, I suspected they would have found me by now. It wouldn't surprise me to learn they had a GPS chip implanted on my body somewhere. For real. Plus, Beach knew my father could very well go ballistic and take it out on the Iron Horse MC, which is the last thing he needed to deal with right now. My dad wasn't exactly known for being sane, which meant I'd have to watch myself around him.

As I pulled into the large concrete circular drive before the first level of my parents' fortress, a rather unassuming two-story, hacienda-style home, I could almost believe that this was just a normal house nestled in the most beautiful slice of Texas Hill Country I'd ever seen. Right now the land was green and lush thanks to weeks of rains that had helped ease the drought. Flowers bloomed everywhere and the goats bleated out as I turned off the car. Over the ticks of the cooling engine came the clucks of chickens somewhere in the distance, and I looked around for their emus, a recent—and weird—addition to the farm, but the corral was empty.

Before I could slide out of my car, the front door of my parents' house burst open and Mimi, my beautiful stepmother, burst forth with her arms thrown wide and a huge smile on her face.

"Sarah!"

As graceful in four-inch heels as she was barefoot, Mimi quickly closed the distance between us, her faded denim skirt flaring about her long legs. As soon as she hugged me, I felt safe—and to my horror, began to cry. Mimi tried to pull away, but I clutched her closer and took in deep breaths of her familiar perfume.

"Honey, what's wrong? Are you okay? Did you and Beach have a fight?"

"No, no, we're good." My stomach lurched and I curled my lips in disgust. "I think I might have the flu."

"Oh, sweetheart."

Mimi went into instant mothering mode, ushering me inside the fully furnished house that no one used, other than the massive kitchen, and down through the double blast doors and into our real home, below ground. I'd seen a few sketches of the colossal underground system my father had built, but it was hard to really comprehend how big it was. When I'd asked my dad, he'd given me a searching look before responding that our home was ten levels, with its own protected water and purified ventilation systems, and that it could house, feed, and keep safe over seventy-five people. Then he'd told me never to tell anyone about it. When I'd asked why, he simply asked me to try to think of which seventy-five people I would save…and what the rest of the world would do to make sure they were one of the seventy-five.

That had been a sobering thought for fifteen-year-old me.

After Mimi got me tucked into my bed, she smoothed the silky eggplant-purple comforter gently with one hand while smiling at me. "While I'm sorry you're not feeling well, it's good to see you. I wish you would have called and let us know; your dad is out on the range right now fixing a bunch of fencing that got torn down by a flash flood a few days ago."

I sank into the softness of my pillows, the lighting turned down low enough that the overhead lights were just a soft amber glow. Mimi's dark hair gleamed as she tossed it over her shoulder, studying me intently. I resisted the urge to squirm beneath her gaze, feeling like her laser mom sight could detect not only my pregnancy, but all the other shit I was currently in up to my neck.

"Have you lost weight?" She brushed my hair back from my cheek. "Or is it just this adorable new cut you're sporting?"

I gave her a tired smile, exhaustion pulling at me, urging me to close my eyes. "Thanks, my hairstylist put a bunch of jagged layers in, says it's the new thing to have."

Laughing softly, Mimi ran her hand over my hair again, the stroking incredibly soothing. I have no idea what it is about a mother's touch, but I swear it heals you when nothing else will. Her gentle petting put me to sleep before I knew it and I fell into a dreamless slumber.

I managed to sleep for fourteen hours before waking up and chowing down on some oatmeal with raisins. It was one of the few foods I could keep down and I even traveled with some instant stuff in my purse, just in case I needed to eat to stave off being sick. While trying to find my mother, I'd also spent a great deal of time researching being pregnant. At this point I was okay without seeing a doctor, but I'd have to go again in a few months to check on the baby. Hopefully by that time this shit would be over with.

Speaking of shit I wanted to get over with, Stewart sat stiffly on the other side of the room from me, neither of us saying a word. He was a handsome man, tall and blond with pretty-boy good looks that would land him a modeling contract in a heartbeat. From his sculpted lips to his chiseled jaw, he was perfect masculine beauty, and I could see how my sister would have been distracted by his good looks. But it wasn't his looks that'd had Swan falling in love with him, it was his brains. Both Stewart and Swan were brilliant, and I'd often listened to them theorize about different things, inventions he was working on and weapons he was tinkering with.

See, much like my father, Stewart was an arms dealer, but a little different. While my father had nothing to do with the manufacturing process of weapons, Stewart was known in the criminal world for his customized toys. What a lot of people didn't realize was that not only was Stewart a mechanical genius, he was a skilled hacker who had a thirst for knowledge, along with a curiosity to explore the forbidden that was likely to get him killed one day. Still, it was that curiosity I was counting on to get him to help me.

Mimi was out of earshot, and my dad was out on the range fixing fencing to keep our dairy cows from wandering off, but I knew I didn't have much time, so I cut to the chase and laid everything out for Stewart, starting with, "I need your help."

After I finished my slightly abbreviated version of events, Stewart stood and began to pace. "Where's Swan?"

I wanted to snap at him that she was none of his fucking business, but I swallowed my anger and pride. "She's safe with Iron Horse."

His glare cut through me. "You really believe that? If what you say is true, Sarah, you're already dead, you just don't know it yet."

My stomach lurched and I forced myself not to throw up, ignoring the burn in my throat. "I need to find my mom, Stewart. Please, please help me."

"I don't know what I can do." He paced back and forth, his long legs eating up the flooring. "Jesus, Sarah...this is just so fucked."

"I know."

He froze. "Your dad knows what's up?"

"No."

"Why not? Shit, he can help you more than I ever could."

"Because he'll kill her, Stewart. Think about it."

My whisper was full of shame and he stopped pacing. "Yeah...fuck. Fuck. Okay, first things first, you think someone is tracking you, right?"

"Yes."

"What have you had with you this whole time?"

"Ummm, my purse, my car, my guns and some other stuff."

"Your parents may get suspicious if your car disappears, so we'll leave it here for now. But give me your phone."

"Iron Horse has some badass tech guys on their payroll that make sure my phone is secure."

"Still, I may find something they might have missed."

"Fine." I stood and stretched out, my back cracking before I went to my purse and got my phone. "Here."

He took the sparkly purple phone with a raised brow.

"What?"

Shaking his head, he put the phone in his pocket. "If I show up here again your parents are going to suspect something. They know we don't get along and the last thing I need is Mimi pissed at me. I happen to like my dick still attached to my body. If I find out anything, I'll send Lyric."

At the mention of the sweet girl who was one of my sister's best friends, I smiled. "Thank you, Stewart. I know you have no reason to help me, so I owe you one, and I always pay my debts."

He shook his head, a red flush coloring his high cheekbones. "Nah, we're good. I...things didn't end well between Swan and myself, as you well know, and I owe it to her to do this. You know, karma and all that mumbo-jumbo Mimi's constantly talking about."

Shaking my head, I bit back tears as the reality of the truth of how utterly fucked I was at this moment crashed over me. "Help me find my mom, Stewart, please. I know I screwed you over with my sister, and I'm sorry, but you wouldn't come clean and I was afraid she wouldn't believe me."

The sun glinted off his golden hair as he gave me a solemn nod. "Yeah, that was really messed up. Pretending that you were giving me a blow job? If Swan wasn't such an innocent, she would have noticed I was as limp as an over-boiled noodle. But you're right...I probably would have married her and made us both miserable forever, so I apologize."

Cocking my head to the side, I took him in as he gazed out the front window, pulling the lace curtain over just enough to see out. "Wow, Stewart, when the hell did you stop being such a giant douchebag?"

"I fell in love." He let the curtain drop then gave me a small smile that was anything but happy. "With a man who won't publicly love me back for fear of being shunned from his community for his sin against a homosexual-hating God."

"Shunned from his...holy shit, Stewart, did you fall in love with a member of Lyric's cult?"

He flushed beet red and angrily fisted his hands at his sides. "Just— forget I said anything."

"No, no, I'm sorry. I didn't mean to offend you, it's just kind of..."

"Ironic?" he supplied with a tight voice. "I am very aware. So maybe I'm hoping some good karma will bring this man that I can't stop thinking about into my life for good. Maybe if I find your mom, Lady Karma will call us even for my toying with Sarah's emotions all those years."

"Maybe," I whispered back.

He abruptly lifted his chin. "Right. Let me get to work on this. You said she might be in Colorado?"

"It's just a hunch."

"Well, at least it's a starting point."

I didn't hear from Lyric until late the next day, and by that time I was more than eager to get on with whatever needed to be done in order to find Billie.

A heavy weight of guilt clung to me, wanting to pull me down into a depression that urged me to stay here, to hide, to let the world burn down as long as I was safe. Of course I resisted it, but it was hard to remain positive when I learned—thanks to a local Austin news station's website—that a member of the MC, someone I knew, had been shot in the back of the head, assassination style. It bore all the hallmarks of a professional hit, and I feared the Russians had grown tired of waiting. Everything inside screamed at me to call Beach, to get a burner from Mimi and contact him to let him know that I was okay, but I couldn't chance it. I had to vanish into thin air or my enemies would tear me apart.

A chime rang through the massive underground living room, with a state-of-the-art gigantic TV screen that took up one entire wall seamlessly. It played live broadcasts from different parts of the world, all set up to look like we were looking out an enormous glass window into some amazing backyards. Right now, the image was of sunset over some distant ocean framed by lush greenery, the darkened colors fitting my mood. The faint accompanying sound of waves helped break up the silence that came from being far below ground and added to the mental illusion that we were in some tropical paradise.

Mimi looked up from her tablet and smiled at me, her dark eyes searching my face. "Lyric's here. She must have heard through the gossip grapevine that you were home."

I swear, if I could lie to Mimi and get away with it, I could fool Satan. Schooling my face into a happy smile, I put the glossy gossip magazine I'd been reading down on the grey couch. After sleeping in, I felt refreshed and my stomach wasn't as queasy as usual. Mimi had been surprised, and happy, when I'd wolfed down two enormous waffles covered with berries and whipped cream. I knew she'd noticed something was off with me, but she tried her best not to push me and I appreciated it more than she would ever understand.

Shoving myself up from the extremely comfy couch, I stretched with a yawn. "Who needs the Internet when you've got the compound's phone tree?"

"True," Mimi laughed before adjusting her stylish black reading glasses. "Tell Lyric she's welcome to stay for dinner. We hardly see her anymore and I miss her."

"I will."

While I made my way quickly to the surface, I tried to tamp down the sense of foreboding that filled me and braced myself for whatever news Lyric had, or didn't have, from Stewart. I don't want to say he was my last hope, but he was my best at the moment, and after days and days of finding absolutely nothing to lead me to Billie, I prayed he could pull a miracle out of his ass.

As soon as I opened the back door, Lyric flung herself into my arms, hugging me tight. She was a little curvy thing, and hugging her was like hugging a super-soft and perfect memory foam pillow. No one on earth gave hugs like this girl, and I gladly squeezed her back, letting her happy laughter soothe something inside of me. Her head only came up to my shoulder and her lovely hazel eyes sparkled up at me as she stepped back, holding me at arm's length. The smile faded from her face as she studied me closer, her strong, dark brows pulling down as she frowned.

"Sarah, have you been sick?"

"I look that bad, huh?"

"No—no, you just seem...tired."

"You mean I look like death warmed over?"

"Pretty much." Pink tinged her cheeks and she motioned to me, her long floral skirt blowing around her brown hiking boots. "Can we talk out by the tree?"

I had to resist the urge to glance over my shoulder at the hidden cameras my parents had all over the house as I smiled. "Sure."

She was quiet while we made our way across the open backyard, heading towards the picnic area set up in a field that butted against a sheer rock cliff behind our house that went up five stories. I can tell you from personal experience that cliff is one motherfucker to climb. This section of my parents' property was used for entertaining, and it was set up to accommodate a large group of people, with over two dozen picnic tables.

One would think that a bunch of prepper compounds of different flavors and beliefs would keep away from each other, but here in our little slice of the Texas Hill Country, it was the opposite. Everyone talked to everyone, and while they may argue about who was right and wrong, they all agreed we were equally fucked and that led to a certain sense of kinship among the crazy. Plus, if the world did implode, everyone knew they could rely on their neighbors to get through the tough times and back to the sweet. Or at least that's how Swan explained it.

We took a seat on one of the well-made pine tables beneath the old sassafras tree that dominated this portion of the yard. A light wind stirred both the leaves and wisps of Lyric's waist-length brown hair that had escaped her braid. She smoothed a piece back then pulled a folded envelope from her dowdy skirt's pocket.

"Here, Stewart asked me to give this to you."

"Did he say what it is?"

She shrugged, her gaze darting away from mine. "I didn't see him. Eli, Stewart's...friend, brought it to me."

I raised my eyebrows as I tried to remember who Eli was. "Eli? The skinny blond kid with all those freckles? He's Stewart's boyfriend?"

"Yes, and the new pastor is totally against homosexuality. Says it's an abomination. Eli's struggling with his feelings right now."

Lyric's father, the old head pastor of the Christian compound where Lyric lived, had passed away recently. Upon his death, a leadership void had been left within the church, but it was quickly filled by some dickhead pastor who'd somehow slithered his way into Lyric's mother's, Evelyn's, no doubt ice-cold and dry-as-a-bone panties.

To make things worse, the guy was a not-so-closeted white supremacist, and he had brought a bunch of new families with him. My dad had been pretty pissed off about that, but he'd had some kind of conversation with the pastor that left my dad satisfied enough that he'd let them stay. Probably had something to do with the fact that Lyric wouldn't leave the compound until her grandmother, who'd pretty much raised her, passed away. The old woman was completely lost to Alzheimer's and weak as a newborn kitten, but showed no signs of departing this world anytime soon, leaving Lyric and her church to care for the old woman.

Lyric looked around quickly, as if afraid someone had overheard us. "You can't say anything. Eli would be kicked out if anyone found out and he's afraid to leave his sisters alone with their parents. He doesn't get along with the new pastor as it is, and I don't want to make things any tougher for him than they are.

"Look, I know this is hard for you to understand because you grew up in the outside world, but for people like me and him—we're completely handicapped by our isolation. We have no idea how to get jobs, or find a place to stay, or even how to use credit cards. I mean, *I* do because you guys showed me how, but Eli is a true believer. He never had any interest in anything but serving the church that took care of him. Now that things are different, he's struggling to adjust his view of the world. Stewart's helping him figure out how to get legal custody of his sisters, but it isn't going to be easy."

I came to a snap decision that felt right. "If he wants out, just let me know. I can set up him with a new identity, him and the girls. He'll have to deal with the fact that he'll be under the protection of a bunch of outlaw bikers, but he'll be free."

Giving a hysterical giggle, Lyric waved her hands around in the air. "Oh sure, that'll totally put his mind at ease. I'm sure he'd love to rescue his two beautiful, sixteen- and eighteen-year-old sisters, only to find them surrounded by criminal bikers instead of racist assholes. I'm sure he'll be totally fine with that."

"Honey, you need to leave."

"Whatever." She wrinkled her small nose at my often repeated advice, a determined expression shutting her heart-shaped face down. "What's going on with you and Stewart? Last I heard you two hated each other after BJ Gate."

I grimaced at the name my friends on the compound have given my rash, drunken attempt to convince Swan her fiancé was no good for her. I'd staged it to look like I was giving Stewart oral sex in one of the stupidest attempts to help my sister in human history. Just the memory of how badly it had all gone made me want to shrink down in embarrassment. "We've got business."

The color left her face. "Sarah, please tell me you're not getting involved in your dad's stuff. You know I love Mike, but what he does isn't safe."

"No, no, nothing like that." I shoved away the taunting thought that Iron Horse most certainly dealt in illegal firearms, like my dad.

She glanced at the utilitarian watch on her wrist before sucking in a hard breath. "Crap, I need to head back before it gets too late and they notice I'm gone."

The worry in her voice alarmed me and I grasped her elbow with the hand not holding the envelope. "So what if you're out late? What are they going to do, ground you?"

Something that really bothered me gleamed in her wide eyes for a moment before she jerked her hand free. "Just extra prayer time. I'm sorry I can't stay longer, really I am."

I wanted to argue with her and try to get her to hang out, but I needed to make sure Lyric gave a message to Swan before she left. Deep in my heart, I knew she was in Iron Horse custody by now, and I also knew she'd come looking for me. Back at my home in Austin, I'd left a message for her in a rather unconventional place, a huge dildo I'd gotten as a joke for Beach. Inside the battery compartment I'd stashed a message for her, letting her know that she needed to go to my parents' house. Like a fucked-up scavenger hunt, I'd leave another message with Lyric, letting Swan know where I was going next. It wasn't like I had my phone and could text her, because Stewart now had my phone.

Shit, he still had my phone—which probably meant something was wrong with it.

"Hold on one sec," I said as I ripped open the envelope from Stewart.

A quick scan had me swallowing back bile as I learned my phone had all kinds of fucked-up shit on it, and that someone had been able to hear and read my every call and text, as well as locate me for who knows how long. As I read on, my palms grew damp with fear. Stewart had done some digging, and like me, he highly suspected there was a traitor—or traitors—in Iron Horse MC, and that they held positions of authority within the club. My hand shook as I scanned the document, trying to process all the information he'd given me.

My mind latched on to the word "Colorado" and my pulse raced as I read the paragraph that changed everything.

Your mom is either in or headed to somewhere around Boulder, Colorado. Word on the dark web is that there will be a major deal going on there soon with multiple buyers bidding on some top-of-the-line weaponry, including missiles. I looked over the manifest for the cargo Iron Horse had been moving and it pretty much matches up, minus a few things. My best guess is if you go there, you're going to find your cargo if you can find out where the sale is going to take place. Oh, and if I was a betting man, I'd say Iron Horse's Colorado clubhouse has some traitors in it as well. I'd avoid going to them for help unless you want to end up being sold into sexual slavery.

"Sarah." Lyric gently grasped my wrist with her oddly calloused and rough fingers. "Sarah, breathe."

I must have worried her because she began to rub my arm briskly, almost like she was trying to warm me up.

For a moment I stared dumbly at her before my I muttered out, "Gotta go to Colorado."

"What?"

Pulling my arm from her grasp, I quickly folded the letter and shoved it in my pocket. "Swan will probably be here in a few days. When she arrives, you need to give her a message for me, it's very important. Can you do that?"

The breeze blew the fine strands of her hair, lifting them in a gentle dance as she chewed on her thumb. "Yes, I should be able to."

As I passed on the information I wanted her to relay to Swan, and probably Smoke as well, because I doubted he'd let her out of his sight, I began to plot my journey that would lead me to my mother, hopefully before it was too late.

Chapter 10

I clung to the sides of the toilet, black spots dancing across my vision as I retched and tried to hold my abdomen. My core muscles ached from all the heaving I'd done and I wondered dimly if the altitude in Golden, Colorado, was somehow fucking with me. All I knew was that in the few days I'd been here, my morning sickness had returned with a vengeance and I was out of my anti-nausea medicine, which left me up shit creek without a paddle. Sweat lay heavy on my skin, and I gasped as I hugged the rim of the toilet I personally cleaned every night like it was a piece of lab equipment in a biological warfare research hospital. I knew, without fail, I'd be slumped over the porcelain throne like I currently was, and I wanted it as clean as possible.

Nothing like heaving into a toilet and noticing a mold stain beneath the rim.

Urk.

My brain was pounding with a massive stress headache that had me seeing more dots and I wanted to just curl up in a ball and weep, but I couldn't. Even though my muscles ached like I'd climbed forty flights of stairs, and even my bones felt brittle, I had to be strong. Giving up was not an option. I had to find my mom, though all I wanted to do was run home to Beach and lose myself in the safety of his arms, but if I did that, people—lots and lots of people—would die. More importantly, the baby growing inside of me would suffer if I gave up under the seemingly insurmountable odds.

When the last wave of nausea passed, I cleaned myself up and stumbled into the bedroom area of the extended-stay cabin where I was holed up in Golden. The worn but clean log cabin butted up against fifteen acres of forest that ended at the back of the Iron Horse MC's main compound, perfectly positioned for spying.

Three months ago, I'd have been over there right now, staking the place out and looking for someone or something to fuck up. I felt, deep in my gut, that there was someone in that clubhouse who knew where my mom was. All I had to do was be patient and I would catch them…that is, if I could ever go more than three hours without puking.

My breath left me in a low sigh as I lie back for a moment and let my poor body rest.

The cabin I was staying in had been built probably sometime in the 1970s, and had been upgraded over time, but bits and pieces of original décor still sat here and there. My wandering gaze went from the floral curtains, faded and slightly stained, to the parquet flooring, and up to the exposed beams of the massive logs that made up the cabin, which someone at some time had painted white. The forest-green comforter on the squishy bed was new, but the chipped, modular wooden end tables had seen much better days. But I didn't choose this place as my hideout so I could vacation in luxury. I needed something isolated, safe, and close to the clubhouse.

As this cabin aged, the wood became stronger, denser, and would become hard enough to stop bullets. The windows looking out into the forest were a liability, but the walls gave me a feeling of security, however false, that I desperately needed. I was exhausted in every way and held on to my panic by ever-dwindling threads. This pregnancy could leave me in serious trouble if I didn't get some kind of medical attention soon.

Right now I was as week as a newborn kitten and out of options. I had to get some more of that anti-nausea medicine and I had to do it soon. The soft layer of fat I'd built up had melted away despite my best efforts to keep myself hydrated and fed. If it went on much longer, I'd need to go to a hospital—and that was a bad idea. Even though I was pretty sure my fake ID would hold up, there was no way I could give them access to any past medical records because they didn't exist. If I had time, I could find someone to forge me a medical history, but I was trying to keep off the radar as much as possible. Besides, other than Marley, anyone could be a traitor. The thought of the men and women I considered friends stabbing me in the back sent a pain of a different kind through my heart.

My options were slim, and that had led me to taking a desperate leap of faith and calling the one person I knew in Colorado who had access to prescription medications that I trusted. Poppy Garcia, aka The Green Goddess. In her late forties, the kind and brilliant woman was in charge of developmental marijuana research for the Iron Horse MC. Beach had seen huge money-making possibilities in the designer marijuana field and had secured Poppy, a brilliant bio-chemist, to develop Iron Horse's marijuana. He'd wanted Iron Horse to have the best stuff around so we could be the go-to regional supplier for high-grade weed. Beach had once again predicted the future with almost scary accuracy and Iron Horse was making money hand over fist at the legal dispensaries we backed throughout Colorado.

Poppy, on the other hand, could give a shit about the commercial aspect of the plant. She did research in her free time on different kinds of medicinal marijuana and her results were amazing. She was a devoted advocate for people with cancer, having survived two rounds of chemo and losing both her breasts in her late twenties. The experience had marked her and gave her an almost mystical calm that never failed to relax me.

I'd met Poppy back in Austin when Beach and I first started dating, and I'd visited her farm every time I came up to visit. I trusted her enough that an hour ago, I'd placed a very short phone call to her, asking for an enormous favor.

Glancing at my watch, I saw it was time to get ready to meet her at the rendezvous point we'd set up. I rinsed my mouth out with a burningly strong mouthwash, then chugged some water and got my barf-bag kit ready.

Because I wasn't able to discuss being pregnant with anyone, I spent a lot of time on a couple of those anonymous online pregnancy sites where they had topics covering just about every aspect of pregnancy, and a lot of good discussions on some of the issues I was facing. One lady had posted her ever-so-helpful barf-bag kit, a brown paper bag with a gallon Ziplock baggy inside of it. Beneath the plastic bag was a small, sealed container with a toothbrush and toothpaste, along with more mouthwash. Bad smells set off my nausea and I didn't want to taste puke in my mouth all day. Just the thought had my stomach roiling.

Forcing my mind back to business, I checked the fit of my dark brunette wig one more time before exiting my cabin, locking the door and heading for the parking lot. My ride tonight was a lovely blue minivan from the early 2000s with a lot of use on it. The vehicle looked like it was used to transport kids around, complete with the interior faintly smelling of French fries. Nobody paid attention to Mom-mobiles. To blend in with the minivan, I'd worn a large University of Colorado sweatshirt that I'd gotten at a secondhand clothes shop, along with a pair of thick-framed, trendy green glasses. They were merely for show, but there were studies proving that glasses messed with a human being's ability to identify a face. I also wore brown contacts and more makeup than usual, aging myself, along with a simple fake gold wedding band.

This look was one of seven disguises I rotated through, and it would work best at the coffee shop I was meeting Poppy at. It was a little strip mall off the beaten track outside of Golden, a place I'd scoped out earlier and found to be sufficient for my needs. Small, clean, and quiet, yet public enough with all the neighborhoods around it that if someone tried to grab me, or there was trouble, enough people around me had cell phones to summon help. I wasn't expecting anything to go wrong, but it was always good to imagine some worst case scenarios before going into any new situation.

I parked in the paved lot the coffee shop shared with a shipping place, a small grocery store, and a hair salon, then scanned the area again. It was busier than I'd expected, and I found myself starting to breathe faster as paranoia tried to rob me of my senses. No, I wasn't going to start seeing enemies everywhere. I would be smart and evaluate the situation like my father trained me to do, not spazz like a spooked animal.

Forcing myself to really pay attention to my surroundings, I looked through the windows of all the places I could see from here and didn't find anything alarming. Bikers would have stood out like a sore thumb among this upper-middle-class crowd, no matter how hard they tried to disguise themselves. There were two motorcycles in the lot, but they were tricked-out, flashy street-racing bikes and men like Beach would never be caught on one.

My heart rate slowed and I took a deep breath, doing everything I could to calm.

As far as I could see, it was just a normal early evening in the natural splendor of Golden. In fact, it was a beautiful. Great weather for going for a ride with Beach. The thought of touring through this town on the back of Beach's bike roared through me and I had to close my eyes and tighten my grip on the steering wheel, fighting the tears. I'd been so proud to be his old lady, so proud of wearing his patch on my back and reveling in being his.

A tingle went up my spine and I instantly went on alert, looking for whatever had caught my subconscious attention.

Nothing looked out of place and I scanned the coffee shop again, looking for Poppy. I didn't see her, but I did recognize her pimp-ass navy-blue Land Rover with its dark-tinted windows parked near the front door. I knew it was hers because it had a happy face daisy sticker sparkling on the back bumper. Only Poppy would put a sticker that looked like it belonged to a seventh-grade girl on her sixty-thousand-dollar custom ride.

The heavy scent of coffee filled me as I left the minivan and stalked across the parking lot, my stomach growling with the desire to gulp down gallons of fresh, hot coffee. Yeah, lucky me gets cravings for strong coffee instead of ice cream and pickles. Too bad I'd already had my quota of one half cup of coffee today, so I wouldn't indulge, but that didn't mean I couldn't torture myself with the smell. The closer I got, the stronger the scent became, and by the time I pushed the doors open I was practically salivating at the thought of one of those big, thick, creamy coffee shakes with caramel drizzle on it.

I scanned the small sitting area with its cute white-painted wrought iron tables and fancy yet folksy chairs. One of the tables was occupied by some hipster dude in a black skullcap typing away furiously on his laptop while bobbing his head to whatever music was playing on his headphones. I ignored him and spotted Poppy next—but she wasn't alone.

My feet took a step back without me even being aware I was retreating as I wondered if Poppy had betrayed me. She was talking to a woman with her back to me. Older, with silver threading artfully through her dark hair, she sat with a poise and grace I would recognize anywhere.

As she turned to face me, my stomach sank as my eyes met Mimi's familiar dark brown ones, filled with anger.

I didn't care how angry she was. I was relieved beyond belief because my mom, my real mom, was here to help save me from the bitch who gave birth to me.

To both our shock, I burst into loud tears and started to stumble to her. Until this moment, I really, deep down, thought I was in this alone, that I would have to do everything by myself. The part of me that had never grown up rejoiced that she was here, knowing without a doubt she'd die to protect me. Her strong, slender arms wrapped around me tightly and I clung to her, sobbing as she shushed me. Various knives strapped to her body pressed against mine, but that only made me feel safer.

Yep, I was officially way overdue for a session with my therapist.

Poppy stood next to Mimi and rubbed my back while whispering, "Shhhh, honey, get ahold of yourself. You're drawing attention that you don't need."

I took in a shuddering breath and mentally cursed my hormones for making me freak out like this. I whispered into Mimi's ear, "I-I'm sorry. I just…I missed you so much. I'm so scared and I missed you so much."

Jerking back, Mimi studied my face, and what she saw there must have been as pitiful as I felt because her gaze softened. "Ahhh, *bambina*, the messes you get yourself into. Come, we need to talk in private."

"I have a cabin."

Mimi's lip curled as she slid her grey suede Dior handbag over her shoulder, the somewhat short skirt she wore inching up a bit in the back as she bent over to leave a tip on the table.

"I have seen your cabin. No thank you."

A man joined us, the hipster writer I'd seen earlier, and I almost reached for my gun before I looked past his disguise to see the familiar and handsome face of my cousin Vinnie. Yes, I actually had a cousin Vinnie. Nice guy, but a real smartass who often got himself in trouble with his grandfather, the head of the Stefano Mafia. Vinnie tried to tone it down, but when God made him, he gave my cousin a huge set of balls and very little common sense. Thankfully Vinnie also knew how to handle himself in a fight, because he seemed to stir up trouble wherever he went.

"What's up, cuz?" He grinned at me, then squinted his eyes. "You look like shit warmed over."

"Thanks."

We left soon after that and piled into Poppy's Land Rover. I ended up in the back with my cousin, while Poppy and Mimi sat up front. "How did you get up here so quick? I only called Poppy three hours ago."

"Lady Karma," Mimi said with a smug smile while Vinnie groaned.

Like most of the Stefano men, Vinnie didn't believe in "woo woo bullshit" like karma and fate. The women, however, were very superstitious and made their men's lives hell because of it. I can still remember my aunt Theresa whacking her husband over the head until he turned around the car we were riding in so she could get a turtle out of the road. She was convinced if we drove past it without offering aid, we'd be cursed. Her husband had been pissed about wasting time over a turtle, but he did it.

"It was fate." Poppy nodded her head in agreement. "Not five minutes after I hung up with you, Sarah, Mimi just happened to show up on my doorstep, letting me know she was leaving Vinnie with me to act as a bodyguard."

"What?"

Smiling at Poppy, Mimi looked into the rearview mirror and met my gaze. "When Mike told me about Poppy being part of the transport deal, and where she lived, I knew where one of our first stops in Colorado would be."

"You think they'll come after her? I mean, she's not really a part of Iron Horse, other than business."

"Possibly."

"Why?"

"Because," Poppy said as she passed a slow-moving sedan, "I'm an expert in about a zillion different plant-related things. There are very few people in the world that have the credentials that I do, and only one or two in the US besides me. While I don't know what kind of saplings they're moving, I do know they're delicate and priceless."

"A priceless plant?"

"Don't look at me like I'm crazy."

Vinnie totally was.

"Think about it this way, what if it's a tree whose fruit cures cancer? Or produces leaves that can eat up oil slicks? Or a new type of apple tree that can grow even in the desert and produces three crops a year?"

"They can do that shit?" Vinnie asked in a low voice.

"Maybe. Science is advancing at an exponential rate, the new discoveries that happened once every fifty years now coming every month. Who knows what kind of crazy shit someone invented." We stopped at a red light and Poppy's worried gaze met mine in the rearview mirror. "Or it could be a biological weapon. A new flower with pollen poisonous to humans, or some type of new disease-bearing tree found deep in the Amazon rainforest. These saplings are with a shipment of weapons; it would seem odd to have a cancer-curing tree amongst so much destruction."

"*Dio dannato*," Vinnie whispered.

Mimi drew in a deep breath and let it out slowly. "We can guess all day long and it won't do us any good. Poppy, can you recall anything else in your instructions that might give us a clue?"

"Nope. I was told my role would be explained to me when I joined the transport crew. If I had a look at the plants I could probably tell you something, but so far I know next to nothing about them."

I looked down at my ragged nails, almost afraid to ask the next question. "Have you heard anything about Iron Horse?"

Mimi stiffened while Poppy shook her head. "No, I've been out of the country in Japan until a few days ago."

I examined my stepmother, who was giving off some really weird vibes. "Meems, do you know something?"

She sighed. "We will discuss it later."

"Mimi, what do you know? And don't lie to me, please, even if you think it's for my own good."

"Last night, two members of Iron Horse were killed in a hit-and-run that we believe was no accident. But that's not the worst part." Her voice cracked as she said, "One of the teenage daughters of one of the members was abducted from her afterschool job last night. We believe it was the Sokolov *Bratva*."

Poppy made a soft, mournful noise as I breathed out, "Who? Wait—Sokolov, like Tom Sokolov?"

"No." Mimi's expression was downright frightening. "Tom Sokolov is nothing like his Russian relatives that now run the Sokolov *Bratva*. They are animals, scum, and he is a good man-nothing like his cousins overseas. In fact, he hates them. Now, I said we will discuss that later and I mean it."

Anger bubbled up in me as my mind ran through the long list of children I'd met who belonged to the members of the Iron Horse MC, hundreds of bright eyes, shy smiles, and happy laughs. One of those sweet girls could be suffering right now, having God knows what done to her by monsters pretending to be men, and Mimi wanted to discuss it later. I struggled to contain myself while Vinnie gave me a weary look.

"A young girl might be being *tortured* right now and that isn't important enough to talk about?"

"No," Mimi snapped, turning in her seat to glare at me. "Because we need to stop the next young girl from being taken, and the only way we'll be able to do that is if we find your mother. Besides, Beach is handling things back in Austin."

"Have you talked to him? Crap, are you going to tell him I'm here? I'd really rather you didn't; if he found out, he'd kill any chances I have of finding my mom."

She slowly shook her head, looking not happy in the least. "No, I'm not going to tell him you are here, but not for the reasons you think. He's keeping Iron Horse from fragmenting beneath the onslaught of its enemies and he needs to focus all his attention on what's going on down there. If Carlos knew you were here, he'd drop everything, no matter how delicate, and come get you."

I slumped back into the comfortable leather seat, my head resting as I looked out the window. "Yeah, he would. He really loves me."

Tears welled in my eyes while Vinnie grunted and muttered something about "chick shit" before saying louder, "I hate to interrupt this Lifetime Movie moment, but Swan is gonna be arriving in town soon with some fuck-up named Smoke—who the fuck names these guys anyway?—and they're stayin' in a place filled with bikers, some of whom are most assuredly traitors. So while I'm all a-fucking-flutter that some stupid biker asshole is sticking his dick in you— Ow!"

His words cut off abruptly as I gave him a titty-twister that left him rubbing his chest and scowling, "Don't talk about Beach like that, ever, do you understand me?"

"Fine! Shit, you nearly ripped my damn nipple off."

I bared my teeth at him as Mimi said in an exasperated voice, "Children. Back on task, please."

Vinnie sneered at me, but returned his attention to Mimi. "Yes, ma'am."

Mimi arched a brow at me and I nodded. "Yes, ma'am."

"Good. Now, we're going back to Poppy's house. Your cousins Mark and Paul are hacking into some of the traffic and security cameras around the city as we speak. They have this new facial recognition software that they swear is the greatest thing since pasta."

I took that in, my thoughts racing as I tried to process everything happening around me all at once. "How did you know where I was?"

"Actually, I followed Swan up here. She told us what was happening and I decided to pay a visit as well. While she's driving up with Smoke, myself, Marco, and Vinnie flew so we could beat her here."

My mouth went dry. "Is Dad coming up here as well?"

"No, your father is working with some of his buddies to try to hunt your mother down."

"Is he mad?"

Vinnie cackled. "Yeah, you could say that. You could also say he's gone off on a murderous rampage, ready to take apart anyone who's harmed his sweet girls. First stop, your boyfriend who loves you soooooo much."

Shit. "He's going to Austin?"

From the front seat, Mimi sighed. "He found out last night about the young girl and went on the warpath. You know your father has a very, very negative view of men dragging children into their dangerous bullshit."

My stomach clenched and I tried to relax by taking a couple deep breaths before I spoke in a faint voice, "Is he going to help Beach or try to kill him?"

The arch look she gave me made me want to hunch down. "Really, Sarah, if your father wanted Carlos dead, he would be. He's going there to help."

A weight lifted from my shoulders. "Really?"

"Yes, really. I know your head was filled with terrible thoughts about Mike when you were with Billie, but Sarah, I promise you, he loves you more than anything in the world and wants you to be happy. We've seen you and Carlos together, we know you love each other, and we're grateful you're with a good man—in his own way. That doesn't mean your father will stop threatening to neuter Carlos, but he doesn't really mean it."

Vinnie spoke up from next to me, his voice cold and hard, without a trace of the usual teasing laughter. "I know the men Beach are dealing with, I've done business with the Russians in the past, and I spent some time with the Israelis. Both will consider it their sacred duty to destroy the Iron Horse MC."

Tears of frustration burned my eyes and I looked away again, training my gaze on the freeway speeding by in orange-ish patches of light followed by darkness as the sun fully set. "I know."

Poppy cleared her throat. "I can't help but notice you don't look very good, Sarah. Have you been to a doctor? Why do you need the Zofran? That's not something they usually prescribe for minor things like the flu."

I considered lying for a moment, but Mimi had to know my limitations right now. Where I'd usually rush into danger like a bull through a field of clover, now I had to protect the innocence growing inside of me. One good kick to my stomach during a fight and I could lose him or her.

I rested my hand on the small baby bump, growing harder and bigger by the day. "It's not the flu. I have super-bad morning sickness."

Silence filled the car and I swear to God everyone held their breath for a few seconds before Mimi shrieked out, "You're pregnant?"

Unsure if she was super-mad, super-happy, super-pissed, or super-excited, I wearily nodded. "Yeah. I'm somewhere between thirteen and fifteen weeks right now. I haven't been to the doc yet for my second trimester visit, for obvious reasons. You don't have to say it, I know I'm a terrible mother already, but I swear I've done my best to stay as healthy as I can."

For a long moment Mimi said nothing, and I became a little worried as she stared out the Land Rover's tinted windshield without blinking. "Meems?"

She held up her hand, then turned as much as she could in her seat, her dark eyes glittering fiercely as she pinned me to my seat with her gaze. "I never want to hear you say that again."

I blinked back tears, confused and stung by her words. "What?"

"You will be the best mother in the world for the baby growing inside of you. So filled with love, so smart and strong, you will be amazing and your child will know nothing but love from you." Her hair fell forward as she tilted her head slightly and gave me a sad smile. "Does Carlos know? I'm guessing not, or he'd have you locked away in some gilded cage on his private island to keep you safe."

Ignoring the truth of that statement, I nervously smoothed back the synthetic hair of my wig. "I—well, I haven't really had a chance to tell him yet."

Vinnie let out a low whistle. "Wait, wait, lemme get this straight. You not only ran off on this guy—who is a hard-case psycho motherfucker, by the way—you also failed to mention that you were pregnant with his kid before you took off after your *puttana* mother who fucked them over sideways. Shit. How long you been gone now?"

"Two weeks," I muttered.

"First, let me say congratulations. Like my aunt, I know you're gonna be a great mother." Vinnie crossed himself before laughing. "Second, lemme know when you tell the proud papa you've been hunting a group of professional killers—alone. I wanna make sure I'm at least five states away when he loses his shit."

With a groan, I removed the glasses and shoved them into my purse before rubbing my face. "You really think he's going to freak?"

The look Vinnie gave me was an odd mixture of sympathy and amusement. "Oh yeah."

Shit.

The next morning, I woke up in a nice room with thick gold curtains blocking the light, wearing what looked like a pair of silky pajamas with cupcakes on them. They were strangely familiar. I flopped back and stared at the textured white ceiling above me, my eyes drawn to the beams of streaming light as I tried to figure out what I was going to do. Even in my dreams I'd worried about what was going to happen, and I'd been haunted by nightmares of girls I knew getting kidnapped as revenge against the Iron Horse MC for losing all that valuable merchandise.

Cupcakes...I was wearing Mimi's cupcake pajamas. I'd had to borrow a pair because I only had the clothes I was wearing with me. They were loose on me everywhere except the chest and I absently rubbed my curved belly.

My wig sat on a white-pine dresser, along with my neatly folded—and no doubt washed—clothes. I'm a light sleeper, odd noises will pull me from a deep sleep to instant alertness, but somehow Mimi had been in and out of the modest bedroom without waking me once. It was either a testament to her skills, or an indication of how worn out I was.

Turning my head to the side, I glanced at the blue digital clock on a distressed wood table next to the bed. There was a picture of a much younger Poppy standing with an older woman who looked a lot like her. They were hugging and looking into each other's faces while laughing. The love they had for each other was evident, and I wondered if it was Poppy's mother.

The clock read just after ten a.m. and I let out a sigh of relief. The extended-release anti-nausea pill I'd taken twelve hours ago had given me the first good night's sleep since I'd left my parents' house. My body thanked me for it and as I sat up, I wanted to cry with relief. Nothing, no urge to puke, just...blessedly normal.

"Well, little one," I said to my belly, "looks like we just might be okay this morning."

From behind me, Mimi said, "Was it that bad?"

I jumped a little bit before I caught myself. "Jeez, Mimi, way to give me a heart attack."

As I turned over, Mimi slid beneath the sheets next to me, dressed for the day in a long black skirt and sky-blue blouse with a big smile on her face. "A baby."

"That's what the doc said." I studied her, my mind rested enough to turn from constant, selfish, protect-the-peanut-at-all-costs mode to look beyond myself, and I took a deep breath then let it out. "Are you okay with talking about…this kind of stuff?"

Tears filled Mimi's eyes and she nodded. "I will always mourn the daughter your father and I had together, the loss of what she could have been, but my other daughter is bringing a new life into the world, and that is the greatest gift any *nonna* could ever want. Plus, it gives my father leverage."

"Uh—what?"

Sitting up, Mimi reached out and smoothed my hair back from my face, sending a wave of comforting warmth through me. "As I am sure you are aware, this is a very complicated situation, but you being pregnant-carrying a baby, allows him more room to maneuver on your behalf. Just about every major crime organization has a finger in this pie one way or another, either as a step on the supply chain or as an intended recipient. My father cannot openly bring the Stefano mafia into it, our enemies would use it as a way to settle old grudges, and our people will die."

"No, I don't want that to happen."

"Hush, of course not. Neither does your grandfather, so while he does not 'officially' know we are here, he has supplied us with some of his top men, who just happen to be family, to help hunt your mother down." She paused, then added almost as an afterthought, "And Vinnie, but that arrogant child annoys me, so I put him on spy duty at the clubhouse. Oh, and Swan arrived last night."

I could easily see the tension Mimi tried to hide from me and narrowed my eyes. "What happened?"

"Your sister had some kind of fight with Miguel, climbed on the roof, sat there and stewed for a little bit before Miguel found her, made love to her on the roof—"

"Ew, enough of that."

Mimi rolled her eyes. "Then somehow Swan found a transmitting device that was sending video and audio of the clubhouse to an unknown destination."

"Holy shit."

"Indeed. My sources within the clubhouse—"

"Wait, you have sources in Iron Horse?"

"Darling, I have sources *everywhere*." I glared at her but she ignored me. "My sources have informed me that word has spread throughout Denver that Swan is there, and there's a team of Russian bounty hunters employed by the Sokolov *Bratva* looking for her."

"Shit. Why the Sokolovs?"

"My sources," she gave me a poke when I rolled *my* eyes, "tell me that the new leaders of the Sokolov *Bratva* who have risen to power over the last ten years control almost all of the human slave trade in Japan, South Korea, and Eastern Russia, along with a good chunk of Siberia. Evidently, the bounty the *Sokolovs* have put on you is much higher than the bounty for your death."

"Well…" I tried to swallow past the pain in my chest. "That's nice."

Mimi grabbed both my hands, hard enough to hurt, and pulled us almost face-to-face, near enough for me to smell her perfume. "It will never happen. I swear it. I will do whatever it takes to keep my daughters, and grandchild, safe."

The fear that lurked behind her righteous fury had me pulling her into a hug. "I know."

I sat up and eased my legs out of bed, waiting to see if my stomach was going to continue cooperating as I walked to the dresser and dug through my purse for another one of those wonderful, amazing pills that spared me the pain of being sick. "So, Swan…are we pulling a detail on her?"

"*We* are doing nothing. You will be going to a doctor appointment at a clinic, someone who is a friend of the family, while your cousins and I guard Swan."

"I'm coming with you."

"No, you're not. You are going to go to a medical professional who is going to make sure both you and the baby are healthy. Sarah, you're just about skin and bones, that can't be healthy for the *bambino piccolo*."

I rubbed my temples as I tried to think of a way out of this. She was right, I needed to see a doctor—the sooner the better. But there was no way in hell I was going to stay home, or wherever I was, while she went out and risked her life for us. No way. But I couldn't challenge Mimi directly on it or she'd know I planned to blow her off.

Woman had a sixth sense for bullshit so I kept my response to one surly word. "Fine."

"Sarah, you've done so much and risked so much already. I've been doing things like this for a long, long time. I can help you, I really can. But first I need you to help *me* by staying safe while I do what I need to do."

Trying to argue with a retired professional assassin about a job was like trying to argue a horse into turning into a fish.

Not gonna happen.

"How about we discuss it after the doctor visit. Are you coming with me?"

"Yes, but I will have to leave afterward. Vinnie and Marco will be staying with you while I go join the men your father has watching Swan. If we're lucky, the bastards behind the theft might be tempted into doing something stupid and go after her."

"Why would they do that?"

"To further destabilize the situation. They're not stupid. At some point anyone with a brain would figure out who your father is, and who I am. We could be a huge asset to the recovery efforts, but not if we were preoccupied with finding you or Swan after you've been abducted. They don't know we're here yet, we've been very careful to stay under the radar, but the longer we stay, the greater a chance of discovery. They could even trade her to the Sokolov *Bratva* for their protection—and that will start a war."

"A war?"

"Absolutely. I will bring down the wrath of hell to keep you safe, and I have many personal contacts in Russia who owe me. I am more than prepared to bring in every single marker I'm owed to keep my daughters safe."

The intensity of her words and the vibe coming off my normally chill stepmom were downright serial-killer crazy. In an effort to lighten the mood, I muttered, "Sheesh, dramatic much? Have you been hanging around Aunt Esmerelda again?"

At the mention of my very overdramatic aunt, a lovely Hispanic woman married to Mimi's brother, some of the death leaked out of Mimi's dark eyes. "Point taken. Now, off you go. Shower quickly because your appointment is in an hour and a half, and you need to eat first."

"Yes, Mom."

Giving me an affectionate smile, she tucked my hair behind my ear. "Brat. Stop being cute and get in the shower, time is of the essence and all that. Go."

I went, laughing softly as the burden on my soul lifted the slightest bit and hope filled me that everything was going to turn out all right.

Chapter 11

AUSTIN TX

The first sign of trouble came in the form of a phone call Mimi received during my checkup. I was cleaning myself of the goop they'd used on my tummy for the ultrasound so I wasn't really paying attention to Meems. I'd been shocked to see how much the little creature on the screen looked like a real baby instead of a peanut. My mind had marveled at the growth, the creation, that was happening inside of me and I couldn't stop smiling, and crying. I wanted Beach here with me, badly, but it helped having Mimi at my side to wipe away my tears while cooing about the little baby. I swear she was as in love with my baby bump as I was.

While I was swabbing at the swell of my belly, Mimi had retreated to the corner of the room, whispering in rapid Italian. I wasn't really paying attention, caught up in staring at the ultrasound pictures the tech had given me. By the time I had my flowing green empire-waist shirt in place, I registered for the first time the rage coming off my stepmother in waves. The color had drained from her face, but her chest was bright red and her eyes were wild with fury.

"Mimi?"

She held up her hand and I didn't dare interrupt her.

After what felt like an eternity, but was really like twenty seconds, Mimi hung up and strode across the room before grabbing my hands in hers. "Brace yourself."

I nodded, trembling as I anticipated the worst.

"Swan was ambushed by a Russian squad."

"No!"

"Calm yourself," she barked, "your sister is a little banged up, but alive."

"Oh my God, I need to go see her, she must be freaking out. I need to protect her from—"

Mimi released my hands then cupped my face. "Sarah, I told you not to underestimate her. You imagine her as much more fragile than she actually is. She took out four professionally trained hitmen, by herself, without a flinch."

"No."

"Yes."

"Where were the guys watching her?"

Mimi closed her eyes and blew out a long breath. "Dead."

"How?"

She ignored my question, releasing my hands as she checked her weapons hidden beneath her designer clothes. "I have to go take care of some business. Vinnie and Poppy are waiting for you outside, along with an escort. You are going back to her house with them, and you're going to stay there. Please, do this for me. I will not be able to concentrate if I think you might be in danger. I want all your trackers on, am I clear?"

I sucked in a deep breath and nodded, grabbing my purse with the gun inside and thumbing one of the straps, turning the tiny device on inside that would send out my location. Next, I fiddled with the small gold earring in my left ear, twisting it so the tracker activated, then the one on my bra strap. Mimi was a big fan of having back-up plans in case I lost one of the trackers.

Putting the strap of my brown leather purse over my shoulder, I secured it with my hand and followed Mimi out of the office, passing by the rather wide-eyed older receptionist watching us from the foyer.

Vinnie met us right away, with a nervous Poppy scanning the nearby road with a frown. Her normally smiling face was grim and her clothing reflected her mood, a dark denim pair of jeans along with a somber grey peasant blouse. She had deep circles beneath her eyes and I felt guilty for dragging her into this mess. Vinnie pulled me into a hug and, surprised, I hugged him back.

"You okay?" he whispered into my hair.

"Yeah, I'm good."

He released me with an assessing look while Poppy wrapped her arm around my waist. "Come on, hot mama, let's get out of here."

I went to look for Mimi, but she was already gone.

Later that night, I sat next to Poppy on her couch while Vinnie lingered in Poppy's Spanish-style kitchen, drinking some coffee and talking on his phone.

I was dozing off as we watched *Tommy Boy*, lounging back into the thick pillows of Poppy's couch. My belly was full of some kind of Italian pasta dish Vinnie had made for us after I let him know that if he cooked or ate steak in front of me, I was going to barf all over him. It seemed to amuse him to no end that I currently found meat nauseating, and at one point he'd chased me around the kitchen like an asshole with a pack of bologna. Idiot.

Still, his antics had kept my mind off worrying over everyone and for that I was thankful.

On the giant TV screen occupying the far wall, the movie played on but I wasn't really watching it anymore.

My blinks became longer and I started to fall asleep—that is, until the gas canisters were thrown through the windows, shattering the glass in a series of loud bangs coming from all around us.

Next to me, Poppy screamed, and Vinnie yelled something from the kitchen before loud gunshots boomed through the night, deafening me.

The smoke burned my eyes and I began to cough, searching beneath the table for my gun. Poppy fell to the floor not too far from me and I was afraid she was dead, but her chest kept moving. I managed to grab my gun, but the increasing smoke made it hard to see anything.

Black boots strode through the fog to the table I crouched beneath and I shot out the kneecap of whoever was approaching me. I could hear his scream even above the ringing in my ears and I strained to see if anyone else was near. I didn't want to fire blindly into the gloom and waste my ammo, or accidentally hit one of the good guys.

My options were taken away from me when someone stabbed the back of my leg with electrical fire.

I tried to scream but the volts from what had to be a Taser roared through me, rendering me mute.

I was fucked. Mimi was off doing something important, Beach didn't know where I was, and my father was focused on helping Beach retrieve the Iron Horse girls who had been kidnapped.

Ungentle hands picked up my still-twitching body and carried me through the gloom. Once we got out to the front of Poppy's house, I could see the dark night sky above but that was about it. Controlling my neck was beyond me, but I did catch a glimpse of Poppy, taped up like a mummy, before they slid me in next to her. I got treated to the same tape treatment and I fought off tears of despair as I wondered if my baby had been hurt.

After a long ride during which I slipped in an out of consciousness, we finally came to a stop.

By this time Poppy was awake and I was completely out of options. I'd been wearing my pajamas so I didn't have my usual weapons on me. While I'd managed to hold back my tears, she was crying as she looked at me and tried to convey something with her gaze. Before I could figure out what she was trying to tell me, the back doors to the van we were in opened and I was hauled out.

The first thing that caught my eye was a leather vest, and for a brief moment I hoped the Iron Horse Mc had rescued us, but when I saw the Los Diablos colors instead, I knew we were utterly fucked.

It was hard to find my balance as they set me on my feet with my thighs still taped together. I leaned against the side of the van while the men discussed me and Poppy in Spanish. I caught something about taking Poppy aside for questioning and keeping me isolated from her until the Russians arrived. Harsh hands gripped me by my elbows and dragged me into a dirty, crumbling adobe house. I had no idea where we were, but it was quiet and I had a feeling even if I screamed, no one would be around to hear me.

We were surrounded by thick forest and I almost choked on my spit when I saw the two U-Haul trucks partially hidden in the thick woods, one with an "Atlanta, GA" motif on the side, the other with "Seattle, WA".

Holy shit, those were the stolen trucks.

I tried to keep myself from turning to take another look, not wanting them to figure out what I saw. A bright sodium security light flooded the dirt yard before the home and dozens of cigarette butts stood out against the dark ground. Some of the butts had lipstick marks on them.

A good many bore my mom's signature color, "Passion Pink".

I must have stopped walking because the guy behind me kicked me in the ass. The man dragging Poppy snarled at the man behind me not to harm the merchandise. Dimly I was aware of what they were saying, but my mind was mostly freaking out over the thought that somewhere inside that home, my mother waited for me. I was scared, more scared than I'd been in a long time, and I wanted to sob with fear, but if I did I might choke due to my mouth being taped shut.

That would be a terrible way to die.

We were dragged into a living room painted a god-awful purple color that made my eyes hurt. Inside the room sat an older man in a Los Diablos vest and long grey hair pulled back in a braid. His face was weathered and grim, his clothing worn, and the big knife strapped to his thigh looked well used. Dark eyes, like those of a snake, studied me before he looked over at Poppy.

"Take the blonde bitch to the slut hut. I've got some questions for Ms. Poppy here."

I began to struggle as they dragged me away, trying to yell behind the tape to leave her alone. She let out a loud cry and I knew they'd ripped the tape from her mouth. Rage burned through me but I was useless at the moment, trapped as I was dragged down the hall. We passed a room where two men were arguing in a harsh language I didn't understand. Before I could get a good look, I was thrown into a small bedroom with a pair of full-size beds and a dresser.

On the bed with the lilac silk comforter, my mother stared at me in shock, and then, without missing a beat, grabbed a needle full of who the fuck knows what and jabbed it into her already mangled arm. She dropped her gaze for a moment while the asshole behind me cut through the tape binding me, none too gently. I considered taking him out the moment I was free, but I had no idea who was around us at the moment and I couldn't risk what could be my only chance to rescue Poppy.

As soon as my wrists were free, I tore at the tape around my mouth, panic filling me with the need to breathe. My mother withdrew the needle from her vein and her bleary blue eyes found mine.

My heart raced as I took in how much she'd aged since I'd seen her last, somehow looking worse than before even though the bruises from her beating had healed long ago. For one, she was emaciated. I'm talking skeleton-thin. Her augmented breasts sat on her chest like weird lumps beneath her overstretched skin, and I could see the bumps of her collarbone as she fell back into the pillows and watched me with heavy-lidded eyes.

The man behind me whispered into my ear in a snide voice, "Say hi to Mommy."

Fucking figures she would take the cowardly way out. Instead of facing me, giving me some kind of answer or explanation, she'd simply drugged herself to the point of oblivion.

"Useless bitch!" someone yelled behind me as Poppy screamed. "What the fuck kind of plants are those?"

I tried to turn instinctively toward her cry of pain, but before I could move, a hood was placed over my head.

With a harsh chuckle, the man behind me said, "Listen very carefully. You're gonna cooperate with everything we say or I will personally go out there and start cutting off your little friend's fingers and toes, then I'll make you eat 'em."

He groped me, his rough hands pinching my labia as I cried out in revulsion and jerked away from him. Before I knew it, I was thrown onto the bed then held down by at least four guys while a fifth expertly tied me up. I wanted to fight, but my belly was so exposed and I'd do anything to protect my baby. Sour bile filled my mouth as despair ran through me, the agony inside of me reflected by Poppy's screams for mercy, that she didn't know anything.

The door slammed shut and I strained uselessly against the ropes, the hood smelling faintly of stale sweat. For a gruesome moment I wondered how many people had died wearing this hood. The ropes pinched my wrists and I stopped struggling for fear of injuring myself.

A moment later someone touched my arm and I tried to jerk away, a cry escaping me before I could stop it.

"Shhh, Sarah, it's me," came my mom's slurred voice.

"Is anyone else in here?"

"No." Her clumsy fingers pulled at the ropes holding me and for a brief moment I hoped she was going to release me, but all she did was loosen it enough that my fingers no longer tingled.

"Please, you have to help me get out of here."

"Can't," she replied and the bed depressed next to me. "Can't, can't, can't. Never ever cross the Chief."

Shit, she'd fried her brain. I'd dealt with her like this before and knew talking to her was like talking to a self-absorbed brick wall. Still, I had to try, so in a desperate attempt to appeal to her as I mother, I whispered, "Billie, you have to get me out of here. I'm pregnant."

For a long time she said nothing, then mumbled, "Oh, that's terrible."

"What?"

"Terrible. Curse of bad mothers, rotting minds, was hoping I was the last."

"What are you talking about? What curse?"

"You'll hurt your baby, won't be able to stop yourself. Bad mother—just like me."

Her voice was growing weaker and I tried to get through to her before she passed out. "Please, at least take off the hood."

"Can't."

"Yes, you can, just lift it a little bit. Please, it's hard to breathe."

For a moment she touched my face, but it was only to lift the hood enough to sit higher on my chin. "Don't dare. Saw what they did to her. Made me watch. Cut her into little pieces, slowly. Died in agony."

"What are you talking about?"

"Thought she could run, thought she could disappear. I told her not to, but she wouldn't listen." Her voice came out in a terrified rasp. "That'll be me if I betray him!"

"Betray who?"

For a moment she paused, then whispered, "Chief."

"Just help me get out of here and I'll keep you safe, I promise."

"I can't."

"Please, Mom, please. Don't you know what they're going to do with me? Don't you care that your pregnant daughter is going to be sold to some psychopath? What is *wrong* with you?" She abruptly stood and my body rolled slightly on the bed. "Mom?"

"I need my medicine."

Shit, she was going to escape reality again by frying her brain with more drugs. Typical response—avoid, pretend it isn't happening, and take a vacation from reality while I was left to clean up her mess. Despair tried to sink its hooks into me, but I wouldn't let it. I was still alive, and as long as I was alive, there was hope.

I had no idea how long I lay there, Billie had stopped responding to me other than the occasional soft snoring sound. My mind kept wanting to show me images of Poppy being raped and tortured, of little pieces being cut off of her, and my emotions flipped between fear and rage.

I hated being helpless like this, hated being at the mercy of monsters, and hated my mother for abandoning me to this. Maybe she was right, maybe I'd become like she was and be a terrible mother. Maybe there was something genetic that made me predisposed to going crazy. After all, at one time, Billie had been the best mother any little girl could ever want.

Faint memories of being cuddled by her, smelling nice and sweet, while she read me stories in bed filled me, and I tried to stop the tears filling my eyes from falling.

The door to the room opened and I tried to sit up out of instinct, forgetting for a moment that I was tied up.

A man's high-pitched voice yelled, "Shit. Yo, Fez, Billie's takin' a fuckin' nodder."

"Chief wants Billie down in Texas, now. I don't give a fuck if she's dead; he wants her, he gets her."

"Why the fuck would he want that old, diseased piece of junkie trash?"

"Who the fuck knows, but he's not payin' me to ask questions. *You* carry that fuckin' nasty skank. I don't want all the cum she's taken today leakin' out on me."

I yearned to strain against my bindings, to yell at them not to talk about my mom like that, but I was helpless in my fear. The hood rode up just enough that I could see a line of light and I held on to that illumination, needing to chase back the feeling of being trapped that rode me like a rabid beast. My arms were tied together, and each of my legs tied to what I assumed were sturdy bedposts.

There was movement around me, then silence. I realized Poppy was no longer screaming and found out why a few minutes later, when someone entered the room again. There was a dragging sound, then a thump as someone, or something, was placed on the bed next to mine.

A woman's soft moan of pain filled the room and I bit back an answering cry of sorrow. I was sure it was Poppy, and I was also sure she was hurt, probably badly. Even through the hood I could smell the tang of blood and my stomach lurched.

My heart pounded a punishing beat as I stayed as still as I could, not wanting to draw any attention to myself even as my bound hands shook. I swore I could feel someone looking at me, and the sensation wasn't a nice one.

My suspicions that someone was next to me were confirmed when a high-pitched male voice said, "Look at this, Beach's fuckin' old lady strapped down like a sacrificial lamb. Makes me hard just thinkin' about how much that motherfucker is gonna hurt over losin' you. Thinks he's so fuckin' good, better than the rest of us, bet he ain't feelin' so high and mighty now."

I refused to give him the satisfaction of answering him at first, but when he jerked my pajama top down, along with my bra with the tracker in it, baring my breasts, I gave a small scream of furry, which was met with an explosion of pain as he hit me across the face.

"Shut up, bitch. I ain't gonna fuck you, but I *am* gonna come all over these pretty tits of yours. I wanna know that while you're being broken in by your new Master, you're gonna be covered in my fuckin' jizz. I should pull that hood off and paint your face, make you eat it—yeah, I should make you eat it then my cum would be inside'a you and Chief couldn't get mad about me fuckin' you."

I lurched with the need to vomit, trying with all my might to fight it back. The act of violation the stranger above me was about to commit took backseat to the primal need not to choke and die. The thought of puking inside the hood was terrible enough to give me the strength to suck it back. The edge of the hood came up far enough to expose my mouth and I swore I could feel the brush of air from his movements next to my face. A nasty, sweaty, musky male smell filled the air and I gagged.

"Uh-uh, you puke on my dick and I'll make you suck it off. So fuckin' pretty, shame you're gonna disappear off the face of this Earth. Where you're goin', they ain't never gonna find you."

Helpless tears of rage soaked the fabric clinging to my upper face and I strained to see something. Turning my head to the side and tilting it up, putting his small, dirty dick unfortunately close to my face, I could make out Poppy on the other bed, illuminated by a faint hint of sunlight. She appeared to be passed out, and an alarmingly large amount of blood soaked the sheets around her. All of her shirt was saturated with it, and the wet fabric clung to her flat chest as she drew in faint breaths. She'd been beaten, bad, and her face was all fucked up.

A sob escaped me before I could stop it and the man above me grunted.

"Open up, bitch. Let's see if you suck as good as your mommy. Maybe I'll fuck that skank and make you suck me clean again after."

My mind snapped and I lost it.

He pressed the tip between my lips and before he'd gotten more than an inch inside, I bit down, *hard*, with a savage intent that would have made any predator proud.

Skin, muscle, and veins gave way as I jerked my head, determined to hurt him as much as possible.

Blood filled my mouth and I involuntarily released his now-mangled penis from my death grip, and knew I'd come close to severing his dick in half.

His shrill scream filled the air for a few brief seconds before loud explosions boomed through the house in a rapid burst of gunfire.

The mask had slid up farther and I craned to see what was going on but could only make out a man, probably in his early forties, cupping his blood-soaked groin while he screamed and screamed. Or at least I think he was; I could only see his contorted face as he stared down at his dick in shock. I couldn't see what kind of damage I'd done, but my churning stomach had had enough. Bile filled my throat and I turned my head as much as I could, straining to vomit away from myself.

The lights overhead flickered, but it was bright enough outside now that the illumination coming through the windows revealed the shapes of two people armed with AK-47s entering the room where I was being held with surgical precision. I couldn't see their faces, they wore some kind of black nylon hood that left them totally unidentifiable, but their bodies were well muscled and they moved with the efficiency of trained killers. They spotted me and Poppy, then swung their guns around and onto the man holding up his blood-painted hands.

He was pleading with them, begging them to help him. My hearing was gradually returning and I could read his lips. Something about needing a doctor and me being a psycho.

Another figure came through the doorway and I just about shrieked with relief. The tall, slender woman was dressed from head to toe in black and as she removed the black nylon mask obscuring her face, I began to chant her name.

Mimi.

She swiftly removed the hood then cut me loose while the two men with her split up, one taking the man I'd injured from the room, the other going straight to Poppy's side.

In less than five seconds, I was free and in Mimi's arms.

I was covered in blood and puke, but she hugged me close anyway, her strong shoulders jerking as she cried against the side of my neck. I instantly crumbled and began to keen as I held her close to me, disbelief that I was alive and safe stripping all my defenses bare.

When I began to cry so hard I was hyperventilating, Mimi sat back and coached me through it, calming me down until I was no longer panting and shaking. Once I got ahold of myself, Mimi took me into the small bathroom attached to the room I was in and shoved me into the shower, clothes and all, then washed me like I was a child. I rinsed my mouth out and scrubbed at my lips, wanting all traces of that nasty bastard's blood off me. We didn't speak and I was grateful for the silence that let me concentrate on not going to pieces in hysterics.

When her hand smoothed over the bump of my belly, I stopped her and held her palm there for a moment, our eyes meeting in a look of understanding shared by all mothers.

After I got out, she had me strip off my old clothes and handed me a pair of red sweats with "Princess" in sparkles on the butt and a faded black t-shirt with the logo for some bar I'd never heard of. The shirt was a bit tight, but the sweatpants fit well enough. I almost asked Mimi where she got them, but decided not to. I don't know if my brain could take the idea that I might be wearing my mother's clothes.

Turning to look at myself in the wide mirror over the beige-tile sink, I just stared at my gaunt reflection. Jesus, I looked like the poster child for some natural-disaster movie. Deep circles made my eyes appear sunken and my lips were chapped and puffy from being scrubbed so hard in the shower. My cheekbones stood out more than I'd ever seen and even my throat looked fragile. I was running on empty and about to crash.

But first, the half-full bottle of strong mouthwash on the vanity.

As I gargled and spit about twenty times, Mimi clued me in on what had happened. Evidently she'd gotten a tip from a friend who informed her that the woman she was looking for was spotted up by Klondike Mountain west of Boulder. While Mimi had been formulating a plan of attack with some of my dad's buddies, I'd been snatched up, along with Poppy.

At the mention of my friend, I finally stopped rinsing and faced Mimi.

"Poppy…is she okay?"

Looking me right in the eye, Mimi didn't try to bullshit me. "She's been beaten, possibly raped, and has a couple stab wounds to the abdomen."

"Is she…is she going to make it?"

"I have my doctor working on her right now."

"You brought a doctor with you?"

"Of course." She gave me an odd look. "I know your father trained you to handle all situations solo, but we really need to work on your team-building skills. Things go wrong on missions and having your own trusted medical source nearby is essential. Really, Sarah, give me some credit."

I stared at her for a long moment then nodded. "Right, how silly of me."

"Come. I wish I could spare you this, but we need to question the men that were holding you."

"Oh God, the moving vans, are they still here?" I had to reach behind me to grip the sink, the enormity of the situation sinking into me. "Did—did we find all the stuff?"

The smile lines around her eyes deepened. "The vans are still here, along with what we believe is the majority of the merchandise, including some things that weren't on the ledger Beach supplied us."

It took a great deal of effort to keep from collapsing in relief. "Thank God."

"Very much so, and the Blessed Virgin."

"So what do we do now? Does Beach know we found it?"

"No, he doesn't, and he won't."

"Why the hell not?"

Mimi closed the door then stepped closer to me. "Because there is a traitor we still need to catch, and tomorrow night at the Iron Horse MC clubhouse will be our best chance to do it. According to my sources, the Sokolov *Bratva* was behind the attack on Swan earlier, a desperate move on their part."

"And do you know if…and mentally? Has she gone…is she still with us?"

The memory of my sister withdrawing from me, going nearly catatonic with shock and grief after what had happened with Stewart, haunted me. She didn't just ignore me after my epic blunder; she cut me so completely out of her life that it was like I didn't exist. For a week after the incident she wouldn't talk to or acknowledge anyone, withdrawing completely into herself before she snapped out of it, then took off to live out in the real world. I couldn't handle seeing her disconnecting from reality like that again, and worried that the shock of killing those assassins might have unbalanced her.

"No, she's still with us. Miguel, despite not being my ideal boyfriend for your sister, is very good to her."

"Good." I rubbed my eyes, exhaustion nipping at my heels. "Shit, I'll be so glad when we get this stuff back to its owners and get those psycho Russian fucks off our backs."

"Agreed, but first we must find out who is the one running this operation." She pulled out one of her matte black knives and held it out to me hilt first. "Shall we go question your kidnappers?"

Taking the knife from her, a surge of strength and control fill me, the scared-and-helpless-sheep feeling melted beneath the cleansing heat of my anger. "Absolutely."

Chapter 12
Carlos "Beach" Rodriguez

The smooth, floral scent of Sarah's perfume ghosted through the air around me as I buried my face in her pillow. I'm not ashamed to admit I miss her so much I ache with it, my chest hollow with the loss of her bright presence. Little things gutted me everywhere I went, subtle reminders that she was gone. I'd see or hear something and mentally file it away to share with her when we cuddled in bed that night. Then I'd remember I'd be going to bed alone and I'd get mad, sad, and completely fucking irritated all over again. My heart began to pound and I groaned, pressing my face deeper into the pillow in an effort to escape my heartache. The fresh scent of her floral perfume mixed with the smell of her hair tormented me with a mere ghost of her presence but I didn't give a fuck. It was better than waking up to a nightmare existence.

I'd stumbled through the door late last night in a daze, having been up for more than thirty hours. Every moment of my day had been spent doing shit too important not to be addressed personally by me. I had to shore up my alliances, defend my people, and maintain the club. All without the support of my Master at Arms, who was up in Denver with Swan. I was also missing his second in command, Hustler. He was out talking with Tom Sokolov right now, our source into the wicked ways of the Sokolov *Bratva*. Back in the day, Tom's dad had been heir to the Sokolov *Bratva*, but he'd suffered a heart attack at thirty-five due to an undiagnosed heart defect, and Tom—then eight—had been too young to assume any kind of authority.

This led to an internal battle within the *Bratva* that left Tom somewhat exiled to the United States with his mother, while Tom's cousin—a right evil fuckin' bastard—controlled the Sokolov *Bratva*.

Tom would probably be dead as dirt if it wasn't for the fact that his mother was the sister of one of the most powerful men in Moscow. Petrov Dubinski, head of the Dubinski *Bratva*, had enough power to raise or destroy entire countries. And for some reason, Petrov Dubinski had a great deal of personal affection for my future mother-in-law, Mimi Anderson, aka Lady Death and a bunch of other nicknames that all equaled scary bitch. I'd spent most of the night sitting in on conference call after conference call with Tom, letting him run the show. He was smart, but more importantly, he was Russian, which opened doors that would have been closed tight to an American like myself. The Russians were big on secrecy, loyalty, and they all distrusted outsiders.

With a groan, I rolled over and tried to force my thoughts to just fuckin' stop racing so I could go back to sleep. My brain was fried to a crisp, my body was pissed at me for running myself into the ground, and I missed having Sarah in my bed more than I'd ever missed anything in my life. It was no surprise my thoughts had been of her and only her, my mind giving me fantasies of holding her once again.

In my dreams, I'd had Sarah tied between two giant trees like some kind of sacrifice, just waitin' for me in the woods. A thick silver chain rested on her hips, covered with little coins. It looked like something a belly dancer would wear. Sarah had an extensive collection of lingerie, body jewelry, and all kinds of sexy outfits that she loved to put on for me, but this chain belt was one of my favorites. It made her look like an exotic sex slave, a perfect sacrifice, built to take my cock.

The grass in my dream was soft beneath my bare feet, and the rising sun bathed Sarah's magnificent body in golden light. Naked except for that gleaming belt, she'd smiled at me as I approached, unafraid of me in a way no one had ever been before. The teasing glint in her eyes matched her dimpled grin and when I reached her, I cupped her sun-warmed cheek and gave her a soft, sweet kiss that had her purring in my arms.

No, she wasn't my sexual slave, she was my gift. These ropes weren't holding her here; she'd been bound by her own free will because she knew it would please me. Though she hid it from most of the world, her heart was unbearably sweet.

A light wind blew against us as our lips whispered over each other, her loose hair brushing against my face and her taste going right to my tight balls.

With my other hand I gently collared her throat, loving how she melted against me. For whatever reason, Sarah loved to indulged in some deep D/s occasionally and when she was in the mood, she was the perfect sexual submissive. She'd never be submissive to me in real life, but in the bedroom, after I'd warmed her up with some spanking, she entered a trancelike state that was fuckin' amazing. Sinkin' my dick into her when she was tied up, unable to do anything but let me give her pleasure, drove me crazy with the need to fuck her, own her, possess her.

Tightening my grip, I deepened our kiss and she began to move what little the loose ropes around her arms and feet allowed. The rich musk of her arousal teased the air and when she scraped her bare nipples over my chest, my cock jerked in appreciation. I don't know what it is about her, but the moment we touch, every part of me yearns to be as close to her as I can get. Slipping a finger between the slick lips of her pussy, I find her clit already erect and her hips twitch as I slowly circle her nub with a feather-light touch, her little whimpers making me savage.

I release her throat, only to replace my fingers with my lips. Without mercy, I simultaneously bite her and thrust two fingers into her greedy cunt. My baby girl cries out and I push in and out slowly, loving the way her inner muscles grip me tight, then release. When she's relaxed her pussy is so soft, feels like silk against my cock. Then she'll tighten up and the silk turns to gripping velvet, equally amazing but in a totally different way.

"Mmmm, *Papi*," she murmurs against my mouth.

I reward her by thumbing her clit while I finger her hot, wet pussy. "You gonna be a good girl and come on my fingers?"

"Yes," she moaned and I stepped closer, placing stinging bites all over her breasts but ignoring her jutting nipples. "Oh yes, please."

I took her hard bud into my mouth while I used the heel of my palm to rub her clit and finger her at the same time. She sagged in her bonds, her back arching and her hips ridding my hand with a sexy wiggle that almost had me spraying in the air. The sun shone on her pale hair, turning it almost white as she closed her eyes and cried out my name, my real name, in a way that made me feel proud. Watching my woman come like a banshee never failed to get me off.

The warm skin of her ass felt great against my stiff dick as I ducked beneath her arm to move behind her. A jewel twinkled in the sunlight between her buttocks and I grinned at the sight of my favorite butt plug getting her ready for me. Fuck yeah, I was gonna pound her tight little asshole. She'd walk slowly for a few days, but the harsh orgasms I wrung from her would keep her smiling with every step.

Her legs were already spread wide and she titled forward farther, the ropes holding her weight while she begged me to take her.

I tapped the hilt of the plug in her ass. "You know I'm bigger than this. Does my dirty girl want it to hurt?"

Pale eyes glinting with happiness, she looked over her shoulder at me, her wicked smile holding the promise of all the best sins in the world. "Yes, *Papi*."

I had to take a moment to steady myself, to get my libido under control before I hurt her in a way neither of us would like. The trust she was showing me by allowing to do a little pain play with her humbled me, and I wouldn't fuck it up. No, my baby needed her *Papi* to give her a little discipline, to make it just right.

Smacking her ass, I watched the tight flesh bounce and instantly turn red. I smacked her other cheek, then grinned to myself as I began to slap her pussy. This was something I loved to do, but most women shied away from it, embarrassed by the sound of their wet flesh being spanked. Sarah, on the other hand, fucking loved it and began to sway with my blows, her head dropping forward, her mind spiraling away into her subspace.

The heat coming off her pussy was incredible, but I ignored her wet sex in favor of the tight little ass I was about to fuck. I worked the plug out with one hand while squeezing my dick with the other, trying to keep myself from going off too soon. The need to fuck her pounded into me with every beat of my heart, burning away the thin shield of civilization and leaving behind a beast intent on fucking his mate.

Her cries filled the glen as I eased the golden tip of the plug in and out of her little hole, pre-cum dripping from the tip of my dick.

When I finally removed it for good, her anus was clenching and releasing as her hips mindlessly pumped the air.

She needed to be fucked, bad, and I was just the man to do it.

After spitting on her ass, I shoved my dick into her pussy for two deep strokes, holding still as she came all over me. A full shiver raced down my spine and I tried to do anything but come, anything but empty my balls into her tight body. Shit, she was so warm as I held her to me with one arm, her back to my chest, before I pulled out then guided my dick to her ass.

She tensed and I nudged against her tight entrance. "Open up for your *Papi*."

The muscles eased and I managed to work the tip into her, but she was so tight it almost hurt. My balls pounded as the head of my dick popped through that firm ring and into the softness of her body. She cried out and tried to jerk away despite the ropes, but I worked another inch in as I held her to me.

"Be a good girl, take my cock."

She made a little moaning, sobbing noise that had me grunting as I worked myself in deeper, the almost constant contractions of her inner muscles jerking me off with every breath.

The salt of her sweat burst on my tongue as I gently kissed her shoulder, loving the strong play of her muscles beneath my lips. My heart burst with love for this woman and I softened my thrusts, drawing them out now, making love to her ravaged body while I whispered words of devotion against her skin.

A loud pounding came from my bedroom door in the clubhouse and I lurched from my bed, yanking on my pants as a sense of doom washed away any happy memories from my dream.

Jerking my jeans up enough that I could start to zip them, I reached over to the bedside table and grabbed my gun, putting a round in the chamber before yelling out, "What?"

"Beach," came Hustler's voice, "we think we found the girls."

That had me putting the safety back on as I opened the door. On the other side, Hustler, Dragon, and Thorn all stared back at me with deadly eyes. We were all beyond furious and heartbroken that four little girls belonging to various members of the club had been kidnapped right from under our noses. They were all in a safe house in the southern part of Austin and someone had thrown in a can of military-grade knockout gas that had taken down our guards on the inside.

The men who had been watching the exterior of the building hadn't been so lucky, they'd all been shot in the back of the head execution style.

My gut burned with the need for vengeance and I added it to the ever-growing tab that the traitor in the club had to answer for. While no one knew who it was, the brothers all had their own personal lists of suspects in mind and it was creating tension within the club. Hustler, for example, was certain it was one of his fellow Enforcers, someone who worked at Smoke's security company. He seemed to be particularly focused on Vance, who in turn suspected Hustler was the one selling us out.

It was a huge fucking mess, and yet another distraction from what should be my focus, finding Billie. That slippery bitch was nowhere to be found, and neither was our stuff. The Israelis were two days away from officially going to war with us and if they did...I knew it would be a slaughter on both sides.

But none of that shit mattered right now because Lisa, Stacy, Kayla, and Sophie all needed me to find them as quickly as I could.

"Where are they?"

Dragon let out a low growl. "The old refrigerator company."

I motioned them into the room while I got dressed. "How'd we get the info?"

"Cruz followed up on a tip and said he managed to see Stacy briefly through one of the windows."

A brief image of the little brown-haired six-year-old flashed through my head and I forced it back. "He still there?"

"Had to pull back, too exposed, but he's waiting for us nearby."

I nodded. "We ready to roll?"

Hustler frowned. "Prez, might be a good idea if you stayed here."

The urge to put a bullet in his head was strong, but I bit it back. "You are out of your fuckin' mind if you think I'm not gonna do everything I can to get those girls back."

Holding up his hands, Hustler shook his head, his lip ring gleaming in the light as his normally laughing, but now dark hazel eyes held mine.

"Listen, I know you think I'm a paranoid fuck, but I'm tellin' you, someone is tryin' to take you down. They want you out of the picture and this could be a trap."

"So I'm just supposed to fuckin' sit here while my brothers go out and risk their lives?" I pulled the case for my AK-47 out from beneath the bed with a huff of exertion. "You're crazy."

"He does have a point," Thorn said in a low voice.

"No."

"Maybe—" Dragon started to add, and I gave him a look that shut him right the fuck up.

"Those girls? Their families trusted me, trusted us, to keep them safe and we failed them. So now we're gonna go pay the price, but hopefully it'll be with the blood of our enemies, not our own."

Hustler tried to argue with me some more before I sent him out of the room, ready to punch him in the face if he didn't shut the hell up.

Thankfully none of my other men gave me shit, and after we piled into our armored vehicles—bikes were not good for sneaking up on people—I spent all my time on my phone answering calls that couldn't wait, praying for some word on Sarah while fearing the worst, and praying even harder that those little girls' innocence had been spared.

When we made it to the connecting street that would lead to the abandoned three-story brick building where they were supposedly being held, I scanned the area, looking for some sign of life. This deserted industrial area was a good one for holding someone, off the beaten track and surrounded by stacks of rusting shipping containers. It had also become a dumping ground for the locals, and mounds of crap lay all over the old parking lot surrounding the building. It looked empty, except for the faintest glow coming through one of the windows in the back.

We were crouched behind a crumbling brick wall next to the burnt husk of what had once been a store of some kind. "Is that where they're holding 'em?"

"Yeah," Dragon whispered. "We haven't seen any movement on infrared, but they could be so deep inside that massive place that we can't detect 'em."

"Anything on who's behind it?"

"No. Los Diablos claims they have no idea," I snorted, "and according to Tom Sokolov, the Russian's wouldn't have taken the girls, something about it being dishonorable or some shit. Israelis haven't said shit, but Mr. Dahan, our contact, has said in the past he never harms children."

"Fuckin' hate this cloak-and-dagger bullshit," I muttered as Hustler talked to a few of our brothers with special-ops training while gesturing to the building. "Can't kill shadows until you shine the light on 'em."

Stones grit beneath Hustler's boots as he crouched down next to us, his black bandana pulled down almost all the way to his eyes. "Our teams are set up, waitin' on your word."

"Right, let's do this fast and—"

"That'd be a big fucking mistake," a familiar man's gravelly voice said from somewhere to our left.

Guns came up all around me, but I yelled out as loud as I dared, "Stand the fuck down, it's Sarah's dad, Mike Anderson."

That motherfucker strolled out of the shadows like a magician appearing out of thin air. He barely made a sound in his worn military boots, and the guns strapped to his body, all painted matte black, didn't jingle in the least. He had weathered features, the kind of face that had taken a beating from life and lived to tell the tale. Our relationship was prickly, we both were absolutely confident that we knew what was best for Sarah, but I was glad to see him. While I might not like the crazy motherfucker, I respected the fuck out of him.

"Carlos," he greeted me, refusing to use my club name. "How's your nose?"

That asshole. We'd gotten in a fight during my first visit to their place—out of Sarah's sight, of course. If she saw us settling our differences with our fists, she'd no doubt have kicked both our asses. And Lord help the man who pisses *Mimi* off on her home turf.

"Mimi with you?"

He shook his head. "Nope."

I waited for him to elaborate, but he glanced at the men around me then raised a brow.

"Mr. Anderson," Hustler said in a low voice. "You mentioned something about a trap?"

Mike lifted his hand to his mouth then made a piercing whistle. I wasn't the least bit surprised when more men melted out of the darkness surrounding us. They were all dressed similarly to Mike and a few had full camo darkening their hands and faces as well. All radiated a cold menace, and if I'd been a lesser man, I'd have been feeling a wee bit intimidated being surrounded by my future father-in-law and his highly armed friends. Let's face it, most daddies don't dream about their sweet daughters hooking up with a way older outlaw biker.

A guy to Mike's left, clad from head to toe in black and wearing a mask, adjusted his gun strap. "The place is surrounded by IEDs."

I blinked at him a couple times while the men around me sucked in a collective breath. Hustler's voice came from behind me a second later, telling our men to stand down—that it was a trap, to pull back and touch nothing. My heart raced as I stared at the area surrounding the old building, the broken asphalt, the piles of crap everywhere. We'd never expect it, and no doubt more people would have died.

Thorn took a step closer to Mike. "No offense, but how the fuck do you know that?"

The guy wearing the mask gave a harsh laugh. "Well, why don't you just stroll on over there and find out?"

"What he means," Hustler smoothly interjected, "is can you share with us what you know? I don't think I need to remind anyone that there are still a bunch of scared little girls out there right now waitin' for someone to save them."

Everyone instantly sobered and Mike nodded. "You're right. Ghost over there is an ordinance expert, could blow you up a hundred different ways before breakfast. He said they're a familiar design, the same kind used in Afghanistan by the Taliban."

"The fuckin' Taliban is after us?" Thorn took a step back and his gold teeth flashed as he grimaced.

"No," the man I assumed was called Ghost answered. "Anyone who was deployed over there would have had firsthand experience with these types of IEDs. Hell, you can find designs for 'em on the Internet if you look hard enough, but I don't think the person who did these was an amateur."

Frustration tightened my muscles into knots as I ran my hands through my hair and I turned to Hustler. "Goddamn it. I should've fuckin' listened to you man, I'm sorry."

Hustler gave my shoulder a squeeze, but Mike said, "Let's head back to your clubhouse. Need to have a talk with you in private."

I left Hustler behind along with a couple of our brothers who had firsthand experience with Taliban-style bombs. The majority of the members of Iron Horse had done service in one branch of the military or another, many of them overseas, and knowing our enemy probably spent time in Afghanistan didn't help me narrow down the suspects that much. I could think of about a hundred offhand right here in Austin, and it didn't put us any closer to finding out which man posing as a brother was actually stabbing us in the back.

So we hadn't found the girls, didn't know who the traitor was, and I was once again left spinning my wheels in frustration. It seemed like every attempt to hurt the club I stopped, another three sprang up in their place. We were having all kinds of problems, but luckily our allied clubs and organizations were helping us deal with the bullshit. Both myself and my brothers have had to call in personal favors owed in order to keep everyone safe and out of jail.

These were my people, they trusted me to make this right, and I was failing them. Worse yet, as soon as we entered the clubhouse two of the mothers of the missing girls had been waiting for us, Darla and Sweet Taya. Only Sweet Taya, a tiny Mexican brunette normally quiet and as nice as could be, became like a demon possessed when she found out we hadn't rescued her daughter. She'd screamed and raged to the point we had to restrain her then give her a shot to knock her out before she hurt herself.

The looks of helpless anger on the faces of those watching us only increased my guilt and I'd taken all the abuse Taya had hurled at me, giving her an outlet for her pain.

Her anguished cries still echoed in my head as I trudged into my office and gestured for Mike to take a chair. He ignored me and instead began to examine my office. It took me a moment to realize he was checking the room for bugs, but I ignored him and went over to the small bar standing in the corner of the room.

I needed a fuckin' drink, bad.

Sarah had installed it a couple months ago, tired of finding bottles of liquor leaving rings on the tables. I'd tried to point out that all the furniture in my office was beat to shit, and that I liked it that way, but she'd gone out and got this kick ass corner bar for me instead. It even had a small fridge/freezer. From the rack of glasses going up the wall I selected, then filled a thick leaded glass tumbler with crushed ice before pouring a generous amount of Kentucky Bourbon Whiskey into the glass.

"Want one?" I asked Mike.

"What're you drinking?"

"1792 Ridgemont Reserve Kentucky Straight Bourbon Whisky

He grunted, "Might as well."

After handing him the glass I settled behind my desk, my gaze going to the sharp silver framed picture of Sarah and I. We were sitting on one of the picnic tables out front, both of us straddling the bench with her tucked between my legs with her back to my front. I was leaning down and whispering something in her ear, probably something dirty, and she was laughing while reaching back and cupping my cheek. I could almost feel her soft skin against my jaw, smell the scent of whatever perfume she'd put on her inner wrist. Fuck I missed her.

"Looks like my ex-wife caused you a bit of trouble," Mike said in the understatement of the century.

"You seen Sarah?"

"Not since she stayed at my place for a few days."

I nodded, knowing before I even asked what the answer was. "Any idea where she is?"

"Got my suspicions."

"Then why are you here instead of out there looking for her?"

"Because Mimi sent me to help you."

"And why would she do that?"

"Because of those missing kids." He gazed out the dark window, his shoulders tight with tension. "Nothing worse than fearing for your child's life."

I took a deep breath, striving for patience and wondering who the fuck was rating club business out to Sarah's stepmother. "And how did she find out about the missing girls?"

He smirked, took a sip of his drink, then rested the glass on his knee. "Really? Seriously? You do know who my wife is, right?"

"Yeah, I know who your wife is."

"Then you know she's pretty pissed, and so am I, that you didn't tell us about your troubles." His eyes got really dark and the wrinkles around his mouth deepened. "We respected your and Sarah's privacy by not digging into your life and monitoring you. And how did you repay us? By hiding the fact that my daughters are in mortal danger and not telling me?"

I met his gaze, letting him see that I wasn't intimidated in the least. "Mike, respect you but this is club business. We've got this handled. Now I admit I was wrong to keep what was going on from you, but Sarah took off without my knowing. If I had any idea she was going to go after Billie I would have chained her to a wall, kept her locked up in a safe room until this shit is over."

Mike laughed. "Good luck with that. I tried grounding her a couple times. Didn't work. I'd lock every exit and entrance to our home and she still somehow managed to sneak out."

Remembering Sarah telling me funny stories about sneaking out of her dad's place, I knew exactly what he was talking about. "You know she had a copy of your fingerprints, right?"

His jaw dropped and I could hold back my chuckle as he stared at me. "She did not."

"Oh yes she did. Learned from a friend how to do it and had a full set of yours, perfectly replicated for use on all your fingerprint scanners. Like the one where you kept a set of maps with the current entrances and exits to your place below ground mapped out. You always keep a paper copy of things because you distrust computers and the Internet."

Shaking his head, Mike surprised me by smiling, just a little bit before taking a drink. "That girl, she always was too smart for her own good."

"You underestimate her. Sarah is brilliant, ruthless, and is about as street smart as they come. I gotta trust she'll keep herself safe."

Mike snorted. "If she thinks for one second sacrificing herself would save this sorry ass gang of yours, she would."

"We're not a gang," I ground out. Mike always said that just to fuck with me. "We're a club."

"Please, your *club* is a fucking mess. You're walking blind into obvious traps, and you somehow lost track of my daughter. Now I'll forgive you for the last part because Sarah is very good at vanishing, but I can't believe you almost got your ass blown to kingdom come. That was just plain sloppy, and desperate. Made me break my cover to warn you."

Anger had me itching to punch him right in his smug, judgmental face, but I knew Sarah would be pissed if-no, when she came back that I'd broken her dad's nose so I managed to growl out, "I'm doin' the best I can. You think I'm not tryin' my best to protect my people? You think part of me doesn't die every time one of them gets killed? And the missing girls-fuck man, they're just babies and who the hell knows what kind of sick fucks have them."

Mike's hard gaze softened the slightest bit and he nodded. "Being responsible for the welfare of his people is hard burden for any man to shoulder alone. I've been in that woman, Taya's place. Thought I lost my child when Billie took off with Sarah. Worst feeling in my life to think about my child suffering and bein unable to prevent it. I'm going to help you find them because it's the right thing to do, even if I think you're a stupid fuck unworthy of my daughter."

I drained the last of my drink and sighed as the fumes warmed me. "I don't need your help, you crazy asshole, I've got my brothers."

"True, but one of them is gunnin' for you."

And boy did that burn.

"You got any idea who?"

"No. I've just started to look into it, whoever he is, he has strong ties to your club." He sat across from me then crossed his legs, his foot tapping in the air as his gaze went distant. "Something about this whole thing, the timing, is off. If they just wanted to destroy the club they could have gone for a variety of more permanent ways to get rid of Iron Horse. It's almost like they want to damage the club enough to make it weak, but not destroy it because they have plans for it in the future. Then again, if the merchandise you boys were running isn't found, you yours are dead in the water."

I thought about it for a moment, the alcohol mellowing me out when nothing else, other than my woman, could. As much as Mike and I butted heads, quite literally sometimes, we always managed to put our personal issues aside when it came to Sarah. Even though I thought he was a borderline abusive prick, and he hated my guts for being with his daughter on principal, we both swallowed our pride in order to keep Sarah happy.

Deciding to change the tone of the conversation to something more productive, I laced my fingers together over my stomach then said, "Nobody that wanted to take over the club would make it a target like this. The supreme art of war is to subdue the enemy without fighting."

"Sun Tzu?" Mike asked with arched brows as I quoted the ancient Sun Tzu's *Art of War*, a book written in the 5th century BC. I knew from Sarah he reads that thing like the bible and used to quote from it during long hikes through the wilderness. I also knew from Sarah he liked to use those quotes as an intimidation tactic, to make someone feel dumb because they hadn't read the book. Unfortunately for him, my grandpa—the one who'd help found Iron Horse—was also a big fan of *Art of War*, and passed on his love of the book to me. In the past, we'd gotten so into our back and forth about battle strategy according to Sun Tzu that Sarah would roll her eyes with disgust and leave the room. Mimi would stay, usually with a bottle of wine, in the corner laughing as things got heated between me and Mike, each of us adamant we were right.

The tanned crinkles around Mike's eyes deepened as he leaned back in his chair, giving me that look that Sarah called his "bored old wise man taking a shit while bequeathing his wisdom to you on the mountaintop" look. "But Sun Tzu also said, 'In the midst of chaos, there is also opportunity.' Nothing like war to start a revolution…but that's just my opinion."

I frowned at him, ready to tell him to shove his opinion up his ass, when the door to my office burst open and a smiling Sledge strode in, raised his fists in the air, then shouted, "Vance found the girls!"

Shoving away from my desk, I rubbed my face, unsure I'd heard him right. "What?"

"The girls! They're okay-well a little banged up but not-you know, hurt." His smile fell a little and he lowered his voice. "Vance followed up a tip, by himself-the arrogant bastard, and managed to take out the pieces of shit that had taken the girls and rescue them."

I blinked at him, hope filling my chest. "They're alive, all of 'em? How?"

"Yep." He slapped me on the shoulder. "No idea how-fuckin' miracle. Don't know about you, Prez, but I'm pleased as fuck they've been found. I don't give a shit how Vance managed to pull this magic trick out of his ass, but he did and he's bringin them home. Venom's with 'em, as well as a police escort from a couple of the state troopers we have that are loyal to us. They'll be here in fifteen minutes. We told the families and they're…man they're just fuckin' overjoyed. We all are."

I bowed my head, the weight of the world still coming to rest on me, but just a little bit lighter. "Best news I've heard all day."

As we left the room I thought I heard Mike mutter, "opportunity in chaos," but I wasn't sure.

Chapter 13
Sarah

As I stared at the door leading into the cream stucco apartment building, my mind turned yet again to Beach, wondering what he was doing, if he missed me, if he'd ever be able to forgive me. I was still mad at him for believing that I'd fuck the club over with my mom, but right now I'd give just about anything to have him here with me, holding my hand and making me feel safe and loved. Protectively rubbing the hard bump of my warm belly, I stared at an older, blonde woman in a hoochie dress making her way to her car that reminded me of my mother.

Fucking Billie, I still couldn't believe she'd gotten away. Not that I'd wanted her to be gunned down, but if we'd managed to capture her, she would have been able to give us some information on who the traitors in the MC were.

Most of the men who'd been guarding me and the weapons at that shithole in the mountains had died during the gunfight, and the few who remained hadn't been able to tell us much. The man who'd tried to force oral sex on me, Peter, used to be a member of Iron Horse back in the day before Beach had taken over. He'd been part of Red's crew that had been kicked out of the club and had a grudge like you wouldn't fucking believe against Iron Horse. Peter *hated* Beach, and when a mysterious man had offered him the opportunity for revenge, and money to back it up, he'd jumped on said opportunity. Los Diablos didn't give a fuck what their members did as long as the money kept coming into the club's bank account. All he'd been able to tell us was that he answered to a man who went by the name of "Chief", who kept both his voice and body disguised, leading me to believe Chief was someone well known in the Iron Horse MC.

I was also pretty sure Chief was still down in Austin, as that's where they'd taken my mother, and that worried me greatly.

Billie...fucking Billie. Stupid, stupid me had hoped somewhere down deep in my heart that my mom would find some shred of decency, some shred of humanity in her, and help me escape. I mean, I was pregnant with her granddaughter for God's sake. Once again I'd been proven wrong. Her words about being cursed haunted me and I wondered if maybe there was some truth to her deranged beliefs, that there was some genetic switch that would eventually flip in my mind and I'd go as crazy as she was.

She had to be insane. What kind of mother in her right mind would allow her daughter to be sold into sexual slavery? It was easier to believe Billie had no control over her actions than face the hard truth that she just didn't give a shit about anyone but herself. My stomach curled as I briefly thought about what her life must be like if she was having sex with people like the ones who'd held me hostage for drugs. It didn't have to be this way, if she'd just once gotten sober and stayed that way I would have taken care of her for the rest of her life so she'd never have to have to sell herself for anything ever again.

Jesus, she was so fucking stupid.

And deadly.

She'd sacrifice anyone and anything in order to save her own life.

I had to find her before she hurt anyone else, but first I needed to get to Swan without anyone knowing who I was.

And that required the help of a very unlikely ally.

Frustration made me antsy and I shifted in my seat, ready to get this evening over with.

People came and went as I sat in the parking lot of the large apartment complex in Boulder with a ring of men surrounding me, invisible to the untrained eye, but there nonetheless. No one was taking any chances with my safety, not after we almost lost more of Vinnie than his leg right below the knee.

My eyes started to burn and I bit my fist hard enough to really hurt as I choked back a sob. They shot Vinnie in both legs and he managed form makeshift tourniquets, but the doctors at the private hospital they transported him to had to amputate his right leg below the knee. The bone, muscle, everything had been shredded by two high-caliber hollow point rounds. While I hadn't seen him, I was there as my cousin Paul gave us the rundown on his health.

Mimi, who was also Vinnie's godmother, had lost her mind, and even I made myself scarce as she raged, making my father's temper look like a gentle breeze.

Seriously, that woman was scary.

Poppy wasn't doing much better. Her left hand had been smashed, her body battered, ribs broken, and she'd lost a lot of blood, but there were no signs of rape. She'd recover, but she probably would never have full use of her left hand again. They wouldn't know for sure what had happened until Poppy woke up from her coma, brought on by blood loss. Nobody said it directly, but I knew everyone was praying her brilliant mind hadn't been damaged beyond repair. Mimi said Poppy was at the same hospital as Vinnie and they were sharing a room together, with my mafia boss grandfather personally watching over them both. At least I could stop worrying about them for now; no one was getting through the head of the Stefano mafia without an army…maybe two.

A harsh shiver went through me as I realized how close I'd come to dying myself, how much was still on the line. I gripped the plastic steering wheel hard enough that my knuckles hurt, needing to do something to ease the adrenaline pumping through me. Mimi had secured the help of the Dubinski *Bratva* and was trying to negotiate with the Novikov *Bratva* for our safety, but when I'd left it wasn't going well. I could hear her desperation, something I never thought I'd hear, but she was begging some bastard in the Novikov *Bratva* for help and they kept denying her.

Fury had me clenching my teeth as I vowed revenge against the bastards who made such a proud woman beg.

That anger took my worry and all my fear, all my longing for Beach, and replaced it with a harsh purpose.

Get into the clubhouse, get to Swan, and keep her from getting snatched up, while Mimi swept in behind the motherfuckers who were trying to take my sweet sister and rained down the wrath of God on them.

And trust me, she had a lot of wrath to deliver.

If everything went as planned Mimi and her crew would secure the woods before Iron Horse even knew they were there. The last thing we wanted was people being hurt in friendly fire, and the Enforcers for Iron Horse would shoot strangers first, ask questions later. It was a dangerous mission, but Mimi had some of the best killers in the world at her back.

However, before any of that could happen, I needed to get into the party, and my way in was taking for fucking ever to leave her apartment. I was waiting for her to come out of her surprisingly nice building with a fenced-in pool while I sat in a nondescript black Honda sedan which had seen better days, pretending to play on my phone as I silently cursed her to hurry the fuck up.

The bangles on my wrist covering my "Beach" tattoo clattered in a super-irritating manner as I shifted in my seat and adjusted my short skirt. There were going to be two kinds of women at the party tonight, old ladies and sweet butts. While I couldn't get away with pretending to be some random old lady, I could get away with being one of the ever-changing pieces of ass strolling through the doors of the clubhouse. The guys at the Denver clubhouse were pussy hounds, and they had more sluts than they knew what to do with, but always had room for one more.

I was nervous about my outfit, but as I checked out my reflection in the rearview mirror, I almost didn't recognize myself with the prosthetic nose I was wearing. Having spent lots of time in the chair with professional makeup artists, I've picked up enough tips and tricks to know how to manipulate things like the length and width of my nose and make it look real. Add some colored contacts and a huge auburn wig and I was sure none of the men from Iron Horse would recognize me. That is, if they even looked at my face. I was sporting enough cleavage to stun the average man into drooling submission.

Still, the men of the Iron Horse MC would be on alert so I couldn't just go waltzing in there on my own. I needed someone to vouch for me, and that particular bitch was finally locking her door behind her.

Now, I hadn't known for sure that Nikki Muller, aka Cyclone, was going to the party tonight, but knowing she practically lived at the clubhouse, I was hopeful. She was a sweet butt who'd been with Iron Horse for over five years, who I'd met briefly months ago while visiting the clubhouse. I didn't know much about her, but what I did know was that she was, for whatever reason, totally loyal to Iron Horse and that she could get me in.

Wearing a tight black and red dress which dipped down far enough in the back to show her pink thong, Cyclone stalked across the parking lot with her fringed black leather purse swung over one arm and her dark curls bouncing with her strut.

Before she made it to her car, a purple sporty little number, I intercepted her.

"Nikki, we need to talk."

Right away she jerked back, her stance defensive as she looked around the lot. "Who the fuck are you?"

"It's me, Sarah Star, Beach's old lady."

Her lip curled back in a sneer. "Listen, you crazy bitch—"

I held up my hand, wrist out so the bracelets could move enough to show the top of my "Beach" tattoo. "Shut up, I don't have time for this shit. Last year when you were at the Iron Horse party Khan threw for Beach, you and I talked about your house-cleaning business and we discussed some new marketing options for your website."

For a moment she seemed dubious, then blinked…and blinked again, then stumbled on her heels back a couple steps.

"Sarah? What the hell are you doing *here*? Beach is losing his damn mind—"

"I know, I know." Glancing around, I took a step closer. "I need you to get me into the party tonight."

Her gaze narrowed and she leaned closer as well. "Why do you need me to sneak you in? What's with this crazy-ass outfit? Why the hell are you hanging out in my fucking parking lot, of all places?"

"We don't have time for this. You and I both know the rumors that there are traitors in the club are more than just rumors. If I go in there as myself right now, I won't get two steps before I'm mobbed with people. I need a chance to see what everyone is doing when they don't think anyone's watching other than sweet butts, and you know a lot of those sexist assholes think women are too stupid to understand a conversation they overhear. There is no way you haven't at least heard rumors that there's a traitor."

Red spots appeared on Cyclone's cheeks and I was taken aback by how pissed she got. "I told those motherfuckers there was a traitor trying to start shit. I told them someone called me from the clubhouse and told me Smoke was asking for me! I'd never disrespect him like that."

"What?"

"Never mind," she muttered while rubbing her arm with a weird expression. "You think they're going to do something tonight? Shouldn't we, like, call and evacuate them or warn 'em or something?"

"No, there should be enough security that if someone does try an attempt, they'd be able to fight them off. They won't send in a shit ton of people, they'll send in a few of their best to try and infiltrate the clubhouse and take Swan. And if there are traitors in the clubhouse they might help whoever's trying to take her."

"How do you know they'll do that?"

I shrugged. "It's what I'd do."

"And you need *my* help to stop this from happening?"

"Yeah, I do. And I need you to help me look for weird shit, people that don't seem like they belong. Help me stop them before they hurt anyone else."

For a moment her gaze wavered then she gave me a brisk nod. "Beach will fuckin' kill me, but I'll help you. I'm letting you know right now if shit starts to go bad, I'm getting you upstairs to the panic room. I don't give a fuck what your plans are, but if you die, I'm as good as dead. Understood?"

"Yes, thank you."

"Don't thank me yet, we still have to get you inside."

Hard rock music throbbed into the night through the open doors of the clubhouse as I sashayed my way through the parking lot with Cyclone's arm looped through mine. She'd started to freak out as we pulled up, the realization of how much danger we were in finally hitting her, and I'd slung my arm through hers in both a show of support and warning. There was no way she was abandoning me now, not when I was so damn close.

At the sight of all the Iron Horse cuts, my heart ached for home, for my man, for my people, and I had to blink rapidly so I didn't cry and smear my thick-as-hell mascara.

Men whistled as we sauntered past and more than one request for a blow job filled the night.

Cyclone slowed down and preened a bit, finally losing some of her nerves as all the men called out friendly greetings to her. It was weird looking at the club through the eyes of a sweet butt, especially when I was used to men respecting my personal space. Now they groped me as we walked by, some with a leer, others just in passing, as if it was an automatic reaction. I reminded myself that the party girl I was pretending to be would be eating this attention up, so I laughed and smiled, but not too much. Last thing I wanted was some drunk-ass moron attaching himself to me.

The party was raging and I wondered if they even had the slightest idea how much danger they were in. As I gave the place a quick scan, I noticed men standing against the walls all over the place with their arms crossed, watching the crowd closely. More men with guns stood openly at the top of the wide stairs at the back, past the pool tables, leading up to the second floor. The Iron Horse clubhouse in Golden was big, and it was almost impossible to see the entire room through the crowd.

My hopes of quickly finding Swan died a swift death.

We made it deeper inside and a couple guys called out to Cyclone, but she waved and hustled us to the back of the room where the slut sofas were.

Why do I call them slut sofas? Because all the sluts gather here waiting for men to pick them for the night...or hour...or whatever. Five couches lined the back of the room near the stairs and a variety of women sat on them, drinking and laughing together. If you didn't know what they were there for, you'd think it was just a bunch of women hanging out.

I know people seem to think the girls who come to party at the clubhouses should be a depressing bunch of dumb skanks, but for the most part, except for the hardcore club pieces, most of these women were just here to take an occasional walk on the wild side. I'd never seen anyone forced to be with someone they didn't want and that impression was reinforced when Cyclone told a brother no and he went on to the next woman on the couch without missing a beat. Most of these women were here because they were down to fuck, no strings attached, and there was no better place to find an uncomplicated booty call than a biker clubhouse.

With the dark leather sofa, which had seen much better days, now empty, we sat down. I pulled at the edge of my green dress, wanting as much protection between my skin and the leather as possible. Right away, Cyclone gripped my hand and leaned closer. "Smile, laugh, look natural."

"What?"

"You look like you want to stab someone."

I realized with a start that I was scowling and quickly put on my beauty-queen smile. "Better?"

"Fuck, that's creepy how you do that, but yeah. I see your sister."

"Where?"

"Don't look, she's glancing over here, but she's behind you on the other side of the stairs with…with Smoke."

"I need to get to her."

"Hold on, if you get too close, they'll suspect you right away. We need to figure out a way to ease our way towards her. Lemme find some guys we can go chat up near them."

Little zings of electricity were sparking across my skin, my senses heightening as my instincts flared to life.

Something was about to happen.

"You feel that?"

"Feel what?"

Before I could respond, I swear my sister yelled something about a grenade. I dropped to the couch and curled up into a ball. Less than a second later, a huge boom ripped through the room, along with a flash of light bright enough to sear my eyelids.

For one terrible moment, I feared a bomb had gone off and I was already dead, I just didn't know it. When no pain came, only thick smoke that quickly obscured the room, I knew my time had run out. Screams that I could barely hear above the ringing in my ears tore through the air and Cyclone was cautiously peeking over the side of the couch.

I climbed over Cyclone and the back of the sofa, clearing the crowd as I made my way to where Swan was supposed to be. Another grenade went off and the emergency lights were strobing from the exits, further distorting my perception. The edge of my heel caught on something and I almost fell, at the last moment catching myself while people shoved past me. I needed to find the wall, now, before I got trampled.

I couldn't see shit, but for a moment the haze cleared enough for me to make out Smoke standing out from the crowd, sheltering someone with blonde hair. I fought and slammed my way to where I'd seen them, the smoke too thick to make out much of anything. We were by the stairs, and I hoped Smoke was trying to get Swan up them.

Then her voice came from right next to me and I reached out and caught the back of some man's shirt then let go. My next grab was nothing but air, but as I stumbled forward, I finally grabbed a slender wrist and yanked.

When someone tried to pull her back, I jerked her to me, unsure if it was Smoke who had ahold of her or one of the Sokolov *Bratva's* mercenaries. With my breath choking off into a coughing fit, I hauled her to me, trying to shuffle us along, but she resisted moving. Damn it, Swan could be as hard to move as an elephant when she wanted to.

In an effort to get her to stop resisting me, I said in her ear loud enough to be heard over the ringing in my ears, "Swan, it's me, Sarah. We need to get you out of here. Up to your room, now!"

The stubborn bitch dug in her heels and I wanted to head-butt her. "Prove it."

"Your first crush was Slater on *Saved by the Bell*. You had a pillow with his face on it that you kissed because you're a pillow-molesting pervert."

She didn't argue with me any more after that and we made our way to the stairs.

My back twitched like someone was waiting to stab it and I practically shoved Swan up the steps in an effort to get away from whoever was hunting us. Two guys stood at the top of the steps in gas masks with their guns pointed at the stairway, but they took one look at us and waved us through. The familiar sound of Khan's voice came from nearby as he shouted but I blocked it out. We had to get to Swan's room, now.

My sister started to slow down and I impatiently hauled her behind me, going up another flight of stairs. Men ran past us, all armed, and a few yelled at Swan to get to her room. I wanted to throat punch them for alerting everyone to where we were.

Suddenly Swan stumbled and slumped against the wall. Her face was a pale, cheesy yellow as she muttered, "I don't feel good."

"What? How?"

"Don't...know. Feel weird. Stoned."
"Did someone drug you?"
"Pain meds...did a big shot of Southern Comfort. And beer."
I wanted to smack her on the back of her head, but feared it would knock her out. "You dumbass! I can't believe you did that!"
She made some mumbled noises and I jerked her along as she stumbled against the wall.
Her eyes were super glassy and I clenched my teeth while hauling her up. "Don't you fucking puss out on me, bitch. Get your ass in gear. *Fight*. Never give up."
My instincts were screaming at me to get the hell out of the hallway, and I spotted a guy coming around the corner whose eyes widened as he saw us. I didn't recognize him and the thick layer of greying stubble on his face helped obscure his features. He wore a battered leather vest and his gut hung over the waistband of his pants.

Something about his expression set me on high alert and I bared my teeth at him as he took a step in our direction. He paused, his eyes widened, then took out his cell phone. While he did that, I jerked open Swan's door. I spared a moment to commit his rough face to memory as he began to run towards us, before shoving Swan into her room. As I swung the door shut, Swan was already fumbling for the lock, turning it the instant I had it closed.

Still feeling unsafe, I managed to shove the dresser over with help from my stupid-ass sister. Swan was never a big drinker, but tonight she'd decided to mix painkillers with alcohol, a big no-no. I ignored the knocking on the door, more worried about my sister than anything else. Afraid she was going to kill herself, I forced her into the bathroom and made her puke until her stomach was empty and she was lying on the floor, panting. I washed her up then eased her no-doubt hurting stomach by rubbing the muscles. Lord knows I have nothing but sympathy now for people puking.

After a few minutes, she mumbled that she was fine, just sleepy—and then she passed out, and no amount of shaking would wake her.

I sat on the floor of the bland cream bathroom and kicked off my shoes, my unseeing gaze focused on Swan as I tried to slow my racing heart.

We were alive.

Both of us.

True, I had no idea where the hell Billie was, only that she was headed to Texas, but we had the merchandise so at least we had something to bargain with, though Mimi was handling the negotiations.

I leaned my head back against the wall and took a deep breath, then let it out slowly. The prosthetic nose was itching as the glue lifted due to my excessive sweating and I pried it off my face, breathing deep and removing the remains of the rubber-cement-like glue from my skin with a tired hand. The adrenaline that had been filling me fled, leaving behind weak limbs and limp muscles. I had to get up and move Swan to the bed, nobody wanted to remain passed out on a cold bathroom floor, but my mind had short circuited and I just sat there, trying to pull myself together.

I thought I might have been in shock, the events of the past few days catching up with me, but I didn't know for sure. All I could be certain of was a sense of relief settled into me as I gently rubbed Swan's back. She was here, alive, warm beneath my touch—if passed out.

The knowledge eased my racing thoughts and I took a deep breath then let it out slowly. No rest for the weary. Sometimes I wish I could be one of those women who just zoned out and stopped caring about what happened to them, but I was a survivor, and survivors didn't have the luxury of taking extended mental vacations.

My attempt to motivate myself to move was interrupted by the lock clicking open, then someone trying to shove the door and dresser out of the way.

I quickly stood and removed two of my knives from their sheaths, ready to throw them at whoever was shoving their way into the room.

"Identify yourself!" I screamed in a high, shrill voice.

"Where's Swan?" Smoke roared as the dresser heaved over with a crash and the door opened enough for him to slide through.

"She's in here."

He froze at the sight of me. "Who the fuck are you?"

For a moment I had no idea what he was talking about, then I remembered my disguise. "It's me, Sarah."

"Sarah who?" He took a step closer then spotted Swan on the floor behind me. "What the fuck did you do to her?"

When he pulled out his gun and loaded a bullet into the chamber, I held my hands up, both daggers gleaming. "Wait, wait, it's me, Sarah Anderson, for real! I'm wearing a disguise. I'll prove it—you won't eat goat cheese because you think goats are disgusting and evil."

The gun in Smoke's hand trembled then slowly lowered. "Sarah?"

I took two steps out of the bathroom and tossed my daggers onto the bed before pulling off my wig, then blinking out my contacts. "Yeah, like I said, it's me."

"Why the fuck is Swan passed out on the floor?" A panicked expression tightened his face as he pushed past me to get to my sister.

"She's okay. Her stupid self decided to mix painkillers and alcohol."

He gently lifted Swan into his arms then carried her over to the bed before smoothly placing her on the mattress like she was made of crystal. He brushed her hair back from her face with a deeply worried look then leaned forward and placed a gentle kiss on her forehead. As he lingered there with his eyes closed, his normally harsh face soft, I inwardly gasped.

Holy shit, Smoke was in love with my sister.

A knock came from the door and a man's familiar, and deep, voice called out, "Yo, Smoke, you okay in there?"

Smoke glanced at me, his narrow dark eyes studying my face. "Yeah, we're fine. Got somethin' you need to see, though."

The door opened and the dresser slid farther as Hulk shoved his way into the room. While he wasn't as tall as Smoke, he was wide, built thick with muscle that he'd carefully honed until his body was a testament to the results of living a healthy lifestyle. I'd trained with him in the gym before and his workout regimen was brutal, designed not for looks, but for strength and stamina. With his pale green eyes and dark chocolate skin, he presented an interesting contrast that caught any woman's attention.

Those pretty eyes widened and his jaw dropped the slightest bit as he looked between me and my sister on the bed. "Sarah?"

I gave him a little wave. "Hey, Hulk."

He actually staggered back a step, still staring at me. "No fucking way."

"Yes, fucking way." I grinned at him, the absurdity of shocking a big, mean biker so thoroughly striking me as funny.

Hulk abruptly stiffened, then strode across the room and grabbed me up into a huge hug. "Jesus Christ, woman, you have no idea how glad I am to see you."

Smoke, however, wasn't feeling as happy as Hulk. "What in the ever-loving fuck were you thinking? Of all the stupid shit you could have done, this was by far the fuckin' worst. Do you have any idea what your leavin' did to Beach? You got even the faintest fuckin' clue the problems you caused?"

Oh no, I did *not* endure all the bullshit I'd gone through to deal with this. No way was I going to just bite my tongue and be a good girl while he went off. I'd put up with way too much crap in the past few weeks and I was beyond my limit. My heart raced as he continued to try to lecture me like I was a moron until I was about ready to slit his damn throat.

Hulk must have noticed my homicidal thoughts because he quickly stepped between us. "Sarah, honey, where have you been?"

"Somewhere with her head up her ass," Smoke snarled as he texted something on his phone.

Normally, I love Hulk. He's a good guy with endless patience and a smile that draws you in. We became good friends, and while I was glad to see him, no way was Smoke going to think he had any right to act like my dad. Fuck that.

"Listen, asshole," I pointed right at Smoke so he knew for sure I was referring to him, "I don't know what planet you live on where you think it's okay to lecture me like you're my daddy, but you aren't, and I suggest you back the fuck off before I cut your balls off. I am in no mood for any macho bullshit and I don't have the time or energy to waste on killing you, so kindly fuck off."

Swan's voice groaned from the bed, "For fuck's sake, Sarah, can you stop yelling at Dad for ten damn minutes. Shit. And go get me some orange juice and some aspirin."

We all flew to her side and it took her a few minutes to fully wake up, but as she did and I watched her interact with Smoke, I knew she loved him as well. In fact, it was almost sickening how into each other they were. I'd never seen Swan like that with a man, not even Stewart, so the open adoration in her expression as she gazed at Smoke, the way his normally mean features eased, made me all gooey inside.

My sister was in love with a good man and I couldn't be happier for her.

At least something positive came of this mess.

They began to kiss and I couldn't help teasing Smoke. "Ha! I knew you had a thing for her."

Swan's fair brows turned down as she frowned at me. "What?"

I ignored her, loving the way Smoke looked almost…guilty. "How the mighty have fallen. I bet every sweet butt from here to New Mexico is crying herself to sleep."

He glared, then smiled at me, his dark eyes sparking with amusement as we fell into our usual pattern of shit-talking each other. "Speaking of fallen, Beach is waiting for you to call him back, Sarah. He wanted me to remind you of your agreement with him, one phone call a day, every day. And my Prez also wants you to know that *Papi* is on his way, and that you're his now, princess. Get ready for a life of spoiled leisure after he punishes you for scaring ten years off his life."

It took me a second to figure out what he was talking about, then I remembered a conversation Beach and I had when we'd first moved in together about checking in with each other. This was after he'd disappeared for four days, leaving me frantic to know if he was even alive. After he returned, and we had a pretty big fight, we'd both agreed to contact each other at least once a day. Phone call, text, email, messenger pigeon, didn't matter how as long as we did. At the time I'd sworn I'd do it, that he could keep me locked up in a gilded cage like a princess in a tower if I didn't check in faithfully, and evidently he remembered that conversation.

Then my brain digested the rest of the conversation.

Papi was on his way.

Oh shit.

My knees grew weak and Hulk was there to brace me in an instant. "Always there to catch me. You need to get a new hobby."

They tried to talk to me more, but I needed some alone time with Swan so I brushed the men off and dragged her into the bathroom before shutting the door and turning on the shower to block our conversation from prying ears.

I'm ashamed to say I came almost instantly unglued, my sobbing apology for not having caught our mother coming out in a broken whimper.

Swan evidently had enough of my pity party because she interrupted my babbling apologies for her getting kidnapped back in Houston by Los Diablos. "Hey, it's not your fault. I wasn't paying any attention. I should have seen them. I guess my paranoia was out of practice. Besides, Smoke saved me, and I started to fall in love with him that night."

Her strength bolstered my own, and I forced myself to get a grip. "I'm so proud of you, and so sorry I still haven't managed to nail our mother down. That bitch is slippery, and I can't get too close to her without tipping off her watchdogs. Please forgive me for dragging you into this, but I couldn't do it on my own."

"You didn't drag me into anything; it was our waste-of-space mother. I'm so proud of you for going after her, even if I want to strangle you for putting yourself in danger like that! Where have you been? What have you been doing? And why the hell wouldn't you contact me?"

"I couldn't. Nothing I sent to you could be trusted not to end up in the wrong hands. They have hackers that make Stewart look like a rank amateur. This is the big league, Swan, and they don't play around. I got the jewels; which'll make Hustler happy. I got the codes which'll make the Russians happy. And I know for a fact that we can trade them for our safety. The Russians will not only forgive our mother's debt, they will add their protection to us. That leaves the Israelis, and I'm hoping that'll work itself out."

I hoped she didn't see how worried I truly was, how much I feared for our future, but I didn't want to freak her out so I continued to lie. "Soon we'll have a strong enough shield of people guarding us, the kind of people who will seek bloody retribution on our behalf, that we should, in theory, be able to live the rest of our lives in relative peace."

She stared at me, hope burning bright on her expressive face even as she continued to wring her hands. "Are you for fucking real?"

"Absolutely." A sudden certainty hit me, and this time I spoke the truth when I said, "The Iron Horse MC is my family. Nobody fucks with my family and most especially, nobody fucks with my blood. I love you honey, so much, and I'm so, so happy to see you. I missed you."

We talked some more before I finally got up the courage to reveal my big secret to her. Yes, part of me wanted to not let anyone else know I was pregnant before Beach, but this was my twin, and I needed to tell her. She, of course, was super excited, and before I knew it, I found myself whispering to her about how I feared I'd be a bad mother, like our own. I figured if anyone could understand my doubts, it would be her.

Swan surprised me with her vehemence as she scolded me for ever thinking I'd end up like Billie, and told me with complete assurance that I was going to be a wonderful mother. When I fretted about Beach hating me, she set me straight on that as well, reassuring me that Beach still loved me and that nothing I could do would ever stop that. Not even my past and my mother.

This caused more crying, and she gave me a pep talk like only Swan could.

"Look at you! Fuck, woman, you faced down bikers and the mafia, then managed to save the goddamn world by yourself. You're a fucking superhero. Any child would be blessed to have you as a mom. Your past is just that—your past. And when did Sarah Anderson, *Playboy* centerfold, Pole Dancing Champion, and Ice Dancing Junior Queen of Nevada, give a fuck what anyone thinks of her?"

I sniffed. "When those two pink lines came up on the pregnancy test."

A loud banging came from the door and we hurriedly cleaned up. Khan, the president of the Denver chapter of the Iron Horse MC, was on his way.

I knew I still looked like shit as I strode out to meet him, but I put some steel in my backbone. No way was I showing any hint of vulnerability to what was probably going to be a roomful of pissed-off bikers. The thought of all of them trying to lecture me about how "stupid" I'd been instantly put me in a pissed-off mood, and I grabbed Swan's hand in an attempt to calm myself.

As soon as we stepped into the now crowded bedroom, Khan's voice boomed out, "You scared ten fuckin' years off my life! Where the fuck have you been? Why didn't you come to me?"

I stared him down, taking in the deep lines around his eyes and how tight his lips were behind his long grey-and-black mustache. "That would require trust, and you know I don't trust anyone except Beach and my family."

He appeared genuinely sad as he said, "Should've come to me, trust or not."

I glanced over at my sister, finding Smoke wrapped around her protectively like a living shield. "My goal, Khan, is to stay alive. I will do whatever it takes to make that happen. As will my sister. It's how we were raised."

Smoke's phone beeped, and as he read the text, the corner of his lip curved up in a grin. "Beach will be here in two hours. He says he wants to talk to you in person."

Every nerve in my body seemed to light up with anticipation, even as the worry that I might have pushed him too far, broken his trust in me forever, haunted me. Not to mention the fact I was still a little pissed that he'd been so quick to accuse me of betraying him. That still stung and I whispered, "How can I love and hate him at the same time?"

"Because you're a crazy bitch," Swan muttered.

I was tempted to stick my tongue out at her, but Smoke said in a low voice, "Which one are you gonna embrace, love or hate?"

"What?"

Swan rolled her eyes at Smoke before turning back to me. "Just let go of your bullshit already and marry the guy. You're obviously stupid for each other, so just make it official and live your happily ever after."

She made it sound so easy. "Just like that?"

"Why not?"

"But there's so much between us…"

Smoke chuckled. "Women…always overcomplicating shit. Here's what you're gonna do: When Beach comes in, you are going to tell him you're sorry, then kiss him until he stops trying to talk. I'll clear out the room across the hall, and you can take him in there and remind him how much you love him. Then, you're gonna take your punishment from your *Papi* like a good little girl."

I grinned at him. "Sometimes being a bad little girl is fun."

"Tell me that tomorrow after you've had a night with Beach, knowing you scared the fuck out of him."

"He'll be fine," I said with a pitiful attempt at nonchalance. My whole body was now shaking at the thought of seeing Beach again, of facing his anger. "Okay, he might be a little tiny bit irritated with me, but he acted like a dick."

Smoke nodded with a smirking grin. "True. In fact, I think he might still owe you. Remember to make him beg for it if you really want an apology. Make him hard until his dick hurts and he'll forgive you for anything once you give him that pussy he's been starvin' for."

Looking down at myself, I couldn't help but notice how frail my arms looked, how prominent the bump of my belly had become when I pressed the fabric of my dress over it. With my hair all ratty from the wig, the skanky outfit, and the remains of melted stage makeup on my face, I probably looked like a heroin-addicted hooker fallen on hard times.

"I look like shit."

Swan slung her arm over my shoulder and pulled me into a hug. "Well, let's kick Smoke out so we can get you ready for Beach and get something to eat."

Chapter 14

A little over two hours later, I was cleaned up and wearing an almost virginal white sundress that hid the bump of my belly while revealing a good expanse of leg. I'd washed up, eaten, and even gotten a small nap in while waiting for him to arrive. My skin smelled like Swan's vanilla body lotion and I'd styled my hair the best I could with products borrowed from one of the old ladies.

I was still sickly looking due to all the weight I'd lost, but at least I no longer appeared homeless.

Smoke and Swan talked in low voices while I paced the room, both of them having given up on talking to me while I waited for Beach.

All at once, tingles raced over me in a harsh burn of sensation.

Carlos was here.

I spun to the door, my whole body shaking with the tension, trapped beneath the need to run out there and see if my instincts were right, terrified of finding the hallway empty.

Before I could find the courage to move, my man strode through the door, breaking my heart into a million pieces as his midnight-blue eyes met mine, the grief blanketing his handsome face lifting the moment he saw me.

I raised my trembling arms to him and wrapped them around his strong neck, the press of his body so hot against mine, so real. My fingers plunged into his thick blond hair, finding more glints of silver at the temples than I remembered. The strong muscles of his neck flexed beneath my touch as an almost tortured sound escaped him that tore through my heart. There was so much pain in it, a staggering amount that brought tears to my eyes.

"Sarah," he groaned against my neck, the relief in his voice filling me.

My mind barely functioned beneath the onslaught of my emotions, but I managed to whisper out, "I'm so sorry."

He clutched me tight, not bothering with foolish words as his fingers dug into me. A buzz began to hum through me, the rasp of the cloth of my dress over my sensitive nipples making them bead up tight. The firm grip of his hands on me was heaven and he began to jerk down the zipper holding my dress together while his other hand disappeared beneath the skirt, gripping my ass hard enough to send delicious shards of pleasure racing through me.

Dimly I was aware of male laughter and voices, but I was too entranced by Beach to give it much thought.

The world spun around me and I wanted to laugh, scream, and cry all at the same time as Beach kissed me like he was trying to devour me. Our mingled taste flowed through me, setting my body on fire. My clit throbbed and I wrapped my legs tighter around his hard waist, the strength of his body easily holding me to him. His strong body moved against mine as he moved with me clinging to him like a kudzu vine.

Abruptly he stopped and we broke apart long enough for me to glance around at what appeared to be an empty bedroom. The warm amber table lamps bathed Beach's face in gold light, revealing how much he'd aged while I'd been gone. Terrible things shone briefly in his eyes and I mourned the way all the stress had marked him.

We studied each other and Beach reached up with a trembling hand, cupping my face and swiping his thumb over my lips. "Sarah."

"I'm so sorry," I repeated, unable to put into words everything I was feeling.

His grip on my chin firmed and anger twisted his features as he scowled at me. "I'm unbelievably pissed at you for running away like that, for puttin' yourself in so much danger. Do you have any idea how much I've needed you? Can you even begin to understand how fucked up I've been without you?"

Ashamed, I looked away, fearing his disgust when he learned I wasn't only endangering myself, but also our unborn child.

Part of me wanted to hide it, to avoid conversation that I was scared to have, but I'd never been the kind of person to run from my fears. I needed to tell him, now, before anything else was said.

"Beach, there's something I need to tell you."

"Later."

"But—"

"I said fuckin' later!" he roared as I stumbled a step back, a tiny bit of fear breaking through the wall of guilt I'd built around my hidden pain. "I thought you were *dead*, I thought you were being tortured, that you were somewhere begging for your life, and I couldn't *find* you! Every time I closed my eyes, I would see you broken and bleeding while some animal ended your life in misery."

Abruptly, my emotional pendulum swung the other way and I yelled at him, "Yeah? Well last time I saw you, Beach, you were accusing me of betraying the club. Sorry if I wasn't sure what your reaction would be if I contacted you."

He hunched forward like I'd hit him in the stomach. "I know, I'm so sorry for doubting you, *mi corazon*. So fuckin' sorry."

The pain radiating from him had me braving his defensive rage as I wrapped my arms around him and held on, trying to let go of my anger. "I love you. I'm sorry too."

"Never again," he groaned in desperation against my head. "Sarah, promise me, never again. I won't survive if you do this again."

"I swear it."

My gaze caught something on the side of his neck and I jerked back while tilting his head for a better look. It was a tattoo, a big one, and it spelled out my name.

Holy shit, he'd gotten my name tattooed on his neck while I was gone. I instantly loved the fact that he'd put it someplace so visible, someplace everyone was bound to see. The black ink stood out from his tanned skin proclaiming him as mine and I teared up.

"Oh, Beach." I traced the flowing letters of my name on his strong neck. "It's beautiful."

He grasped my hand and exposed where I'd tattooed his name on my inner wrist. Kissing it softly, he traced the suddenly sensitive skin with the tip of his tongue. "Better or worse, *mi Corazón*. Those aren't just words with us, but a promise. Gonna marry you as soon as we can have a wedding without worryin' about assassins."

I struggled to keep my mind on target, to tell Beach about the baby, even though all I wanted to do was make love to him until we both passed out. "Honey, I really need to tell you something."

"Your dad clued me in on his plan. I got Tom working on it—he owes us, big, and this'll call us even. We're gonna make them an offer they can't refuse."

My breath came out shaky as the scruff around his lips abraded my tingling skin. "What?"

Now licking his way up my arm, he bit the sensitive skin of my forearm before looking up at me with a purely wicked gleam in his eyes. "Later."

"But I—"

My words were cut off as he scooped me up then tossed me onto the bed, his weight following me. He jerked the top of my dress down, the delicate straps snapping easily beneath his strength. I drew in a deep breath to tell him to stop, but he took my now super-sensitive nipple into his mouth and I practically shot off the bed.

Holy shit, I knew they were more tender than usual, but I had no idea it would be like this. A harsh moan ripped from me as he added teeth, and I found myself trying to jerk his head from my breast even as I arched closer to the lush sucking of his mouth. Each pull sent harsh daggers of warmth straight to my clit and I wondered if I'd be able to orgasm like this.

He released me long enough to whisper, "Fuck, I missed these perfect tits."

A giggle escaped me that quickly turned into a moan as he sat up between my legs, his magnificent arms flexing while he ripped off his cut, then his shirt, the absolute perfection of his thick body sending my hormones into overload. When he covered me with his weight again, I took in a deep breath of his familiar musk and found myself growing even wetter. Damn, he smelled like a weird mixture of sex and home, pleasure and safety. The primitive parts of my mind rejoiced at being reunited with my mate.

The coarse hair of his chest rubbed my nipples while he softly kissed my mouth, his busy hands roaming over the parts of my body that weren't pressed tight to his.

When he reached between us towards my belly, I startled. "Wait!"

Looking at me like I'd lost my mind, his lust-filled gaze narrowed on me. "What?"

"Wait…I…Beach…give me your hand."

I took his large, calloused palm in my own and swallowed hard enough that my throat clicked as I slid it over the hard curve of my normally flat belly. "I'm pregnant. Carlos, you're going to be a father."

His gaze grew glassy and he stopped breathing long enough that I grew alarmed.

Then I was pretty sure he fainted for a second.

Honest to God, his eyes started to roll back in his head and he slumped forward, giving me all his weight.

"Beach!" I yelped. "Squishing me."

"The baby!" he yelled as he abruptly came too, his frantic gaze going to my stomach while he lifted himself off me in an impressive plank. "Did I hurt the baby?"

"No, no honey. She's perfectly fine."

His normally dark tan paled as his arms lost some of their ridged straightness. "She?"

"Yes. We're having a baby girl."

Then he closed his eyes and began to pray in Spanish so fast, I worried—until I realized he was thanking God over and over again.

Leaning up, I wrapped my arms around him and pulled him to me, but he remained stiff.

"I want to see."

When his gaze met mine, I nodded, worried and unable to read his expression as his gaze bore into mine with an intensity I'd never seen before. It was like he was looking all the way into my soul, his entire being serious to the point of being dire. My stomach clenched and I hoped the pill I'd taken earlier kept on working. Abruptly the darkness in his blue eyes disappeared and was replaced with an incredible warmth that took away all my fear and worry.

He was overjoyed that I was pregnant.

With a gentle reverence that was totally at odds with his earlier dress-ripping actions, he slowly tore the fabric away to reveal my stomach in all its glory. I made sure to use coconut oil on it nightly and so far the skin was smooth and stretch-mark free. The baby books called this the "pretty belly stage", and Beach seemed utterly entranced as he leaned down and began placing kisses all over my bump while talking to his daughter in Spanish, calling her his little flower and other sweet names.

While he bonded with his baby, I ran my fingers through his hair, marveling at the way the tension seemed to melt off of him, how life was returning to his face.

He began to kiss his way lower on my belly, until I started to squirm as he drew closer to other parts of me that had missed him as well.

I couldn't help but wonder if my lady bits were more sensitive now due to the pregnancy.

Beach answered that question when he gently stroked the panel of my teal cotton panties between my legs. I groaned and right away arched into his touch, desperate for him. When he scraped his thumb nail over my clit, I swear my legs shook and I opened my eyes, needing to see him.

"Naked," I begged, "please."

When he didn't do as I asked, I tackled him.

The look of surprise on his face would have been comical if I wasn't so desperate to have him inside of me. I pawed at his pants, yanking and jerking them while Beach laughed, the warm sound bringing an answering ring of joy through me. It was such a vital sound, so filled with life, and when I managed to yank down his pants enough to pull out his cock, he didn't fight me.

"Anything you want, *mamacita*."

Wise man.

I held his length in my hands, ready to plunge myself down on him, but he had other ideas. With a growl and a surprising show of strength, he plucked me from his hips and brought me up to straddle his mouth instead. I lurched forward until he steadied me with an impressive display of raw strength before grasping my hips and pulling me down onto his ravenous mouth.

At the first lash of his tongue, I fell forward, my hands tearing at the pillows as he nuzzled between my legs, hungry noises escaping him as he feasted on me. Warm tingles raced from my pelvis down to my toes, and back up again as I began to rock against his mouth, eager to come. He knew just how to eat me right and when his tongue circled my clit, slow, hot, and wet, I tensed then exploded with a scream. My orgasm was so powerful, rocketing through me while Beach kept licking, gripping my hips and forcing me down on his face.

My inner muscles clenched and spasmed when he thrust two fingers into me, and soon I was coming again while he finger-fucked me hard enough to make my breasts shake.

When he finally removed me from his face, I was useless, totally limp and pretty much unresponsive with my happy glow.

Beach, however, was ready to fuck.

He rolled me onto my back then rubbed his cock over my sensitive clit, making me hiss and writhe against him. It was too much, too soon, but he made me endure the painful pleasure. When the wide, pierced head of his cock pushed into me, I rolled my head with a bone-deep sigh, and his hard length filled me perfectly.

"Shit," Beach hissed. "You're so fucking hot and tight."

"Pregnancy," I muttered. "More blood flow."

"Fuck. Shit." He gave an experimental stroke. "So good. I ain't never leavin' this pussy, gonna have you knocked up all the time."

If I'd been able to think of anything beyond his fat cock inside of me, I would have argued with him about being used as a broodmare, but holy crap could he fuck.

Beach worked his hips with each thrust in a way that sent bursts of pleasure through me, my body heating up until our slick skin slid together. He hunched over me, careful to keep his weight off my stomach, and began to kiss me deeply while we moved together. A deep climax flowed through me and I sucked his tongue into my mouth, loving the way he began to grunt as my pussy squeezed him tight again and again. Moving faster now, Beach fisted my hair and forced me to look at him, his eyes boring into mine.

For my final orgasm of the night, we went over together, and I was asleep before the last waves of release moved through me.

Chapter 15
Carlos "Beach" Rodriguez

I'd anticipated Mimi's arrival, but not at the break of fucking dawn. Sarah and I had spent the night going at it again and again until she'd passed out. Evidently pregnancy had her starving for my dick and I wasn't complaining about the lack of shuteye. Being tired this morning was a fair price for the amazing orgasms I'd given her last night. Just the memory had a satisfied smile curving my lips as I chowed one of the breakfast burritos Mimi brought with her when she showed up at the clubhouse with two of Sarah's Stefano cousins.

Satisfaction and profound relief filled me as I glanced over at Sarah sitting next to me, doing her best to finish off a second giant breakfast burrito.

Safe, thank God she was safe.

Every touch, every taste of her last night had been magnified by my overwhelming relief at having her whole and well in my arms again.

Her and my daughter.

Dear God, I'm going to be a father.

Unable to help myself, I reached out and stroked the back of Sarah's neck, smiling to myself as her cheeks went pink. When her sparkling pale blue eyes met my own, I could see her love for me shining bright. I wasn't the only one happy about our reunion and I was so fucking thankful she'd forgiven me for being such a giant dick. I should have ignored Vance and his conspiracy bullshit that Sarah was somehow involved. Motherfucker almost had me believing his bullshit. True, he'd been right about where the girls were being kept and had managed to rescue them, but that didn't mean he was right about Sarah. She was loyal with every ounce of her formidable heart, and she was all mine.

We were seated in a small conference room in the clubhouse, about half the size of the room where they held church here. Smoke sat next to me on the right, while Sarah cuddled into me on my left. I'd tried to get her to go back to bed, but she'd ignored me once she learned her stepmother was here. Swan was still sleeping and Mimi wanted to keep it that way.

I personally thought they were underestimating Swan's ability to deal with shit, but both Mimi and Sarah were overprotective of Swan to the point of going a little overboard with it. Sarah had explained her paranoia by saying that once, when Swan was ten, something had happened to frighten her badly and she went almost catatonic, retreating from the world until Mike and Mimi feared she'd never resurface. Eventually she'd snapped out of it, but the experience had led to Mike and Mimi becoming even more overprotective of Swan.

Normally I'd fight for Swan's presence here because she deserved to know what was going on, and it was dangerous to keep her in the dark, but I bit my tongue. Smoke was here and that pussy-whipped bastard would tell his woman everything. Like the fact that we were getting ready to head into what could be a deathtrap.

So far, Mimi hadn't told us dick about what was going on, other than to say she could now openly help them as a representative of the Stefano Mafia as they attended the meeting we'd all be heading to soon. When Sarah had questioned her about the Novikov *Bratva* getting involved, Mimi had refused to say a word, but I was pretty sure the news wasn't good. She had something up her sleeve, I can't believe she'd leave her daughters' collective asses hanging out in the wind, but whatever it was, she was holding her cards close to her chest.

Sarah took another huge bite of her breakfast, then chugged a gulp of milk. "So I'm going to ride with you, Mimi?"

"Yes."

I started to protest that Sarah wasn't leaving my sight but Mimi held up her hand and gave me such a hard look that I bit back my words.

"Carlos, you will be riding up front, but Sarah and I will be in the rear of the SUV with the privacy panel up. This is not because we will be plotting your murder, but rather so I can coach my daughter on the meeting ahead. If you are there you will distract her, and we cannot afford that."

"Fine," Sarah said quickly while squeezing my thigh. "But once we're at the meeting Beach is sitting next to me. I don't care what anyone thinks or says."

Mimi's lips twitched, but she nodded. "Agreed."

The door to the room opened and Swan came in, a confused frown on her face that melted away the instant she saw her stepmother. "Mimi!"

My woman gave a small sigh as she watched Mimi and Swan hug.

"You okay?" I whispered against the silk of her hair.

She wiped a tear away, but nodded. "Yeah, I'm good. Just happy to see them together. I was afraid…well…I was afraid."

She didn't need to say any more. I was all too familiar with fearing for my loved ones, and I wouldn't wish on anyone the sick feeling of knowing the woman I adored beyond reason was in very real danger. Once again my hand found the back of her neck as I stroked her skin, more to soothe myself this time than her.

Across the table, Mimi and Smoke spoke to each other in low voices, but my attention was focused on breathing Sarah in, on feeling the heat and life emanating from her.

I placed a gentle kiss on her temple, the faint scent of her makeup reaching my nose. She wore a sexy black business suit with a shimmering gold top beneath that was at once classy and sexy. Paired with some sleek black heels and conservative gold jewelry, she reeked of elegance and class. Mimi had supplied her with the outfit, and I had to admit my future mother-in-law knew her shit about dressing a woman in what amounted to the female version of armor. I don't care who you are, any heterosexual man is affected by the sight of a drop-dead gorgeous woman, and Sarah's about as pretty as they come.

Swan was a stark contrast to my woman's sophisticated beauty. She wore a pair of dark brown pants with almost bell-bottoms and a loose cream sweater belted around the waist with a gold chord. As the sweater pulled tight on her hips with her movements, I noticed what was probably a gun on one side and a knife on the other. I couldn't help but grin as I thought about the weapons Sarah had, no doubt, strapped to herself as well.

The conversation switched to Sarah's pregnancy as the other women fawned all over her. Right now Swan was holding Sarah's hand as they leaned together and whispered while Mimi talked to Smoke. A piece of me that'd been torn away was finally filled again by my soon-to-be wife and baby. My gut clenched as the thought of all she'd been through, all the dangers we still had to deal with, threatened my self-control. It was only with a great deal of effort that I was able to suppress the urge to snatch Sarah up and disappear with her, never to be seen again. I could do it, but she'd hate me, and I'd rather gut myself than lose her love.

By the time we arrived at the meeting with the Boldin *Bratva* and the Israelis, the other representatives were already there. Mr. Dahan, a big player in the international criminal underworld, was representing the Israeli Multoz Criminal Family, a huge smuggling organization that controlled much of the Middle East trade routes. A dark-skinned man with a bold nose, Mr. Dahan was in his early thirties but he'd lived a hard life. His light brown eyes studied everyone, constantly, like he was expecting an attack at any minute. An aloof distrust radiated from him, but when he looked at Mimi, a small muscle on the side of his neck would begin to twitch. He was good at being a cold motherfucker, but Mrs. Mike Anderson scared him.

Not that I blamed him, right now Mimi was as lethal as a great white shark surfing the cold ocean depths in her pretty business suit that showed off her toned legs to her advantage.

Sarah sat next to me with Swan at her side. Smoke was somewhere behind us, along with a bunch of Mike's stone-faced friends, each a legend in his own right. Ghost, the associate of Mike's who kept me from getting my ass blown up, was there as well, a surprisingly normal-looking guy with dark brown hair and thin lips. If it wasn't for his calculating, cold blue eyes, I wouldn't have recognized him without his camo makeup.

From across the wide wooden table, Mr. Loktev, a thick, balding man with bad acne scars on his cheeks, stared at Sarah as she laid out her terms.

The tension in my woman was growing, but so far she'd managed to keep her cool. The tips of her ears turned red and I inwardly groaned, urging her to hold her temper in check. A wave of what I can only describe as sparking anger came from her a moment before she said in a smooth, almost seductive voice, "You and I both know that your reputation hasn't been harmed, because not only did you find the items she stole from you, I know there were some very expensive, very interesting toys there as well which will make you a ton of money. And don't try to bullshit me. I saw them with my own eyes, and I know what they are worth."

Mr. Loktev wasn't a man used to anyone defying him, let alone a woman, and he glared at her. "You do not know this for sure. Since you were not there, you can only assume that the extra weaponry was where you said we'd find it."

Mr. Dahan's gaze met mine across the table as the situation rapidly began spiraling out of control. I held those deadly eyes, letting him see the merciless animal that lived inside of me who would kill anyone and anything to keep my woman and baby safe. His lids lowered just the faintest bit, then his attention turned to an increasingly agitated Sarah as she gripped her hands into fists on top of the table.

"We had an agreement."

"If," Mr. Loktev said with a grim smile, "you paid the interest, dear Sarah."

All at once, the professional muscle on the other side of the table all focused their attention on Mimi, and I wondered which of them she was going to kill first.

Blood was about to be spilled, and I'd already planned the best way to get my woman out intact.

I might not make it, but she would, and that was good enough for me.

All I needed was Mimi to start this shit show and I'd destroy these motherfuckers, starting with who I deemed the greatest threat, Mr. Dahan.

Before we reached that fatal point of no return, the doors behind me opened and I followed everyone else's gaze as we all turned to see who the fuck would dare interrupt this meeting.

I bit back a bark of laughter as Tom fucking Sokolov breezed into the room looking like he'd just stepped out of a *GQ* magazine.

The dark blue suit he wore stood out in a sea of camo, leather, and jeans, as did his thousand-dollar haircut and thick black-rimmed glasses. Built with slabs of muscle like a linebacker, he was big enough that no one would ever tease him about his slightly nerdy looks. He spotted Smoke and paused for a moment to talk to him. Sarah glanced over at me and the confusion in her gaze probably matched my own. We both looked back at Tom as he took a seat next to Mimi, who glared at him like he'd just taken a shit in her rose garden. He merely grinned at her, then winked over at Swan and Sarah before lifting his chin at me.

Voices whispered all around us, and not all in English, as Tom took a moment to adjust his jacket before meeting the gazes of the men across the table.

The smug, cocky smirk he gave Mr. Dahan and Mr. Loktev had me raising an eyebrow, hoping his arrogant ass wasn't about to get us killed.

Instead of reaching across the table and smacking the smirk off his face, Mr. Loktev paled and stammered out, "Mr. Sokolov, it is good to see you again."

For a moment my view of Tom was blocked by Sarah and Swan, then he leaned forward and tapped the table with a large manila envelope. "We would like to propose a trade."

Mr. Loktev blustered, "I don't—"

"This is not a trade for you, but for your boss, Mr. Boldin." The teasing grin fell from Tom's face as he abruptly switched to Russian.

I studied Mr. Loktev while Tom spoke, and I would have given my left nut to know what my friend was saying to the older man because he looked like he'd just been kicked in the gut.

Loktev switched back to English, his voice strained. "You would make this trade? What do you want?"

"It's not what I want; it's what Ms. Anderson wants. Agree to all of her terms and drop all penalties. I'm aware of exactly what you received in addition to the missiles." Tom leaned back in his chair while Sarah reached under the table for my hand, then squeezed it hard. "We're taking care of your import, and you will split the profit fifty-fifty with the Anderson sisters. None of these terms are negotiable. Do we have a deal?"

With an almost eager look, Mr. Loktev nodded. "Then it is done. Ms. Anderson, the Boldin *Bratva* agrees to your terms. We will discuss payment arrangements with Mr. Sokolov."

To my surprise, Sarah stood, then reached into her blouse and removed a folded piece of paper before handing it to a rapidly blinking Mr. Loktev.

"The codes," she said in a cool voice, and Loktev nodded.

Damn, loved it when my baby went all badass on people.

"That is all wonderful," Mr. Dahan said in a flat voice, "but there is still the little matter of what your mother owes us, Ms. Anderson, that priceless item she stole so easily. Unless you have it. Do you have it, Sarah?"

Sarah glanced at Mimi, who was staring at Mr. Dahan, and whispered, "I...no."

I slowly moved my hand to where my gun was stashed, the mood in the room plummeting as Tom laughed. "I was wondering when you were going to speak up, Mr. Dahan."

The look he gave Tom was apologetic, but cold. "I am sorry, but even for you, Mr. Sokolov, this is out of my hands."

I'd forgotten about the envelope on the table before Tom, until he tossed it over to Mr. Dahan with a flick of his wrist. "Inside you will find something better than the product.

"And what would that be?" Dahan asked in a bored tone, his hand beneath the table, no doubt resting on a weapon of some kind.

"The person who made it."

I resisted the urge to look at Sarah, wondering who the hell she was talking about, but now was not the time or place. In the brief moment we'd had to talk before walking into the meeting Sarah had shared with me that Mimi had a plan, a complicated one, but a plan none the less. Mimi had obviously coached Sarah through this, and I wasn't going to screw it up by appearing clueless. The silver stuff belonged to the Israelis, as well as the trees, and I wondered what had happened to them since Sarah was obviously pretending we had no idea where they were.

His dark brows rose the slightest bit, and I could see a ripple of movement going through his bodyguards. "A very generous offer, but it will take at least a year to make. Even this will not save them from paying the price for their mother's sins."

Sarah leaned over and whispered, "Easy, Beach. Get your hand off your gun."

I hovered on the edge of violence. "On my mark, we leave."

She must have seen how close I was to losing it, to saying fuck it and getting her out of here, because her hand clamped down over mine beneath the table, pinning it to my gun as she whispered directly into my ear, "No, just wait. Mimi told me in the car she's been working with Tom and his uncle, Petrov Dubinski, but she didn't know if Tom would arrive in time. Please, honey, just give him a few more minutes."

Rubbing at his jaw, Tom leaned back far enough in his chair that I could see the small smile he gave Mr. Dahan. "My cousin, Dimitri Novikov, is calling in his marker."

My mind raced as I tried to place that name. Obviously Russian...ah yes, the Novikov *Bratva*. One of the most feared criminal families in the world, ruled by a monster, and Dimitri Novikov was one of the monster's sons. I'd heard of Dimitri, that he was a dangerous yet fair man, but most of my business was done with the Dubinski *Bratva*.

Smoke was my main connection to the world of the Russian Mafia, he'd been over there a couple times on club business with Tom and had some connections. I stole a glance at him and found my stoic Master at Arms looking a little shocked. Mimi hadn't moved and she still had her gaze locked on the Israelis.

When I looked across the table, I found one of Mr. Dahan's bodyguards eye-fucking my woman and her sister as they whispered together, their pale blonde hair blending as their foreheads touched.

If I didn't notice the pulse pounding in Mr. Dahan's neck, he would have appeared utterly bored with the whole situation. "I will have to verify this."

Smoke made his way over to Swan and squeezed between her and Mimi. I couldn't hear what he said to her, but whatever it was, his words calmed her down. Around us rose and fell the soft hiss of low whispers.

Mimi met my gaze and for a brief moment she allowed me to see how worried she'd been, and how relieved she was, before her gaze closed back up. Sometime in the near future, me and her were gonna have a long talk about what had happened here, because I was out of the loop of information and I didn't like that one bit. Still, if whatever she had done worked, I was gonna buy her a diamond tennis bracelet the size of boulders for saving my soon-to-be wife's and child's lives.

Sarah moved into my line of sight, breaking my gaze with Mimi.

Whatever she saw in my face must have disturbed her because she whispered, "It's going to be okay. Mimi saved Dimitri Novikov's life, he owes her big. We're going to be okay."

Before I could respond, Mr. Dahan started speaking to someone on the phone in Russian, his manner congenial and an actual smile cracking his normally serious face. Smoke and I exchanged a curious look before turning our attention back to Mr. Dahan. His bodyguards had backed off a few steps, allowing their boss to pace while the Russians silently looked on. Mr. Loktev was texting as he watched Mr. Dahan, the look on his ruddy face positively stunned.

Turning back to the table, Mr. Dahan smiled at my woman in a charming way that set my teeth on edge. "Ladies, it is a good day when two beautiful women such as yourselves are given a second chance. Your debt to us is forgiven and you are now under our protection. Congratulations, Sarah and Swan Anderson. You have become untouchable."

For a moment there was total silence, then I found myself clutching an armful of warm woman pressed against me, her lips finding mine as we kissed long and deep, celebrating this moment in a way our words couldn't. All around me people were talking in an excited rush, and I heard Mimi's laughter as it rang through the room, the relief in it evident.

Sarah tore her lips from mine, tears streaking mascara down her face as she both smiled and cried. "We're going to be okay."

"We're going to be okay," I reaffirmed, holding her as tight as I dared with our baby between us.

Chapter 16
Sarah

It was one day after we'd returned from Denver and I was on the back of one of Beach's antique Harley-Davidson motorcycles, riding out of town to Birdie's ranch for a Sunday brunch.

They'd demanded Beach share me with the world, and though he would have liked to ignore them and keep me tied down to our bed for another day, for real, he'd bowed to the combined pressure of Birdie and Mouse threatening his life if they didn't get to see me. Only we didn't know word would spread about our brunch plans, and when we arrived at the sprawling ranch north of Austin, with a large escort of armed-and-dangerous brothers spread out behind us, the huge circular drive was already filled with motorcycles and a few other vehicles.

Beach slowed his bike then pulled off onto the terracotta pavers lining the side of the massive concrete drive. He quickly turned off the engine, which rumbled to silence beneath my legs. Confused as to what was going on, I frowned as people began to exit Birdie's house, but my field of vision was limited by the full face helmet Beach insisted I wear. He was taking no chances with my safety and I was lucky he hadn't insisted on a bulletproof vest as well. I didn't blame him, I was feeling a wee bit overprotective of him as well, but there was no way in hell I was wearing a heavy-ass vest in this heat underneath enough clothes to disguise it.

As I was pulling my helmet off, I heard what sounded like clapping and cheering.

Once I could see again, I turned to find the driveway and massive front porch of Birdie's ranch house filled with familiar faces.

And they were all smiling and cheering.

When I turned to Beach he was grinning, with happy surprise bringing out the light blue flecks in his dark navy eyes. "What the heck?"

"Looks like we got us a welcome home party, *mi amor*."

I glanced at the growing crowd then back at Beach. "Is it too late to turn around and go home?"

He laughed out loud then held my hand as I climbed off. "My mom threatened to disown me if I didn't bring you."

"Did you know everyone would be here?"

He grinned, not bothering to answer as Mouse yelled out, "Carlos! Sarah! Come here right this instant."

Beach smiled at me again as people cleared a path for us, patting us on the back as we walked past them.

The look Mouse gave me held a fair amount of anger, as well as happiness, and I whispered to Beach, "Is she mad at me?"

"She wasn't too pleased when she found out you'd run off." Wincing, I tried to slow down our walk but Beach chuckled and tugged me along. "But I think she's going to be too happy that you're alive, and that you managed to save the club, to give you too much sass about it."

He was right, because Mouse was already running down the steps, her tanned arms held wide as she engulfed both me and Beach in her hug, or as much as she could. Despite having a giant son, Mouse was only a little bit over five feet tall and her short, silky grey hair brushed my chin as she held us close. Her back hitched for a moment before she let out a deep breath, and I shot Beach a panicked look as I worried she might be crying.

"Mom," Beach said as he patted her back. "Get it together. You're freaking Sarah out."

With a scowl that threatened to break into a grin, Mouse stepped back and put her hands on her hips, glaring at Beach. "I hope you feel like a right asshole for what you said to Sarah."

Beach blinked twice, as stunned by the verbal attack out of nowhere as I was, then said, "What?"

Shaking her finger in his face, Mouse, snapped, "You thought Sarah betrayed the club, don't deny it, and you accused her of it in front of everyone. That was an asshole move and I raised you better than that. Anyone with eyes can see she's the best thing that ever happened to you, and it's time you started treating her like it. You'll be lucky if she doesn't make you sleep on the couch for the next two months."

The crowd around us roared with laughter, and Beach narrowed his gaze at me as I couldn't hold back my giggles.

"Really? After all this shit, I gotta come home to my mom busting my balls?" He grinned as he said this, and Mouse shook her finger at him.

"I didn't say anything while all that trouble was going on, but now that you're both safe and alive in front of me, I can remind you how to treat your future wife. If your father was alive right now, he would be mortified."

Next to me, Beach rolled his eyes and muttered, "Ah shit, here we go."

"I heard that!" It was getting harder to hold back my laughter as fierce little Mouse tried to stare Beach down, without much success.

When I made a choking sound, his gaze switched to mine and a snort of laughter escaped.

"Mom," he said in a silky tone while holding my gaze with a smirk. "Sarah's pregnant. You're going to be a grandma. It's a girl, but we don't have a name yet."

Inwardly I cursed at him for throwing me under the bus like that, and the best I could manage when everyone turned to stare at me like the baby was going to suddenly explode out of my body was a squeaked out, "Surprise!"

The crowd around us rang with voices as word spread to those in back that Beach had "knocked his old lady up" and that there was a new "club princess" on the way.

"Oh my sweet God!" Mouse screamed and everyone in a ten-foot radius winced. "Oh my God, a baby! You're pregnant with my little girl grandbaby!"

At that point, everything descended into madness as the entire club lost its mind.

Deep down I knew that, while they were happy for us, the baby was also an excuse to celebrate and take their minds off of the terrible events of the last few weeks, something everyone needed. Kegs were pulled out of the cold-storage building next to the main bunkhouse where the single men who worked the ranch lived. Before I knew it, the fairy lights Birdie kept strewn around the place were on and we were having a party. Everyone seemed determined to fatten me up as quickly as possible, and I found myself grazing on calorie-loaded food. Thanks to the miracle pills, or being in my second trimester, I was craving meat again and ate the hell out of some killer ribs until I was so full I could barely move.

It hadn't taken me long to find myself sprawled out on the couch with my feet up and a glass of homemade lemonade in my hand. I'd protested everyone catering to me, but Mouse whispered they needed to do this, needed to thank me somehow. Even though I hadn't even come close to saving the club—it was mostly Mimi's actions that had given us a blanket of protection—it seemed the members of the MC liked the idea of me single-handedly saving them. While I had their loyalty for being Beach's old lady, the fact that I'd risked everything, on my own, to save the club had earned me their trust.

The women had driven the men from the large living room and they all sat on the couches around me, while I squished onto a brown leather couch with Birdie on one side and Mouse the other, wide-eyed as the ladies chatted about pregnancy and raising kids.

Apparently, I had all kinds of interesting things to look forward to. Like sore and leaking breasts, babies screaming for hours if they were gassy, and my vagina tearing all the way to my rectum. Oh, and if I was really lucky, I'd poop on the delivery table.

Then there were stories of the sweet smell of a baby's hair, the heartbreaking pleasure of your child sleeping in your arms, and a love beyond comprehension.

I guess that made up for the stretch marks.

I was so intent on listening to Birdie's advice on baby names that I missed the fact the chatter around me had silenced.

It was only when Beach stood before me, an immovable wall of leather and denim, that I realized everyone had stopped talking and were staring at the men.

Venom made his way into the room then, and Birdie pushed herself up from the couch with a little help from me, her silky black slacks with their silver stitching rustling as she hurried through the crowd of ladies over to her husband.

Beach stood before me, his hands clenched into fists. "Babe, need to talk to you."

My skin prickled as a negative energy filled the room. "Okay."

He helped me up and I was grateful for his assistance, my fear redoubling as I scanned the room and saw people talking together in small groups with shocked faces. More than a few women were crying, and the men were just flat-out pissed. The earlier good mood had vanished, and I startled when a woman made a loud sobbing noise.

"Beach?"

He pulled me upstairs and into a guest bedroom with a pair of bunkbeds covered in colorful cartoon-animal-festooned quilts. After flipping on the overhead light, a cute rocket-ship-themed ceiling fan, Beach sat me down on the edge of the bottom bunk. Stress deepened the grooves on his face, making him look weary beyond words. I cupped his cheek with my hand, silently lending him my strength.

"Hustler's been arrested for murder."

"What!" I dropped my hand and shook my head. "I don't understand. Murder?"

"Someone shot Veronica, Smoke's sister-in-law and Hustler's ex-piece, in the back of the head, then dumped her on his back porch."

My hands covered my mouth, as if by not speaking I could somehow stop this from happening, make it not true.

While I didn't know Veronica well, she wasn't one of my favorite people at the club. She was one of those fake women who'd grown up in normal suburbia but liked to pretend she grew up in the Spanish ghetto. Her brother, Tricks, had married Smoke's sister Julia—a really nice woman with three little girls who I did like. While Julia went out of her way to help others, including animals at her veterinarian clinic in Austin, Veronica was about as selfish as they come.

And she was trashy.

Not because of her large fake breasts and tendency to wear stripper clothes, I cast no stones there, but because she liked to play with men's emotions. She was kind of like a sweet butt, only she long-term dated a string of brothers, monogamous relationships that always ended with them getting sick of her shit, no matter how hot she was in bed. And none of them had ever put their patch on her. That's how she'd ended up with Hustler. I'd warned him not to get mixed up with her, but he has a hero complex for damsels in distress, so crazy-ass Veronica was right up his alley.

Now, just because I personally didn't like her and all the drama she loved to surround herself with, doesn't mean I don't feel badly about her dying in such a terrible manner.

"That's horrible."

Beach nodded sadly. "Yeah. I talked to Smoke and got him and Swan a flight out. They're on their way back and Julia's going to pick Smoke up, but the government is still trying to find Tricks so he can come home. They stashed him deep behind enemy lines and I'm guessin' they can't get to him easily."

"Poor Tricks, to lose his sister like this." I took a deep breath and let it out slowly. "Whatever you need me to do, I'm here for you. Just let me know."

He closed his eyes and rested his head against my chest. "Fuck I missed having you at my back."

I cradled him close, realizing my strong man needed me.

Threading my fingers through his hair, I cherished every moment we had together, memorizing the feel of him in my arms, the slight citrus of his cologne, the scent of his hair and the feeling of his breath on my skin. I loved him in a way that consumed me and when our lips met, I melted into his kiss, our tongues stroking each other in a slow, wet caress that had my nipples hard and my clit waking up. He pulled back and his gaze roamed my face as I stared at his before he stood with a sigh.

"I'm havin' Thorn and Scarlet take you home. I don't give a fuck who it is, you don't let anyone into the house without my direct say so. Understood? Anyone tries to get in, shoot 'em in the face. Do as I say-no sass."

Do as I say? No sass?

Evidently, my man had lost his damn mind.

The snark was heavy in my voice as I said, "What if it's your mom?"

He gave me an exasperated look, but some of the tension fled from his mouth. "I trust you to use your judgement."

"Then why bother forbidding me? Why not just tell me to be on alert?"

A knock came from the door as he lowered his head and licked his lips in a way that had me wishing I was back in his arms. "When I get home, we're gonna discuss that smart mouth of yours."

Instead of being frightened, I smiled back at him. "Promise?"

A few hours later, my world imploded.

Beach broke the news to me that Smoke and Swan had been kidnapped from the parking lot of the airport. Julia's minivan had been stolen and she'd arrived late at the terminal, only to find Smoke and Swan gone. We'd searched for them, then an informant told us Los Diablos had them. I was ready to invade every single one of their homes and scorch the Earth until I found my sister and the man she loved, even though the Los Diablos protested that they didn't have them.

My beautiful, sweet sister who had just found love had been kidnapped.

I was sick with rage at the thought of some depraved asshole having her and my heart ached like I'd been hit in the chest with a mallet.

Beach stared at me from across the big table in the conference room, then glanced behind me. Two big men suddenly flanked me on either side but I ignored them, waiting for my fiancé to give me word on my family. The desperate need to vent my rage on the people guilty of taking her burned through me, and I wanted so badly to just leave and do my own thing, but I couldn't. I was shackled by both my word and my child.

That didn't mean I was happy about Beach's refusal to attack Los Diablos at their clubhouse.

Hustler leaned over and murmured in my ear, "Listen to me, Sarah, please. Attacking Los Diablos is a trap."

His words startled me enough that I stopped glaring at Beach while fingering the big knife strapped to my belt and turned my attention to him.

Hulk stood at Hustler's side and when I glanced at him, he nodded slowly. "Listen to the man, sweetheart."

I burned with frustration for action, but I'd heard from Beach how Hustler's instincts would have saved him from endangering his men, if he'd only listened. You can say many things about the differences between men and women, how we think and act, but one thing is for sure—in general, women are better listeners. We pay attention to people when they speak, dissecting their body language in a way men usually don't. Plus, despite his asshole sense of humor, Hustler was wicked smart. His usual joking persona had been burned away by the harsh reality of Veronica's death, revealing the serious man beneath all those teasing smiles.

It suddenly occurred to me that I hadn't seen Hustler smile once since I'd returned. Not even at the announcement of my pregnancy.

Drawn out of my crippling worry for my sister, I paid more attention to Hustler as he pulled me into the corner of the room, away from everyone. Hulk stood a few steps away with his arms crossed over his chest, looking every inch the intimidating biker that he was. Since I'd seen him last he'd gotten new ink, but his skin was so dark it almost seemed to absorb the intricate pattern, then reveal it as his muscles flexed and the light hit his smooth skin. Seeing the Iron Horse MC patch on his back brought me back into focus and I realized I wasn't handling myself that well.

In fact, I think I might be on the verge of a mental breakdown.

Swan...they could be touching her right now, breaking her spirit merely by placing their hand on her bare arm.

I almost started sobbing, but a tiny baby foot kicked me from the inside, or I had a gas bubble, and I pulled my shit together.

Placing my hand over my stomach, I jerked when a distinct little body part pressed against my palm and Hustler gently grabbed my arm. "You okay?"

"Yes." I gave him a tired smile, then took his hand and placed it on my abdomen where my little one was moving. "She's kicking."

The dark sadness in Hustler's eyes lifted as his gaze met mine and she gave my belly a good thump. "*Jesucristo.* You have a feisty little girl in there."

"Get your hands off my woman," Beach growled out from nearby with barely contained fury.

I wanted to kick him in the ass for making the small amount of happiness in Hustler's hazel eyes vanish, darkening them again and making me sad. "He's feeling the baby kick."

Right away, Beach shouldered Hustler out of the way, his anger forgotten as he placed his hands reverently on my belly and whispered, "Hey, *chiquita*, it's your daddy. How's my beautiful girl doin'?"

I wanted to stay mad at him and wished our daughter would ignore him for being a jerk, but she gave him a couple good punches that made his face light up in the most beautiful smile I'd ever seen.

My heart melted even as I scolded myself for letting him distract me from being pissed. "Any word?"

The baby had finally settled, but he kept his hands on me as he looked up, the smile fading. "Your dad and Mimi are on their way, but they were in Russia when I spoke to them."

I blinked. "Russia?"

"Yeah. Had some meetings." I gripped his wrists and he shook his head. "Nothing bad, at all. Said they were visiting personal friends."

Closing my eyes, I tried to calm myself before I said, "What about Swan? Did you find out anything?"

"No."

The fear I'd been holding back burst through me and I started to cry, hot tears falling from my closed eyelids and dripping down my face. Beach stood then gathered me into his arms, holding me close and kissing the top of my head over and over. I clung to him, crying without shame as my emotions overwhelmed me. Through it all, he rocked me in his arms, wrapping himself around me and giving my poor battered heart a place to heal. My sobs wound down to sniffles and I gave Hulk a pathetic smile as he handed me a bunch of bright white tissues.

Beach took a step back as I blew my nose, repeatedly, the corner of his mouth lifting as I honked.

"Shut up," I said in a thick voice. "I'm an ugly crier."

"Nothin' you do could be ugly," Beach replied with such gentleness that it brought tears to my eyes again.

My phone started to ring and I almost ignored it, but pulled it out when I saw Hustler and Beach having a low conversation together.

The number was unfamiliar but I answered it anyway.

"Hello?"
"Sarah!" Swan sobbed on the other end of the line.
For a moment my fingers went numb, then I screamed, "Swan? Oh my God, Swan! Where are you?"
"I don't know. I need help. Mom's dead, I don't know where Smoke is, and there are bad guys on their way."
My stomach lurched and I barely forced out the words, "Mom's dead?"
"Yeah. She OD'd."
Beach snatched my phone away and I sagged against Hulk, my body numb.
Death had finally caught up with my mom and I wasn't sure how to feel about it.
I focused on Beach's tense face as he gripped my phone tight. "Swan, where are you?"
He listened for a moment, repeating what she said to Hustler, who'd grabbed a pen and a notepad from somewhere and was writing shit down.
"Help's on its way," Beach said in a tight voice. "You just stay alive and we'll find you. Do you know who took you?"
Whatever she said hit Beach like a punch, because he physically flinched, then started to freak out.

A moment later he was yelling at Swan not to go, then cursing more.

He looked at Hustler, the rage in his expression freaking even *me* out. "Cruz is a traitor. He's the one who picked them up at the airport then delivered them to someone named

Chief."

Hustler stared at Beach like he was crazy. "Cruz?"

"Yeah." He thrust the phone at Hustler. "Get Dragon on this, I need the location where this call is coming from, *now*. She kept the phone on and hid it where it can't be seen, so keep it on mute just in case anyone can hear it. Got me?"

"On it."

"Hulk," Beach barked out.

"Yo," he said from behind me as he briskly rubbed my arms.

"Take care of my woman."

"Wait," I managed to spit out even though I was beginning to tremble. "I'm going with you."

The hard look he gave me had me biting my lip. "You're staying here, in the panic room, with Hulk."

"But—"

Grasping my chin with one hand, he lowered his face to mine. "You. Are. Staying. Here. Do not fight me on this, Sarah. The more of my time you waste, the longer it'll take to find your sister and my brother."

I wanted to argue, but he was right.

Not long afterward, they took off, at least thirty men, all armed to the teeth and heading forty miles south of Austin—while I sat in a steel box with Hulk.

It was comfortable in there, had a couch and some easy chairs, as well as a cot and a small kitchen. The safe room was located on the ground floor, behind the kitchen and next to what we called the infirmary. One whole wall of the twenty-by-thirty-foot room was filled with monitors that showed different cameras all over the clubhouse. I was antsy as could be, with no outlet for my nerves, so I constantly surfed through the different cameras to try to get some idea of what was happening out there. Right now it was a whole lotta nothing, just guys talking but the cameras weren't positioned for me to read their lips other than the occasional word.

Hulk was silent, stretched out on the couch while he watched the monitors with me.

The men had been gone for over two hours by now, and I was frustrated by the complete lack of communication.

"Would it kill him to call me?" I griped as I spun around on the wheeled, high-back leather chair set up before the monitors.

"Just might," Hulk said in a mellow voice.

I stuck my tongue out at him, making him chuckle. "He could be dead right now."

"Or he could be alive, Debbie Downer." The corners of his eyes crinkled and he cracked his neck. "Come on, little mama, take a load off. Rest. I know when my ex was pregn…"

He trailed off and I wanted to slap myself in the forehead for not being more sensitive to the fact that Hulk had lost his daughter not too long ago. His dipshit ex-wife drove wasted with their little girl in the car and got in an accident. Ex survived, little girl did not. I could not imagine the devastation he felt every day without someone else's pregnancy being thrown in his face.

Tears welled in my eyes and Hulk abruptly sat up. "Sarah, you okay?"

I didn't want to bring up sad memories for him, so I sniffed out, "I hate being so emotional. This isn't me! I don't cry like this. Yesterday I lost it over a freaking ice cream commercial featuring a gay married couple. It was so sweet; they were sharing a shake that looked really yummy."

More tears came at the memory of how cute the commercial was while Hulk laughed. "Shit, woman, you're gonna drive Beach insane. Glad I'll be around to watch."

I wiped at my eyes with some tissue I grabbed from the box on the small table, then blew my nose. "We're happy to have you here, Hulk, really. Beach said you have a brother nearby?"

"Yeah, lives down by Waco with his wife and my nephews."

"Well, that'll be nice to visit them."

He gave me a tight smile. "We're different men, got along like oil and water as kids, but maybe we've grown up enough to be around each other without constantly fighting."

My phone rang with the song I'd assigned for Beach, "A Whole Lotta Love" by Led Zeppelin, and my skin tingled.

"Hello?"

Beach's deep voice rolled into my ear. "Baby, we found them. They're hurt, Smoke's been tortured, but they're alive and on their way to the hospital."

I have no idea what else he said because my mind had had enough and I fainted.

My sister lay in her hospital bed sleeping while I held her hand. It was a few days since they'd brought her in suffering from a gunshot wound to her leg bad enough that she would always walk with a limp. She'd been shot while shoving Smoke out of a fucking second-story window, from a burning barn—then dived out after him. This was all after our…our late mother shot Swan full of heroine.

My skin crawled at the thought of what my sister had been subjected to and I forced those negative thoughts from my mind.

Mimi was a firm believer in a positive attitude in the sickroom, so anyone who was hanging out with Swan, or Smoke in the bed next to hers had to check their sorrow at the door. Swan had thrown a fit about seeing Smoke and Beach had quickly gotten Smoke and Swan into a private room together. I think he was a little scared of Swan, which only made me even more proud, because it turns out Beach was right, we didn't give Swan enough credit. Beneath her innocence lay a hardened warrior who would do whatever was necessary to save her man and family.

Thank goodness, because the bastard who had taken her, the man known as Chief, had tortured Smoke to within an inch of his life. He lay in the bed behind me, sleeping heavily. They'd cut him, burned him, beaten him, had broken bones, but he'd survived. Swan had freed him in time to save his life, but he'd always bear the scars of his time in captivity.

The only thing we knew about Chief was it appeared he was the source of the attacks against the club, and that he went to great lengths to disguise himself, all the way down to his voice. That meant he was either insanely careful, or he was a public figure among Iron Horse—a brother people would recognize. I honestly had no idea who he was, but I made had my suspicions.

Speculation about who Chief was burned like wildfire through the club, and right now the popular moron vote was Hustler. He suspected Vance, still—despite the fact that Vance saved the girls *and* shot the man about to kill Smoke and Swan after they'd jumped from the barn.

I mean, yeah, the guy was an asshole, but it didn't make sense for him to do those things if he was the traitor. Hustler had his theories, but he'd kept them to himself, not trusting anyone.

Unfortunately, that feeling was becoming mutual with some of the brothers. There were whispers about Hustler, rumors that Veronica had found out he was the traitor and he'd killed her before she could blab. Not to sound like a psycho, but Hustler would have done a much better job of killing her in a way no one would know than leaving her body on his porch in clear view of the early-morning dog walkers.

A dead blonde wearing a sparkling neon orange dress and only one shoe, with a hole in her head, tended to draw attention.

Plus, the lack of blood indicated she'd been killed somewhere else and dumped there.

A headache threatened and I rubbed my face, glancing at the new diamond-encrusted women's Rolex Beach had gotten for me. Birdie would be here soon to sit with Smoke and Sarah. We never left them alone—well, in addition to one of our Enforcers standing constant guard outside the room. I'd learned early on that in this world, money could buy you a lot of things, and Iron Horse had a lot of it, so when they wanted a private room with a big-ass biker standing outside and scaring the fuck out of the nursing staff, they got it.

I picked up the huge baby bible I was reading and sat back in the surprisingly comfortable reclining chair. It flattened out into a small bed and I knew it was cozy enough to sleep in because I'd conked out myself a time or two. While I no longer wanted to puke, I was sleeping at least twelve hours a day and my stomach was expanding so fast, I sometimes swore if I stared at it enough, it would grow before my eyes. My baby was now the size of a Banana, but I still called her peanut. Beach had started referring to her as that as well, and I wondered what we would name her. Of course, everyone had an opinion, but I'd already told Beach her middle name would be Mimi, and he'd readily agreed.

Right now he'd agree to pretty much everything I said. Like the fact that once my sister was out of the hospital and safe back at Birdie and Venom's ranch, where she and Smoke would be cared for by both professional nurses and the terrible twosome of Birdie and Mouse, we were on the next plane out to Las Vegas so we could get married, just the two of us, at my favorite spot outside of Las Vegas. I know a lot of people think a quickie Vegas wedding is the ultimate in tacky, but having lived in the city and been to a handful of weddings, I knew there were some venues that were beyond amazing.

But we weren't getting married in the city. No, we were taking a 45-minute helicopter flight out to the Grand Canyon and getting married alone. Just the two of us, a justice of the peace, and a wedding photographer on the rim of the Grand Canyon. That's it.

We'd made the decision after I'd been bombarded with all these elaborate wedding plans from everyone. Even the men had opinions about how we should get married, and when one of them had mentioned having the reception at the clubhouse after we'd gotten hitched at a bar, I put my foot down. This was about me and Carlos, and we'd earned the right to focus only on each other on our special day. That didn't mean we weren't going to throw a massive party and have a huge reception after we got back from Las Vegas, but while we were out there, it was just me and Carlos.

I reclined my chair and pulled the green and grey afghan Mouse had made for Smoke over me. Swan had a matching one done in shades of pale pink and grey folded over her feet. Well, her foot. A giant cast encased her broken leg. They'd done surgery on, putting a steel rod, pins, and all kinds of hardware in to try to mitigate the damage the bullet had done. My throat burned as tears filled my eyes, but I blinked them back on the off chance either Smoke or Swan would wake up. I didn't want them to worry about me because I was the world's worst leaky faucet when I was pregnant.

The dim hum and beep of the machines monitoring Smoke and Swan's health soothed me, and as I lay back in the chair, I picked up my phone and began to scroll through wedding websites, back to planning the ultimate wedding reception with the man I loved beyond all reason.

Epilogue

Carlos "Beach" Rodriquez

One Year Later

I sat beneath a gigantic white silk tent, which rippled in the warm Texas evening breeze as the crystal chandeliers, festooned with wisteria and lilacs, swayed and threw rainbows of light which fascinated my daughter. Though right now, she was conked out in my mom's arms as she chatted with her friends. Mouse cradled my daughter close as she laughed and I couldn't help but smile at how obviously happy my mom was.

My sweet baby girl, Kylie Mimi Rodriquez, pursed her little rose-colored lips, breaking my heart for the millionth time today. Voices rose around us, joy filling the air as our friends and family had a hell of a good time. Sarah had spent months planning this party, wanting it to be the perfect reception for both herself and Swan. While Smoke and Swan had just tied the knot only a few hours ago, Sarah and I had been married long enough for me to feel like I couldn't remember a time when she wasn't a part of my life. When I turned to look at her, I found her smiling at me, her pale blue eyes sparkling like snow in the moonlight.

Unable to help myself, I carefully slipped my fingers beneath her hair, not wanting to risk her wrath as I gave her a light kiss on the lips. I would have loved to tongue-fuck her in front of God and country, but it wasn't a fear of her mafia cousins shooting me that stopped me. No, I'd watched my woman freak out about this fucking party until I feared for her sanity, so there was no way I was messing up her makeup that had taken two hours to apply by her theater friends flown in from Las Vegas. Normally Mike would balk at having this many strangers on his homestead, but he'd do anything for his daughters and had enough of a reputation to ensure no one fucked with his land or property.

When I pulled back, she gave me an odd look and tilted her head to the side. "Why are you kissing me like a scared fourteen-year-old on his first date?"

Lyric, who was sitting next to Sarah, giggled loudly, the sound musical enough to draw the attention of everyone around her. She flushed when she noticed people staring at her and grabbed her glass of champagne, sipping at it like a nervous hummingbird. I made a mental note to have my guys keep an eye on her tonight. She was like a fluffy little sheep among hungry wolves. Already I'd noticed more than one man giving the curvy brunette an interested look, but so far they'd kept their distance. Might have to do with the fact that Sarah had announced, back in Austin, that she'd gut any man who laid a finger on her.

Unfortunately for Sarah, that'd only made Lyric even more interesting to my boys, and that's not counting the looks the Stefano men were giving the shy young woman.

"Beach?" She glanced over her shoulder at Lyric, who was now talking to a tattooed Asian woman named Indigo who was more than a little crazy.

The pretty, tattooed, young woman attracted her own share of attention, but I wasn't worried about her. Indigo Yazuki struck me as the kind of chick who broke men's balls for breakfast and she was keeping a close eye on Lyric. One of the Stefano boys—Sarah had at least one hundred male cousins—kept giving Lyric these creepy fuckin' eyes that I think was his attempt to woo her. He was young, early twenties, and obviously hadn't learned how to attract a woman. It sure as hell wasn't with that goofy-as-fuck pout. I was waiting for him to make a move on Lyric, but so far Indigo's glares had kept him at bay.

Placing her hand against my face, Sarah turned my gaze back to her. Her bright blue eyes were highlighted by some kind of sparkling pink eyeshadow that perfectly matched the flowing, lacy, pale pink gown that she wore for the reception. I liked the latter because it was a halter top and showed a good deal of her beautiful, tanned cleavage. And since she was breastfeeding, her already big tits were enormous. Just looking at them made my dick hard and I tried to force away images of her nude, tanning on the beach. We'd spent the last week down at the Iron Horse island in the Caribbean. Mouse, Mimi, and Mike had come along, but I didn't mind. I had a family now, and I'd never deny my daughter the attention of the people who loved her.

Plus, having grandmas and grandpas around had allowed me to steal Sarah away to a private lagoon, where I'd fucked her with the sun burning down on our naked bodies.

"Honey, don't worry about Lyric, she'll be okay." Her full, pink-frosted lips, curved into a big smile. "You're such a good daddy."

If I wasn't sure Mimi would throw a dagger at my dick, I'd bend Sarah over right here and spank her pert ass.

Her smile grew until her teeth gleamed against her tan. "Hold that thought, it's time for our first dance."

We'd had our actual first dance on the edge of the Grand Canyon while the sun had burned purple, orange, and blazing red, framing my woman in God's fire.

The memory grew stronger as we walked out onto the dance floor, Smoke and Swan on the other side.

Our women had wanted to share their first dance, and we were more than happy to accommodate them.

When the first haunting strains of "The Sound of Silence" cover by Disturbed filled the tent, people stopped talking and the tent dimmed until we were bathed in warm golden light while surrounded by darkness, spotted here and there by candles.

Sarah slipped her hand into mine and I placed my arm around her, the smooth rasp of the singer's voice serenading us as I swept her around the dance floor. We kept clear of Smoke and Swan, who were more swaying than dancing due to Swan's bum leg. My friend wore a custom-made tux, which he wore well, while Swan had changed into a knee-length, sparkling white dress that flared around her as Smoke picked her up and spun her around.

Sarah watched them as well and when she looked up at me, she smiled so brightly it stunned me.

Never in a million years would I have imagined that night back in Sturgis would not only start a chain of events that led to Iron Horse almost being wiped off the map, but that it would also be the night I was fated to meet my future wife.

Singing along quietly with the song, Sarah gazed into my eyes as we slowed down, our bodies moving together in perfect rhythm as the music wound down.

By the time the last notes ended, I couldn't keep myself from kissing her, hard and wet, while everyone around us lost their minds.

I was forced to come up for air when Mike Anderson tapped me on my shoulder. "Mind if I cut in?"

The light strains of "What a Wonderful World" began and I grinned, bowing out. "Be my guest."

I'd promised this song to another lady.

Turning, I found my mom waiting with a now-awake Kylie. As always, my daughter smiled when she saw me and reached for me. She had barely any hair, but Sarah had put a cute, frilly white baby headband on her with little pink silk flowers that matched Sarah's dress. Kylie squealed happily as I took her in my arms and began to sway across the floor with her. Swan had taken a seat on the edge of the dance floor, draped over Smoke's lap while he kissed her, much to her nearby cousin Vinnie's disgust.

I hadn't seen him much since the events in Colorado that had led to him losing his leg, but Sarah said he was dealing with it.

Right now he was making disgusted faces while Mimi laughed and smacked his arm.

Kylie, mad that she didn't have my attention, whacked me on the mouth with her little fist, laughing when I smiled at her. Not gonna lie, she's a daddy's girl through and through. Oh, she loves her mommy, but no matter how cranky she is, I can get her to calm down. I grab her little fist before she can hit me again, kissing the tiny fingers that hold me with all their strength. Her eyes are still a bright, light blue, and I hope they stay that way. Love having Sarah's stunning eyes looking back at me out of Kylie's chubby little face.

The song ended and when the next began, Sarah joined us, Kylie diving from my arms and into hers. Holding our daughter between us, we danced together and I was happier than I ever knew was possible. Kylie rested her head on my shoulder and I held them both close to me, willing to destroy anyone and anything to keep them safe.

Exquisite Karma(Iron Horse MC, #4)

Keep reading for a sneak peek at ***Exquisite Innocence*** **(Iron Horse MC, #5)**

Lyric Ashton

Music pounded into the night as the wedding reception began to grow wilder. The older people and the kids had all left, and those who remained partied how I imagined Vikings celebrating a successful raid would party. Lots of drinking, roaring, and women. Energy pulsed in the air and the champagne I'd downed made my blood fizz. The table I sat alone at was away from the dancefloor and I'd turned down the men who'd asked me to dance. I didn't want to draw any more attention to myself than I already was and I certainly didn't want word reaching Pastor Middleton that I'd been acting like a harlot in public.

The thought of enduring another one of his screaming lectures on chastity had me slugging back more of my orange juice and vodka.

Unfortunately, no matter how much I drank, I couldn't help but wonder what kind of fate awaited me when I returned home. I'd snuck out, and even though I'd left a note explaining I'd be attending Smoke and Swan's wedding, and I'd arranged for one of the women I trusted, Mrs. Klein, to watch over my frail grandmother. There should be no reason for any drama over my attending Swan's wedding, but I knew there would be a price to pay when I returned.

I took another drink, trying to rid myself of the taste of fear. It was ridiculous, I was nineteen years old, no longer a child, and I should be able to leave the church grounds if I wanted. They had no reason to assign me any punishment chores, or—the Good Lord forbid—penance.

Goose bumps rose along my arms and I startled when someone sat next to me.

A quick glance up showed it was an older man with grey hair and a tattoo on his neck. His blue eyes were cold and I wanted to scoot away, but I was afraid of offending him. It wasn't his fault I hadn't been exposed to a great many people. He was probably a perfectly nice man. After all, he'd been invited to the reception. For a long moment he studied me, then gave me a smooth smile.

"Hello, pretty girl. Name's Vance. Who're you?"

I wondered if I should shake his hand, but my palms were sweaty so I settled for clenching them into the shimmering silver fabric of my bridesmaid dress. "Lyric…Lyric Ashton."

He blinked at me, then something in his face changed and his gaze became intent, probing. "You live around here? How do you know Swan? You guys close?"

"Uh…" I tried to figure out a polite way to avoid his question. "Yes."

"That's not an answer."

"Pardon me?"

He leaned forward, capturing me with his gaze and I could smell the alcohol and cigarettes on his breath. I felt like a bird mesmerized by a snake and leaned back as he closed the distance between us. My skin prickled as he invaded my personal space, and my mouth went dry when he placed his hand on the back of my chair, almost touching me.

Now, I haven't had much experience with men, but I wasn't ignorant about sex, and I knew the look on his face was lustful.

"When I ask you a question, I expect an answer. Am I clear?"

I drew farther away from him but didn't know how to respond.

Thankfully, I was saved from my inability to speak by a strong, tanned hand grasping mine as a deep voice said, "Come on, sweetheart, you promised me a dance."

I most certainly hadn't promised anyone anything, but I was thankful for the excuse to get away from the older man, now staring at someone behind me with open hatred.

"Go away, Hustler. She ain't your kinda girl."

Wanting to avoid a scene—the last thing I needed was word getting back to the church that two rough men had been fighting over me—I quickly stood. "I'm sorry, but I did promise him a dance."

Vance's upper lip started to curl in a snarl before he caught himself and gave me a smooth smile, reminding me a lot of the racist jerk currently running what used to be my parents' church. Pastor Middleton, the current thorn in my side, and his son were the bane of my existence. They were up to something, I didn't know what, but my church didn't have enough money to support their lavish lifestyle. Part of me wanted to know what they were doing, but another part just wanted to keep my head down until my grandmother passed and I could leave.

At the thought of my sweet grandmother, trapped in the fog of Alzheimer's, I worried again if maybe I should leave early. I'd promised Swan I'd stay the night at her parents' place, but I had an uneasy feeling about being away from home. It wasn't that I didn't trust Mrs. Klein with watching my grandmother; I just didn't trust Pastor Middleton and his people. While he had no reason to hurt my grandmother, or me, I still didn't like the way his gaze lingered on me a little too long when my mother wasn't looking.

Kind of like Vance's gaze crawling over my semi-exposed breasts. I never showed this much skin, but Swan had refused a more modest cut to the top. The sweetheart neckline displayed the beginning of the soft mounds of my breasts and I had to resist the urge to tug it up while.

"Come on, darlin'," a smooth male voice purred behind me, sinful enough to persuade an angel to flirt with evil.

When I faced him, I had to hold back a gasp—because it was the groomsman who'd been devouring me with his gaze as I'd walked down the aisle in Swan's wedding. Just the memory of his burning, light brownish-green eyes staring into mine had my heartbeat picking up. I'd been slightly disappointed he'd ignored me after the ceremony, but now, with his pretty hazel eyes staring into my own, I grew slightly lightheaded. Little prickles of excitement raced over my skin and I swear my heart skipped a beat as something powerful, primal and seductive, moved through me.

What in the world was wrong with me? I was swooning like one of those ladies I liked to read about in naughty historical romances. Thank goodness for the invention of the eReader, because I could read my tawdry novels without being judged as a whore. As if reading about people falling in love somehow made me mentally unclean. *Please.*

Pastor Middleton was big on chastity and virtue, on clean bloodlines...whatever the heck that meant.

I didn't say anything as he led me away from Vance and onto the dance floor.

He placed one hand on my waist, then used the other to lift my arm around his neck. While he wasn't as tall as Smoke or Beach, he was perfect for my shorter height. He still towered over me, but it wasn't like my face was at his belly button.

I had no idea what music was playing as I wound my fingers together behind his thick neck, the silk of his black hair brushing my skin and making it tingle. A pencil-thin goatee lined his perfectly full lips and my gaze returned to his pretty eyes again and again, a little spark racing through me each time that settled between my legs in a low throb.

"Thank you for rescuing me Mr....?"

"Hustler."

I stopped swaying against him, unaware that I'd even been moving, and tilted my head in confusion. "Your name is Hustler?"

Amusement sparked in his gaze. "Yep."

I flushed, remembering Swan telling me about road names. "Oh, yes, I see. It's your club name, correct?"

Now his lips curved in a smile that made a dimple pop out in his cheek.

Goodness, he was extremely handsome.

"Glad you think so, sweetheart."

I stumbled when I realized I'd said that aloud, thinking I might have had a little too much alcohol. "I didn't—"

The music changed, became a deeper and faster beat, and I found myself pressed fully against Hustler as he grew tense against me. "My real name is Lorenzo."

His words held an interesting accent as he said that and I repeated him, rolling my R like he did. "Lorenzo."

"Mmm, like it when you say my name like that. You have the sexiest voice I've ever heard."

Blushing, I looked down, and became aware that my breasts were pressed to his hard chest, that his thigh was close to brushing between my legs. The cologne he wore reminded me of oranges and spice, a very masculine smell that made a woman wonder if it smelled even better closer to his skin. Everywhere he touched on my body heated and grew sensitive and needy.

Despite the fact I grew up on a compound that highly discouraged dirty dancing, I'd learned how to do it over the years while visiting my friends on other compounds. I was by no means good at it, but I knew enough that I could move easily with Lorenzo. No—Hustler. My body relaxed into his and he was very, very good at showing me what he wanted, how he wanted it. There was something thrilling about a man so confident and controlling, at least for me. I know it's probably a result of my upbringing, but I've been raised to follow a man's lead and I found it…comforting. And arousing. Darn it, I probably shouldn't have had that vodka.

I felt the distinct bulge of a rather large cock pressed into the softness of my stomach and shivered, that ache back between my legs. The song beat through my blood and the crowd around us was filled with people dancing way closer than we were. In fact, people were making out with drunken abandon as they ground against each other. It was a wild crowd and normally I'd be freaked out by being in the middle of them, but in Hustler's arms I felt safe. He was so big, broad, and even though he wasn't the tallest man in the room the hard pressure of his muscled frame against my much softer one had me panting.

Curious to know if he was feeling the same intense arousal that I was experiencing, I looked up at Hustler through my lashes and internally combusted at the heat in his gaze.

In a completely seductive purr, he murmured, "Fuck, why'd I have to meet you now? Perfect, so sweet I got a toothache, so hot you make me burn. And the way you melt for me…shit."

"Pardon me?"

His look was almost sad as he cupped my cheek with one rough hand, stroking his thumb over my lower lip. "Soft, like peach skin. Love havin' you pressed up against me. Makes a man wonder what it would be like to own a sweet beauty like you. Bet you don't know how irresistible you are, how many men are wishin' they were in my place. You walk through the room and men can't help but follow the sway of your round hips and full ass."

The deep timbre of his voice had my nipples stiffening as I soaked up his praise-even if it was dirty praise. I'd had men compliment me before, but nothing this raw, this visceral. A little pang of guilt went through me that I was allowing a man to speak to me like that in public, but the dirty girl who lived at the heart of me secretly loved it.

I didn't know what to say to him, didn't have his way with words, so I settled for, "Thank you."

His face dipped down next to mine, the tip of his nose running over my ear and making me want to straddle his leg and seek some relief from the ache he started inside of me.

"Look at you, that pretty pink blush." In one smooth move he lifted my skirt high enough that he could slide his thigh between mine, only my panties and the thin fabric of his tuxedo pants protecting my heat from his flesh. "Fuck, I can feel how hot you are, how wet."

That embarrassed me, pulled me out of my arousal a bit, but Hustler wasn't letting me put any space between our bodies. He grasped my hips and rocked me up and down his thigh, rubbing me against him in a way that had me seeing stars. His erection thrilled me, proof that he found me attractive, and he let out a groan of his own as I sank my fingers into his hair and pulled lightly. His soft moan had me making an almost matching sound of desire.

"Yeah," he whispered into my ear, "harder. I like it rough."

Goodness, what was I doing? I was so far out of my league with this man, it was laughable. He liked it rough, and I hadn't even had enough experience to know what I liked at all. I mean, yes, I've read my erotic romance novels, and Sarah's a good friend of mine so I'm not naïve about sex, but reading and doing are two different things. I wasn't prepared for the burning craving to kiss this man I barely knew, this devilish temptation wrapped up in a tuxedo with the collar unbuttoned enough to reveal a raven tattoo on the side of his neck.

Curious, I traced it with my fingertips and he moaned softly, turning me on even more. "Shit, I like it soft with you just as much. Dangerous. Triple threat."

"What?"

He licked the side of my neck and I rubbed myself on his leg. "Dangerous, make me want things I can't have right now, not with that asshole gunnin' for me."

"I don't understand." My voice came out all deep and breathy and I swore I was turned on enough to climax if he kept grinding my clit against his thick thigh.

The strong thump of his pulse met my fingertip as I traced my way from his throat to his jaw, unable to stop touching him. With the music, the lights, the crowd of strangers around us, I felt like I was living in a dream where my actions didn't have consequences. Fascinated by his plush lips, I traced my fingertip over the bow of his mouth, dipping it lightly inside when he parted his lips on a soft snarl.

I should have realized the risk of teasing a man like Hustler.

I should have run away from him that instant.

I should have paid attention to Vance staring at us with pure hatred in his gaze from the edge of the dance floor as he talked into his phone.

Instead I succumbed to Hustler's gentle urging and titled my face up to his, softening my mouth in anticipation of his kiss.

When the tip of his tongue tasted my skin, I made one of the biggest mistakes of my life as I yielded to him, because a moment later his arms were wrapped around me, my body exploding into tingles while he lowered his delicious mouth to my own and sealed my fate with a kiss as delicate as a butterfly's wing.

Lyric and Hustler's story will be continued in Exquisite Innocence (Iron Horse MC, #5) coming late 2016.

Still craving more of the Iron Horse MC? Did you know my biker series crosses over with my Submissive's Wish series? Yep, and Mimi has a role in both. ;) If your curious about the rather kinky and wild world of the hot Russian Doms who run the *Bratvas*, check out the first book in my Submissive's Wish series, Ivan's Captive Submissive. Fair warning, it's steamer than Iron Horse, but I think my bitches can handle it.

Ivan's Captive Submissive

When Gia Lopez signs up for the Submissive's Wish Charity Auction she has no idea that she's about to be bought by a Russian Dom who will do anything to make her fantasies come true. Including staging an elaborate kidnapping that Gia believes is real. Ivan is instantly drawn to Gia and he wants to be the best Master she's ever had. As he spends time with Gia he begins to have intense feelings for the strong, independent, and sexy American woman. He's only won a week of her service but wishes to keep her forever.

Unaware of Ivan's true feelings, Gia fights her growing emotional attachment to him. All she wants is to settle down with a nice Dom in the United States, continue her career, and live a normal life. However, Ivan sets a plan into motion that will push Gia to all of her limits and take her on a global journey of self-discovery, extreme pleasure, and love.

Warning: Contains Erotic Spanking, Subspace, f/f situations, a devastatingly sexy Dom who knows what he wants, and a submissive who just might be ready to give him what he needs

Chapter

Gia Lopez stood in a staging area for the submissive auction with a line of women covered in sheer black robes. Her long, light brown hair was twisted back into an intricate braid that was a work of art, but she desperately wished she'd gotten plastic surgery to take care of her big nose before agreeing to this. The other women scheduled to be sold off with her were beautiful, each perfect and lovely in their own way.

She felt like a sparrow surrounded by peacocks.

While Gia possessed enough self-worth to admit she was cute with her dimples and big brown eyes, she'd never be breathtaking like the auburn-haired sex-bomb submissive next to her. Gia had a slender figure from her daily jogging, but with her small breasts she felt like a boy when compared with the curvy submissive.

Why couldn't Gia have gone after someone who wasn't a pinup girl?

Mistress Alice, a tall, blond Domme, walked down the line of submissives. They were gathered in what looked like a parlor with all the furniture moved out. Elegant watercolors still graced the walls and a tasteful chandelier bathed the room in a low, golden light. The door to the room where the auction would take place was currently closed, but from her orientation earlier, Gia knew that on the other side there was a curtained area to hide them from the audience. Then, the scariest of all, a stage where she would be sold to the highest bidder.

Mistress Alice paused now and again to point out something she wanted changed with a submissive's hair or makeup and took a moment to speak with each woman. Up at the front of the line, a few men in brown leather loincloths presented a nice visual treat as they were oiled up by a trio of giggling submissives.

Mistress Alice stopped before Gia and slowly inspected her from head to toe. When she spotted the gold barbells piercing Gia's nipples through the sheer cloth of the gown, she smiled. "Lovely touch against your nicely tanned skin. The gold works much better than silver."

"Thank you, Mistress Alice." Gia curtsied as she'd been trained, and Mistress Alice's gaze warmed.

The Domme tilted her head and studied Gia's face. "You're Mistress Viola and Master Mark's girl from South Carolina, Gia."

"Yes, Ma'am. Mistress Viola and Master Mark were my trainers."

"Lovely couple. I met them once at a Domme convention in Las Vegas. They told me to keep an eye on you, that you have quite a temper and are very high-spirited."

Gia flushed and dropped her gaze. "I'm working on that, Mistress Alice."

"Well, don't work on it too hard." She leaned closer and whispered, "Some of us like a sub with fire in their veins. We like the challenge and the constant battle for your submission."

Gia started as the other woman gently bit her earlobe before leaning back. "Am I understood?"

A soft rush of desire went through Gia and she licked her lower lip. "Yes, Mistress."

The desire unfurled gently in her belly as she relived her training and how she owed her trainers a debt she could never repay. It had been a unique experience to work with Mistress Viola and Master Mark. Together they'd helped her start her transformation into the kind of submissive she yearned to be. They'd also given her glorious orgasms that swept the world away and left her existing as a being of pure pleasure. Not only did they train her physically, they helped her learn how to love herself just the way she was.

Mistress Viola was a plump, curvy, delicious armful of woman. By today's standards she was considered overweight, but back in the 1950s she would have been the ultimate in female beauty. Gia had yet to see a man who didn't gravitate to Mistress Viola in a room, no matter how many other women were there. The fact that her husband, the more traditionally handsome Master Mark, loved her beyond reason helped more than anything else to make Gia believe that maybe there was a man out there who could love her just as she was and give her the confidence to become the woman she wanted to be.

Beautiful, elegant, and loved.

Well, she wasn't loved yet, but she would be. She had faith her Master was out there, looking for her. The thought of him being here tonight, maybe waiting for her in the audience, sent an ache of longing through her. The practical part of her mind scoffed at the idea of soul mates and fate, but the romantic side of her nature insisted anything was possible.

A petite mahogany-skinned woman who reminded Gia of a pixie came up to Mistress Alice and knelt at her feet. "Mistress, Master Martin wishes me to inform you we have fifteen minutes until we begin."

Mistress Alice nodded. "Thank you, Tilly." She smiled at Gia. "Have fun, sweet girl. Whoever gets you is going to have their hands full."

"Thank you, Mistress." Gia bent into a graceful curtsey.

The pair went farther down the line and Gia tried to slow her breathing. The redhead in front of Gia turned around and gave her a warm and dazzling smile. "First time?"

"Yes. Is it painfully obvious?"

"Yep. First timers are pretty easy to spot. You're the only ones who aren't excited. My name is Iris."

"Gia. Nice to meet you." Gia smiled and smoothed her hands against the sheer robe. "I take it by your lack of panic attacks you've done this before?"

"Oh, yes. This is my third time." Iris gave a dreamy smile. "After the first auction, I was bought by a lovely Dominant couple. At the second auction, I met my husband, who is also my Master."

Gia tilted her head in confusion. As far as she knew, this auction was for single, uncollared submissives. "If you have a Master, why are you doing this again?"

The woman laughed and fingered her collar. "Because he wants to win me all over again."

Gia couldn't help a small stab of envy. "That's very romantic."

A chime sounded three times, silencing all conversation. All of the submissives turned toward the sound, and the redhead leaned over to whisper into Gia's ear, "Don't freak out. Whoever you end up with is going to be one of the best Masters in the world. If you click, great. If you don't, then you will, at the very least, come away from the experience as a better submissive. Besides, all of the Masters have your fantasies available to them, and only a Master or Mistress interested in fulfilling your fantasies will bid on you."

Gia laced her fingers together, trying to keep her anxiety at bay. She didn't want to start shaking like a scared puppy. "That's what worries me." She lowered her voice and leaned closer to Iris. "I shared a bottle of wine, or two, with my girlfriend before I filled my form out, and I'm afraid the fantasies I submitted are a little more…frank. Let's just say I was super honest about what my deepest, darkest desires are. Like, embarrassingly honest. When I read what I had already submitted the next morning, I couldn't look myself in the mirror for the rest of the day without feeling like a pervert."

Iris giggled. "Oh, that does sound interesting. Care to share what one of those fantasies was?"

A stern man's voice rang out over the crowd. "Ladies, eyes on me."

They turned and Gia recognized Master Martin, the man who ran the Submissive's Wish Charity Auction and owner of this elegant mansion. Tonight, the distinguished man wore a dashing black tux with an expertly tied red and black bowtie that nicely set off his graying hair. His presence filled the room and all conversation stopped.

Raising his arms, he smiled. "Welcome to the twenty-eighth annual Submissive's Wish Charity Auction. Some of your faces are well known to me as members, and others are delightful new additions to our evening. Whether new or old, I encourage all of you to make the most of the opportunities presented to you tonight. Allow yourselves to embrace your submission and give yourselves the freedom to enjoy the fantasies your Masters or Mistresses create for you without useless shame or misplaced guilt. For the next week, you will be at your Masters' or Mistresses' beck and call. You will find yourselves challenged, pushed beyond what you thought you could endure but, in the end, it will all be worth it."

ABOUT THE AUTHOR

With over forty published books, Ann is Queen of the Castle to her husband and three sons in the mountains of West Virginia. In her past lives she's been an Import Broker, a Communications Specialist, a US Navy Civilian Contractor, a Bartender/Waitress, and an actor at the Michigan Renaissance Festival. She also spent a summer touring with the Grateful Dead-though she will deny to her children that it ever happened.

From a young Ann has had a love affair with books would read everything she could get her hands on. As Ann grew older, and her hormones kicked in, she discovered bodice ripping Fabio-esque romance novels. They were great at first, but she soon grew tired of the endless stories with a big wonderful emotional buildup to really short and crappy sex. Never a big fan of purple prose, throbbing spears of fleshy pleasure and wet honey pots make her giggle, she sought out books that gave the sex scenes in the story just as much detail and plot as everything else-without using cringe worthy euphemisms. This led her to the wonderful world of Erotic Romance, and she's never looked back.

Now Ann spends her days trying to tune out cartoons playing in the background to get into her 'sexy space' and has accepted that her Muse has a severe case of ADD.

Ann loves to talk with her fans, as long as they realize she's weird and that sarcasm doesn't translate well via text. You can find her at:

Website
http://www.annmayburn.com/

Facebook
https://www.facebook.com/ann.mayburn.5

Pintrest
http://pinterest.com/annmayburn/

Twitter
https://twitter.com/AnnMayburn

Other Books by Ann

Prides of the Moon Series

Amber Moon

Emerald Moon

Onyx Moon

Amethyst Moon

Opal Moon

Club Wicked Series

My Wicked Valentine

My Wicked Nanny

My Wicked Devil

My Wicked Trainers

My Wicked Masters

Virtual Seduction Series

Sodom and Detroit

Sodom and the Phoenix

Submissives Wish Series

Ivan's Captive Submissive

Dimitri's Forbidden Submissive

Alexandr's Cherished Submissive

Alexandr's Reluctant Submissive

Long Slow Tease Series (FemDom)

Still

Penance

Emma's Arabian Nights (FemDom)

First Kiss

Second Touch

Third Chance

Fourth Embrace

Bondmates Series

Casey's Warriors

Jaz's Warriors

Paige's Warriors(Novel Coming Soon)

Iron Horse MC Series

Exquisite Trouble

Exquisite Danger

Exquisite Redemption

Exquisite Karma(Coming Soon)

For the Love of Evil Series

Daughter of the Abyss

Princess of the Abyss

Chosen by the Gods

Cursed

Blessed

Dreamer

Single Titles

Blushing Violet

Bound for Pleasure (FemDom)

Sensation Play

Peppermint Passion

The Breaker's Concubine

Guarding Hope

Scandalous Wish

Pursued by the Prisoner

The Bodyguard's Princess

Summer's Need

Wild Lilly

Diamond Heart

Sam and Cody

Made in the USA
San Bernardino, CA
28 May 2016